Others Available by dk holmberg

The Dark Ability

The Dark Ability
The Heartstone Blade
The Tower of Venass
Blood of the Watcher

The Cloud Warrior Saga

Chased by Fire
Bound by Fire
Changed by Fire
Fortress of Fire
Forged in Fire
Serpent of Fire
Servant of Fire

The Lost Garden

Keeper of the Forest
The Desolate Bond
Keeper of Light

THE TOWER OF VENASS

THE DARK ABILITY
BOOK 3

ASH Publishing
dkholmberg.com

The Tower of Venass

ISBN-13: 978-1523967810
ISBN-10: 1523967811

ASH Publishing
dkholmberg.com

THE TOWER OF VENASS

THE DARK ABILITY
BOOK 3

CHAPTER 1

Rsiran Lareth stood before the sloped roof of the
freshly painted wooden building. It was new construction,
and unlike most buildings in Elaeavn, made of wide rough sawn
timbers rather than block or stone. A building like this was meant
to be temporary.

"You don't need to do this."

Rsiran turned to Jessa. Her face still hadn't lost that haunted expression, the aftermath of what she'd gone through when Josun had
abducted her, and her normally flushed cheeks looked pale. Brown
hair hung longer than it had since he first met her, passing her shoulder. A length of ribbon tied it back. She pulled on it, bringing it around
her shoulder and twisting it between her fingers. Another nervous tick
she'd acquired. A yellow flower was woven into her lorcith charm, the
first day she'd worn one in many weeks.

"I haven't come here since I learned."

"It's not like you haven't been busy," she said.

Rsiran sighed. Since returning from rescuing Jessa from Il-phaesn, he'd spent his time fortifying the smithy he'd taken over. Bars of the heartstone alloy now lined the inside of the walls, worked together as a barrier. He'd not risk Jessa's safety again and let someone like Josun reach her. Now, no other Sliders would be able to enter the smithy, keeping them safe from the threat from the Forgotten for now. As far as Rsiran knew, only he could Slide past the alloy.

"I still should've come before now," Rsiran said.

She grabbed his hand and turned him toward her. Her green eyes seemed especially bright under the full moonlight. Were he Sighted, like Jessa, he might see the tight lines of worry around her eyes that had been present since he'd rescued her from Josun. Instead, his ability was different. Once thought to be a dark ability, he'd finally come to accept his gifts from the Great Watcher.

A hard-packed path led away from the building, winding back toward the rest of Elaeavn. This was separate, almost on the edge of the Aisl Forest, and surrounded by enough trees that you had to know where to look to find it. In spite of that, the steady sound of crashing waves carried even here, bringing the scent of salt air to mingle with the earthy odor of decay.

"Why? What has he done to deserve that?"

Instead of answering, Rsiran checked the knives stuffed into his pockets. He didn't need to touch them to know where they were. The lorcith pulled on him, connecting to him in a way he still didn't fully understand. Like his father, he had lorcith in his blood. That was part of the reason he'd come tonight.

"I need answers. Della only has so many." He thought about what Della had told him of his ability and of the Elvraeth, remembering her hesitation. "And some she won't share."

"You think she's trying to hide something from you?" Jessa didn't chide him as she once would have. Neither of them felt completely comfortable with what had happened to them. Risks taken that had kept them in the dark and pulled them into a fight that was greater than either of them.

The lorcith charm he'd made her hung openly from a small chain of the heartstone alloy around her neck. That had been the first thing he'd made after rescuing her. Delicate work that he'd asked the lorcith allow. After losing her once, Rsiran would do anything to keep Jessa safe.

"I'm not so certain of that anymore."

"Rsiran—"

"How much did Brusus keep from us? He knew what he had me doing… he knew the risk he asked of me and did it anyway."

"Would we have done anything differently?"

He sighed again and shook his head. Brusus was family to him.

"We shouldn't do this. Let's return to the city. By the time we get back, maybe Haern will be at the Barth. We can dice and have some ale—"

He shook his head. Since Lianna had died, the Wretched Barth hadn't felt the same. Maybe that wasn't right; since learning that Josun hadn't died as he thought, nothing about the city felt the same. The Elaeavn he'd known was different now. Darker. The only place he felt comfortable was the smithy. Even there, he jumped every time he heard a strange sound.

"I need to see him. He deserves that much."

"Does he? After what he did to you?"

Rsiran squeezed her hand. "If he hadn't, I never would have met you." He tried to keep the bitterness out of his voice. Meeting Jessa was one of the few good things that had come from what his father had done to him.

"I think I would have found you eventually. The Great Watcher would have seen to that."

Rsiran didn't argue. Only the Servants claimed to know what the Great Watcher intended. After everything that had happened to him, how could the Great Watcher have a plan with him? "Ready?"

She squeezed his hand, signaling that she was.

Rsiran Slid past the door.

There came the familiar rush of stale air, reminiscent of the bitter scent of lorcith. Flashes of color streaked past him as he felt movement, though took only a single step.

Such a brief Slide took little energy. Since facing Josun again, he'd taken to Sliding everywhere, building up his stamina so that Sliding great distances wouldn't challenge him. When alone, he practiced Sliding rather than walking. In the weeks since he'd left Josun trapped inside Ilphaesn, he Slid everywhere.

Bringing Jessa with him took only a little more effort. From the beginning, he'd Slid with her. First, throughout Elaeavn as they made their way through the city. Later to Ilphaesn and back or out to Firell's ship. Usually, having her along comforted him. Today felt different. Today, she would meet his father.

Rsiran emerged from the Slide to see a shadowed room around him. Hard-packed dirt formed the floor, more evidence of the temporary nature of the building. A lantern with weak orange light streaming from it rested on the floor near the far wall. A small raised platform for a bed tucked into the corner. A low counter served as a makeshift kitchen. The place stank of a mixture of smoke and sweat.

Everything seemed more welcoming than the man living here deserved.

A small fire pit set away from the wall. Three logs that had burned down to glowing coals sent smoke drifting toward a hole cut in the roof. A stump rested near the fire pit and a lean man sat atop it, staring into the coals.

"Are you sure about this?" Jessa whispered.

"There's nothing more he can do to me," Rsiran answered.

He took a step forward, Sliding without thinking about what he was doing. Jessa held his hand as they Slid, but said nothing. She had grown accustomed to him Sliding everywhere. Often, she preferred it.

"They said you would come."

The voice came from behind him and Rsiran spun. He should have realized there was someone else in here with them. Brusus wouldn't leave him unguarded, not until he fully understood why his father had been in Asador. The Forgotten had taken him there, but they still didn't understand why.

He didn't recognize the man near the door. Brown eyes looked back at him. Not of Elaeavn.

Dressed in thick leathers, he carried a short sword—forbidden in Elaeavn except for the constables—made of steel. Rsiran frowned at it, thinking it might be one of his forgings, though it was difficult to tell. Working with steel gave him a way to practice the skills lorcith taught him, to see if he could carry it over to other metals.

"What else did they say?" Rsiran asked.

The man grunted. He wore hair shorn close to his scalp, revealing the end of a long scar. He shrugged. "That I wasn't to interfere with you."

Rsiran narrowed his eyes. Did Brusus actually think this man *could* interfere with him? "And that's it?"

A smile split the man's face and reached his eyes. "Also said I should run if I saw one of your blades. Figured that was a joke." He shrugged again as he studied Rsiran.

"How do you know Brusus?"

The man tilted his head, considering him a moment. "We've worked a few jobs together."

"In Elaeavn?"

The man shook his head. "Mostly in Thyr."

Rsiran tried to hide his surprise. Thyr. One of the great cities, though far enough away he'd never thought to be able to visit until he learned he could Slide. Rsiran knew little about the great cities. He'd only Slid to Asador once, and that was because he searched for Jessa. Like Asador, Thyr was home to a university. This man looked nothing like a scholar. But how had Brusus managed to reach Thyr? He couldn't Slide like Rsiran, which meant he had to travel using more conventional methods. He'd never heard Brusus mention leaving the city before.

"What's your name?" He wanted to know who Brusus assigned for this duty. Until recently, he'd felt removed from Brusus's work. Even now, he didn't think he fully understood everything Brusus had in motion.

The man tipped his head slightly, revealing more of the scar. It stretched from the top of his forehead all the way back along his skull.

How had he survived a blow like that?

"Thom L'alin." The man waited, as if expecting Rsiran to recognize his name. When he said nothing more, the man chuckled again. "And you must be Rsiran Lareth." He turned, eyes slipping over Jessa. "Jessa?"

Rsiran frowned. How much had Brusus shared with Thom about Rsiran? Enough to know he could Slide. To Thom, it would appear as if Rsiran simply appeared in the room. Had Brusus said anything about Rsiran's other ability?

"I'd like some time alone here," he said to Thom.

A dark hunger shone in his eyes as he looked at Jessa. "Guess we'll be going then?"

She shook her head. "I stay."

Thom shrugged. "Tell me when you leave."

Rsiran nodded and Thom turned to the door, twisting the lock quickly and slipping outside. Jessa released Rsiran's hand long enough to hurry to the door and lock it again.

Now they were alone with his father. Perhaps Jessa was right—maybe he shouldn't have come.

"You finally come to finish me?"

Rsiran turned and looked at his father. He stared at the glowing embers. His face appeared long and gaunt, wasted compared to the muscular man Rsiran knew, but the beard that had been there the last time he'd seen him—the beard that prevented Rsiran from recognizing him—was gone. Lantern light reflected off eyes that had once been a brighter green.

"Finish you? I'm the one who brought you out of Asador," Rsiran said, Sliding forward a step. "I saved you."

His father still didn't turn. "You should've left me there. Then I wouldn't have to see what you've become."

Rsiran blinked slowly, hating how his words could still sting, even after all this time. "I've become what you made me. What the Great Watcher made me. Nothing more."

His father finally looked toward him. His eyes were deep hollows. "If that's what you wish to believe, but don't think to lie to me. I've seen your work. The forgings you made. Dark works, things the Great Watcher never intended a smith to make with lorcith."

Rsiran tensed. How had his father seen his forgings? "I make what the ore requests."

He snorted and looked back toward the fire. "You should be better than that, but I've seen what you've made. Was forced to study it. 'Recreate it,' they said." He shook his head. "Lorcith never calls like that unless you want it. Had you stayed and learned, you'd have understood."

Without thinking, Rsiran Slid forward to stand in front of his father. He would make him look at him. He felt Jessa as she neared, the lorcith charm pulling on his senses. Even the heartstone chain around her neck pulled at him, though its call was soft, and barely there. He had to focus on the heartstone to hear it fully.

"Anything I learned of lorcith, I learned by working with it. Had you only been willing to listen, you might have understood how I made my forgings. The lessons the ore taught—"

"Dark lessons," his father snapped. "Dangerous and forbidden." His eyes looked past Rsiran and over at Jessa, lingering on the heartstone chain. They widened slightly.

"Forbidden by who? The Elvraeth? Or the Great Watcher?"

He looked back at Rsiran. "Yes."

Rsiran shook his head. Why did he let his father push him like this? "The Elvraeth only want to keep power. That's why they control the lorcith so tightly. That's why they created the myth of the dark ability." He Slid forward, just a step, remembering when Josun told him how the Elvraeth worked to eliminate Sliding. Identifying the ability as a curse went a long way toward that end. Rsiran had lived nearly a year thinking he needed to hide what he could do… and when his father had learned of it, he punished him. "I've learned much since you banished me."

His father blinked. "And forgotten much, as well, it seems."

"What does that mean?" Rsiran heard the word "forgotten" and thought of everything he'd feared since learning of his ability. Banishment from the city, sent away from everything he knew. But by sending him to work in the mines, it was his father who had banished him, not the Elvraeth council. Exiled from everything he'd ever known. Forgotten, just as much as if he'd been sentenced by the council, until he'd decided he wouldn't accept the exile.

More than that, he thought of the Forgotten. He knew little about them other than that they were out there, searching for a way back into Elaeavn and back into power. Josun had worked with them to achieve their goals, until Rsiran left him in the mine he and Jessa had discovered on the other side of Ilphaesn, chained, unable to escape.

His father leaned forward. Once thick arms had lost much of their muscle. Skin seemed to hang where before it had been taut and youthful. "You reach too far, Rsiran." Was that a note of concern in his voice? "There are things we weren't meant to make. Had you chosen to listen—to learn—rather than being so stubborn, you might have understood. Instead…" He shook his head and turned his eyes back to the fading fire.

Rsiran sighed. Arguing with his father would not get him the answers he sought. Better to confront him directly. Rsiran no longer needed his approval.

Drawing on the sense of the lorcith knife in his pocket, he *pushed* it out and hung it suspended over the fire. The knife was simply made, the blade solid lorcith and forged in such a way the dull grey metal still appeared liquid. The knives he carried with him were weighted for pushing. Small enough to flick with a thought but dangerous enough to harm.

"Could you teach this?" he asked his father. Rsiran knelt, leaning so his father had to meet his eyes. "Did you keep this secret from me?"

His father blinked. For a moment, Rsiran thought he felt pressure on the knife, but maybe that was simply his imagination. Then his father's eyes flickered up to Jessa, brighter than they'd been before. "You're with him?"

The question carried a certain weight, but Jessa didn't hesitate as she nodded.

"Then it falls on you to keep him safe." He looked at the knife but made no other movement.

"From who?" Jessa's voice came out like a whisper. Rsiran heard the uncertainty in it.

"From himself."

Rsiran *pulled* the knife back toward him and snatched it out of the air. He thumbed the smooth edge of the blade, running his finger along it. Why had he come here? To taunt his father? To find the answer why he'd been pushed away from his family? He glanced at Jessa. Those answers didn't matter anymore. Not like they once had.

But there were other answers he did need.

"Who took you to Asador?" Rsiran asked, wanting confirmation that it was the Forgotten. He slipped the knife back into his pocket, feeling foolish for letting his emotions get the best of him. Seeing his father took him back to all the times spent within his smithy, times when he'd feared making any wrong move while hoping to impress him enough that he'd allow him to work the forge. Now it didn't matter. Rsiran had his own forge and access to a supply of lorcith his father once would have longed for.

His father stared at the crackling coals and said nothing.

Rsiran stood and took a deep breath. He wouldn't get angry—not again. "Why were you trapped there? What did they want with you?"

Moments passed with the only sound that of the coals snapping. Finally, his father shook his head. "They wanted you." He spoke softly and didn't look over at Rsiran.

"Why? What would they want with me?"

"Because you started this. You began making weapons of lorcith again. For centuries, that had been forbidden." He looked up, and a distant look crossed his eyes. "You think you control the lorcith? You think me cruel for forcing it to become what I want rather than letting the ore work through me? You think you have learned so much, that you know what it means to have the blood of the smiths run through you, but you are nothing more than a child playing at the forge."

Rsiran swallowed and leaned forward but felt Jessa's hand on his arm. She squeezed, pulling him back before he did or said something more foolish than he'd already managed. He looked over at her, saw the way she bit her lip, her chin tilted toward her flower as she sniffed softly, and knew she'd been right. He shouldn't have come.

He took her hand. "This was a mistake," he said.

"You've made plenty," his father said.

Rsiran sighed. "Maybe I should have left you in the cage in Asador with the Forgotten. You would have been happier then, if you've ever been really happy. At least I wouldn't have to wonder if I did right by bringing you back to Elaeavn." He turned and looked at Jessa. "Let's go."

She looked over at his father as if she wanted to say something but bit her lip again. She held his hand, squeezing.

Rsiran Slid toward the door. He wouldn't give his father the satisfaction of hiding the ability from him. Not after everything he'd been through. At the door, he hesitated. Without looking back, he said, "Alyse thinks you left her and mother. Should she think you're dead too?"

His father sucked in a quick breath. "You've seen Alyse?"

It hurt that Alyse meant so much to him. "I've seen her. She works in Lower Town now."

"How... how was she?"

Rsiran snorted and shook his head. Perhaps he should have started with word on Alyse. Maybe then, he would have gotten the answers he wanted. "Angry. But well." Rsiran looked back. His father stared at the wall rather than the fire. "If I see her again?"

"Whatever else happens to them, it's better for them that I be dead." He looked over to Rsiran, and his eyes softened. "Let them have that," he begged.

Rsiran stared, debating his answer. Finally, he nodded and then Slid past the door.

CHAPTER 2

THOM LOOKED AT RSIRAN AS HE EMERGED. His brown eyes flickered from Rsiran to Jessa before looking at the door. "You left it locked."

Rsiran looked over at the door, cursing to himself. In his haste to leave, he'd forgotten that Jessa had locked the door. As he readied to Slide back inside, Jessa signaled him by squeezing his hand.

"You have a key in your pocket," Jessa said to Thom.

A tight smile pulled at his mouth, and he nodded slightly to Jessa, the scar atop his head gleaming against the moonlight. "Sighted then?" he asked.

Clever, Rsiran realized. Thom knew enough about Elaeavn to wonder what abilities each of them had. And by simply Sliding into the hut, Rsiran had announced his ability. At least his other skill remained hidden.

Jessa said nothing.

Thom fished the key from his pocket and held it up. "Wouldn't be much use if I didn't have a key. Gotta piss sometimes and can't leave him there unlocked."

Rsiran laughed softly. "What does Brusus plan for him?" It was a question he hadn't dared ask Brusus yet, fearing the answer. He hadn't seen much of Brusus in the last few weeks. Safer to stay within the smithy.

Thom shrugged. "Don't know. Sometimes there's different levels to what he intends, you know? He tells me one thing, but means another."

Rsiran couldn't help but note how similar that seemed to the way Brusus had once described Josun. "Has Brusus been here?"

"Not that I've seen. But the old man mostly just sits quietly." He snorted. "Tried asking questions but got nowhere. One time, I asked about his family, and I had to hold him back."

Rsiran frowned, having a hard time envisioning that happening.

Thom shook his head and turned to the door. As he slipped the key into the lock, he said, "The old man has got a temper with questions. Surprised he didn't jump you too."

"It wouldn't matter."

Thom looked over his shoulder as he twisted the key. "No. From what I've seen it wouldn't." He opened the door a crack. "So who is he?"

Rsiran debated answering. He knew nothing about Thom, just that Brusus trusted him. Once that would have been enough. Now he wasn't as certain. "Neran Lareth."

"Lareth?"

"My father."

Thom smiled wide and laughed. "Strange families you have in Elaeavn." Thom hesitated. "So have you been to my homeland too?"

Rsiran frowned. "Homeland?" Did he mean Thyr? Or did Thom come from someplace else?

Thom tipped his head. "Sithlan. Your father said he'd..." A smile pulled at the corners of Thom's mouth. "No. I can see you haven't." He disappeared inside, closing the door behind him. The lock slipped into place with a loud *click*.

Jessa stared at Thom before pulling on Rsiran's hand. "Do you feel better that we came?"

Rsiran frowned. What had Thom meant that his father had been to Sithlan? As far as Rsiran knew, he'd never been anywhere other than Elaeavn. Why had he never said anything about leaving the city?

He sighed. Did it matter how well he knew his father? After everything that had happened between them, perhaps the mystery of their experiences was the difference. Rsiran had long ago given up on the idea that he might learn to understand his father, perhaps even have his father understand him.

"Not better," he admitted. "But I needed to come."

"To have him do that to you? Do you still think you deserve that? After everything your ability has let you do, you still think you deserve to be treated like that?"

The way his father treated him went deeper than his ability. The ability to Slide had surprised and scared Rsiran. When he first awoke on Krali Rock, not knowing how he'd gotten there, he'd gone to his father for answers and hoped for support. Instead, everything changed. To his father, Sliding was a dark ability, one for thieves and criminals. And Rsiran had used it to sneak places he should not have been—places like the Elvraeth palace or Firell's ship—but he'd also used it to help his friends. For his father, what Rsiran had done was worse than that. He'd turned away from his apprenticeship, as well, leaving no one to take over the smithy that had been in the family since the founding of Elaeavn.

"It doesn't matter what I think," he said.

Jessa punched him gently on the shoulder. "You're still an idiot." She pulled him along the path leading away from the wooden hut.

Massive trees quickly stretched overhead, blocking much of the moonlight, leaving dark shadows hanging around them. "If you think it doesn't matter, then it doesn't. I think it matters. Brusus and Della too."

Rsiran shook his head. "Brusus hasn't been exactly honest with us."

Jessa shook her head. Her short brown hair swished as she did, and she grabbed it with her free hand, pulling it back over her shoulder. "He's got his reasons. We can't know what it was like, what he's gone through knowing where he came from, but unable to reach the palace. I'd think you would understand more than most."

Rsiran understood. Brusus thought to learn about the Forgotten, but in doing so, he'd pulled Rsiran—and Jessa—into something more.

"I can Slide us—" He wanted to get back to the safety of the smithy. Out in the Aisl, he felt safe enough, but once they reached Elaeavn, the familiar anxiety would return. Fear of what could happen—had almost happened—to Jessa.

"Let's walk," Jessa said.

Rsiran didn't push. Besides, standing beneath the sjihn trees of the Aisl, a sense of peace washed over him, different from what he felt while in the city. Standing here, he could almost imagine what it must have been like before their people moved to Elaeavn, when they'd lived among the trees.

"What do you think it would have been like?" he asked.

Jessa frowned. "What?"

"Living among the trees. In the Aisl. How would it have been?"

Jessa looked at him, amusement twisting her face. "Cold. Wet. I'd rather have a roof over my head."

Rsiran considered the heavy canopy and wondered whether it would have mattered. "Sight would have been useful. Listeners. Probably Readers too." He thought about the other abilities, but those seemed the most useful in the forest.

"You don't think Sliding would have been helpful?"

He shrugged. "Sliding from tree to tree? That seems as dangerous as…"

"Sliding onto a moving ship?"

He laughed. That had been dangerous. But it had worked. If he hadn't gone to Firell's ship, he wouldn't have found Josun. He would never have found Jessa. And he might never have learned about his ability with the heartstone alloy. "Didn't you once tell me that sometimes you have to take risks to be rewarded?"

Jessa slipped her arm around him and pulled him close. She laughed softly. "Haven't I rewarded you for what you did?"

Rsiran smiled. He loved the way Jessa felt against him, her warmth pressing through his clothes, the way her hips curved toward him. "You never can have enough thanks."

They reached a small clearing in the Aisl. A circle of rocks surrounded a soft mound of earth on the other side of the clearing. Grass had overtaken the mound, deep green in the daylight. At night, it looked practically black. Rsiran had first thought it strange that Brusus would build the wooden hut out here in the forest, so close to the place he'd buried Lianna, but suddenly realized why. He missed her and did what he could to be near her again.

Jessa turned toward him and put both arms around him. She leaned into his chest and rested her head. As they stood for a moment, Rsiran smelled the clean scent of her hair, the crisp bite of the sjihn trees, and the damp earth beneath his feet. He could stay like this and be happy, he knew.

A low howl echoed through the forest and made him jerk.

Jessa laughed and pushed away, the moment ended. She pulled on her hair and bent her face toward the flower in the charm. "What now?" she asked. "Now that you've seen him. What do you plan?"

Rsiran hadn't thought that far ahead. Since rescuing Jessa, he'd focused mostly on fortifying the smithy, making it so he couldn't be surprised again. During that time, she'd mostly watched him. Jessa would never admit it, but since Josun took her, something had changed in her. Some of the independent edge softened. Rather than roaming Elaeavn without him, she preferred to stay nearby. The only times she didn't were when he Slid to Ilphaesn for more ore.

"I don't know. I told Brusus that he would have to explain everything he knew about the Forgotten, but he hasn't. Not yet. We can't be stuck in the dark, forced to wonder what might happen next."

Jessa shrugged. "I'm never really in the dark."

Rsiran wondered again what it must be like to be Sighted like Jessa. Never isolated in the darkness. With his ability to Slide, he could always escape, but he needed to know where he Slid to take the next step safely. "I know. I'm like a blind babe."

She laughed. "At least you finally admit it."

The howl came again, closer this time. This time, Jessa stiffened. From his time spent in the Aisl, the sound always came at night, never during the day. He'd never seen what made the sound, but imagined some massive wolf prowling through the treetops. Had they feared the creatures when their people lived in the trees?

"Still want to walk back to the city?"

She punched his shoulder. "Get us out of here."

He grabbed her hand, focused on the smithy, and Slid.

Sliding into the smithy now was a different experience than it had been. Before, he'd been anchored to the smithy. With enough of his forgings there, he barely had to exert any energy to reach it. He'd managed it even when weakened and fatigued. After the fortifications he'd built around the walls, he didn't think he could manage the same anymore, but that was just as well.

Rather than a rush of wind and color, what he felt was more of an oozing, his body stretching as it slipped between the bars of heartstone alloy. So different from Sliding anywhere else. Not painful, but not comfortable or easy. A barrier designed to keep them safe, and similar to the one the Elvraeth used for the palace.

They emerged from the forest to the dimly lit smithy. The blue heartstone lantern sat atop one of his long tables, the light drifting out enough to easily see everything in the smithy, especially with eyes adjusted for the moonlight. The air had the familiar bitter tang of lorcith, but after all the work he'd done, it now mixed with the strangely sweet scent of the heartstone. The alloy seemed to have no odor of its own.

Once inside, Jessa let go of his hand. She tossed a log into the hearth built into the far wall, and flames slowly built around the dried wood. She stood staring at the flames, reminding Rsiran of how his father had looked back at the hut.

He stepped up to the table and twisted the knob on the lantern. More of the blue light spilled into the smithy, pushing back the shadows. Except for near the hearth. There, shadows seemed to linger, almost as if swirling around Jessa. Another trick of his imagination, he figured.

Rsiran took the knives from his pockets and set them on the table, counting as he did. He'd taken to inventorying what he'd made. After what ended up on Firell's ship, he wanted to know where his forgings went. And he'd stopped sending knives to Brusus that he could trade for information. So far, Brusus hadn't challenged him on that.

Two dozen of the slender knives rested on the table. Made from only three separate lumps of lorcith, he could feel the bindings between the blades made from the same lump. The contours of the blades shared a similarity as well. Rsiran *pulled* on the knives, lining them quickly without ever touching them. After seeing his father, he wondered if others could push with lorcith, as well, especially those who could hear its call. The boy from the mines. His father. Other smiths.

Had his father had a glimmer of recognition when he'd *pushed* on the knives? He'd certainly become more agitated at that point, and Rsiran could almost imagine he'd felt pressure on the knife, but maybe that had been just his imagination.

In addition to the knives, Rsiran had a few other implements on the table. An iron pan. Steel tongs for holding metal he forged. His attempt at making one of the heartstone lanterns. Another failure, but he felt he was getting closer. Those were more difficult than anything else he'd made.

"Come sit by me," Jessa said.

He turned, scanning the walls of the smithy. Long slender bars of heartstone alloy ran from the smooth floor planks to the ceiling every few paces, creating a perimeter. Rsiran had experimented with the spacing until he felt comfortable that another Slider couldn't easily pass through, but ensuring he wouldn't have to strain too hard to enter his smithy. It was a delicate balance, and one that took the better part of two weeks. Each time he forged one of the heartstone alloy bars, he found it easier to do.

At first, he'd struggled mixing the alloy. Different from working with pure lorcith, adding heartstone to it required asking the ore to allow it. He didn't think the ancient smiths who had made the alloy for the palace had forged it the same way, especially considering the strange forge Shael had asked him to make, but it was the only way that Rsiran knew to do so. In some ways, his method worked better. He didn't fight with the alloy, not as he would if he tried to force it. That was the reason that making the necklace for Jessa had gone as easily as it had.

He couldn't talk to anyone about the process—who'd understand that he spoke to the ore in a way?—which left him feeling more isolated than ever. Even with Jessa sitting watching him. There was a part of him that wished he didn't have to ask such a forging of lorcith, but to keep Jessa safe, he would do what he needed.

Rsiran made his way over to her and took a seat on the floor. She'd swept the floors clean, her contribution to keeping the smithy tidy, but they still hadn't managed to get any chairs to sit on. The bed was little more than a low pallet with a thin straw-stuffed mattress. Neither minded so long as they were together.

"You're distracted," he said. He pulled her hand into his and squeezed. Slender fingers felt so small and delicate, all the better to pick locks he suspected. An old scar worked across the top of her hand, slightly raised and smooth. He ran his finger along it.

Jessa looked over at him. Firelight reflected in her green eyes, looking like dancing flames. "I'm not the one who's been distracted, Rsiran." She swallowed and leaned away from him, looking around the smithy. "This… place worries me."

"You shouldn't worry. With the bars of the alloy, no Slider should be able to get in here. We're safe here."

She turned back to him. "Are we? This is safe?" She shook her head and closed her eyes. "After what happened, I feel safer being with you, but this is something else."

"What then?"

Jessa took a deep breath. "I know you needed to see your father. I don't understand why, but I know you did. And I was happy to go with you, because it finally got you away from here. This smithy—everything you've done to it—makes it feel…" She shook her head. "I don't know. Less like we're keeping others out and more like we're trapping ourselves inside."

Rsiran frowned as he looked at the walls, thinking of the Elvraeth in the palace, the bars of the alloy over the windows. They had been there to protect the Elvraeth, hadn't they?

"What should I do?" he asked her. "I can't lose you again. Not like that."

Jessa smiled and leaned toward him again, taking his hands. "You won't lose me, Rsiran. I'm more worried about you losing yourself."

After chasing Firell and then Josun, Rsiran wondered if he knew who he was anymore. Once it had been a simple answer, but the days of being the son of a smith were gone. Now? Was he Brusus's private smith or was he something else?

"What do we do then? The Elvraeth—"

"Not the Elvraeth. The Forgotten. And you can't blame Brusus for what happened. You have to forgive him, and I don't think you can move on until you do."

Rsiran sighed. For some reason, that had been more difficult than he expected. Secrets kept from him, secrets that had put Jessa in danger. But what else was there? Brusus had taken him in when Rsiran had no place else to go, gave him a purpose, friends.

And if he didn't try? What would happen with Jessa? He saw the strain on her face, the anxious way she pulled at her hair and sniffed the flower. He'd thought that was because Josun had captured her—possibly tormented her—but what if that wasn't it. What if she worried about him? He couldn't be the reason she was unhappy.

Rsiran forced a smile onto his face. "Should we go to the Barth?"

Jessa smiled and pulled him toward her. "Well… maybe not tonight," she said. "But tomorrow. We need to see our friends again."

As Jessa pressed against him, he couldn't help but feel the familiar pit in his stomach, that fear of stepping too far outside the smithy and risking losing her again. He forced it down and away as he focused on her.

Chapter 3

Rsiran stood on the rocky slope of Ilphaesn Mountain gripping a heavy burlap sack. Fading moonlight gave enough light for him to see. Cool mountain air gusted around him, fluttering his thin shirt and tasting of bitter lorcith and a hint of the sea. Nothing else moved around him.

Lorcith pulled on him from every direction. It came most strongly from the mountain itself. The vast mines working through Ilphaesn were filled with ore. Some nights, Rsiran still dreamed of the way the ore pulled on him when he'd been exiled to the mines by his father. In those dreams, the steady tapping he now understood to be other miners working in the hidden section filled his head, pushing out everything else until he could think of nothing more. Those nights, he awoke soaked in sweat.

But he felt lorcith other places as well. Standing here, away from Elaeavn, he recognized the sense of his forgings from within the city. The hidden sword tucked into his smithy pulled on him the most, even through the heartstone alloy barrier. Other forgings were scattered around the city as well. Many were knives. Rsiran had been surprised to discover that his forgings had made it into the palace until learning how Brusus traded his knives for information. Others were things like the bowl he'd once made Lianna or gifts he made for Della to thank her for all the times she'd Healed him.

He clung most strongly to his connection to the charm he'd made Jessa. Keeping an awareness of it in his mind kept her close to him, even when he Slid elsewhere. He would not lose her again.

Rsiran pushed away his sense of lorcith. Doing so was no longer difficult as it once had been. As he did, he felt the soft pull of the alloy. This sense was not the same as the way lorcith pulled on him. Not so much muted as harsher, as if harder. Much like the alloy itself.

With it filling him, he recognized the bars he'd placed in his smithy and those blocking the palace. There were others, though nothing with a pattern. He had a vague sense of the necklace he'd made for Jessa, too distant to sense it well. None of that was why he'd come here.

Rsiran turned to the closer alloy he felt. High overhead, and nearby, the bars barricaded access to the hidden mine. And, once, had prevented him from accessing them as well.

He closed his eyes and Slid, emerging past those bars and in the mine.

No light made it into the mine. With the sense of lorcith pushed away, he sensed another forging of the alloy. Usually when he came, he sensed it deeper in the tunnels. Tonight it was nearby.

Rsiran turned to Josun Elvraeth and tossed the burlap sack onto the ground. "Supplies for the week," he said. He didn't worry about whether Josun would find it. As one of the Elvraeth, he was gifted with all the Great Watcher's abilities. His Sight would allow him to see what Rsiran had brought.

"What will happen when you don't come?"

The voice sounded as if it came from a hundred feet away, but Rsiran knew he was barely ten paces from him. A trick of the mines.

"I will come."

Josun grunted. Light suddenly flared in the mine, a soft orange light from the lantern Rsiran had brought when he first visited to bring food. With the light, Rsiran saw Josun leaning against the wall. The heartstone alloy chains that had once been used on Rsiran, what he'd learned were considered Elvraeth chains, cuffed each wrist, dangling between them. His face had grown lean and haggard, a wild beard growing where none had been before. Few in Elaeavn wore beards. Dirt and debris coated his once neatly kept black hair. His deep green eyes flickered around the cave wildly.

"And if you don't? You would let me die?"

Rsiran hesitated. "Yes."

Josun turned toward him, eyes focusing more clearly for a moment. Then he laughed. The sound filled the cave, deep and edged with anger. "You're not a killer, Lareth. You've proven that time and time again."

"And if something happened to me?" Rsiran asked. "No one else knows you're here. What would happen to you then?"

Josun leaned forward, one hand touching the wall. Rsiran tensed. Even chained as he was, Rsiran prepared to Slide if needed. Josun had proven himself dangerous too often.

"You're not the only one who knows I'm here," he said softly as he slowly picked up the sack of food Rsiran had brought. There were a few skins of water, as well, enough to keep him alive for the next few days. Eventually, Rsiran knew, he would have to decide what he'd do with Josun. He couldn't leave him here forever.

Rsiran frowned. "Who else knows?" Did he have to worry about someone coming to rescue Josun? Would he have to worry about another attack? The Forgotten who Elvraeth Josun worked for might know, but would they have any way of reaching this mine?

Josun cackled and shook the chain connecting the cuffs. "Your girl knows."

Rsiran took a step forward. "You will not touch her again."

Josun laughed again and turned his back on Rsiran. "Or what? You'll bring me more food? What is it this time, jerky and dried bread?"

"You should be thankful."

Josun turned to look over his shoulder. Shadows swirled around his eyes as he did. "For what? That you brought me food? That you continue to *let* me live? I imagine you see yourself as having great compassion." Josun turned back to the cave wall and touched it with his open hands, sliding his fingers across the rock. He sucked in a deep breath. "It would be better were you to leave me to die. That would be compassion."

"You haven't earned that compassion."

Josun snorted. "Maybe you are harder than I realize, Lareth. Could it be you leave me here to torture me? That's more like what one of the Elvraeth would do." He took a few steps away, disappearing from the lantern light. "How long will you keep me here? How long before someone comes looking for me?" He smiled, and the shadows played across his face. "You know of the Forgotten now. Will you be ready when they return? Will your friends be safe?"

"I will keep them safe."

Josun hesitated. "Can you?" he whispered. "Can you really keep them safe? You didn't keep your girl safe, if I remember."

"I found you."

"You did. But I haven't decided whether that was because of what you did or what they did."

Josun continued away from him and the lantern went dim, flashing out slowly and leaving Rsiran standing in the darkness.

He'd let the sense of lorcith return as he spoke to Josun, and now he felt it all around him, creating the space of the cavern. Rsiran could walk through the mine without needing to see anything, but as he stood there, he feared what would happen were Josun to reappear next to him.

"What who did?"

Josun didn't answer, only laughed, his voice trailing into the darkness.

Rsiran prepared to Slide away and return to Elaeavn. As he did, he heard Josun again. "I hear it sometimes," he said.

Rsiran paused. "Hear what?"

Josun laughed again, the sound carried strangely down the caverns, bouncing off the walls and mixing with the call of the lorcith, but he didn't say anything more.

Rsiran shivered and then Slid from Ilphaesn.

CHAPTER 4

RSIRAN SAT IN A HIGH-BACKED CHAIR at their usual table, leaning against the brick wall of the Wretched Barth. From where he sat, he had a good vantage of the entire tavern. Jessa sat next to him wearing a pale blue flower plucked from a spindly bush outside the Barth tucked into the top of a simple dress she managed to find. As they sat there, she leaned forward and sniffed at the flower.

Compared to the last time he'd been here, the tavern was busy. Mostly men, some wearing leathers that reminded him of Thom, others in faded and dirty shirts, all sitting in pairs or more at tables scattered around the tavern. A few sat alone along the counter near the kitchen. Tucked into Lower Town but near enough the docks to have a variety of patrons, the Barth had been like a second home to him since banished by his father. When Lianna ran the tavern, it had been a homey place where soft music and savory smells greeted him each time he came. Since her sister took over, the music remained, but the focus was more on the ale than the food. Rsiran left the steaming mug untouched in front of him.

A stack of ivory dice sat next to Jessa, and she idly grabbed them, stuffing the dice into the leather shaker embossed with the logo of the Wretched Barth, that of a spindly old man, back bent as he leaned over a cane.

They had been in the tavern for nearly thirty minutes but so far, no one else had come.

"We can go," Jessa said.

Rsiran shook his head. "You're right. We need to be out of the smithy more. I haven't seen Haern in…" He thought about it, realizing it had been when they'd broken into the alchemist guild house. "A long time."

"You're not even touching your ale."

He looked down at the mug. He wanted to take a drink, but hadn't done more than sip. Were he honest with himself, it was because he feared dulling his senses. "It's not the same," he said, flicking his eyes toward the kitchen. Once, Lianna had been there, always bustling around, making certain to welcome everyone. Gillian was pleasant, but it really wasn't the same.

Jessa nodded, saying nothing as she took a long drink from her mug.

The door pushed open and a gust of cool sea air whistled into the tavern. Rsiran looked over, not really expecting anyone he knew. The Barth had always been the place they congregated, but with everything that had happened, he didn't know if any of the others had still been coming.

Brusus walked in. Other than his dark tunic and pants, clothes more formal than usual in Lower Town, he looked mostly the same. Dark hair streaked with grey. Pale green eyes—a glamour of sorts hiding his true abilities—scanned the tavern before settling on Rsiran. A wide smile split his face.

"Haern said you'd be here. 'Bout time you returned," he said as he approached the table. Brusus threw himself into one of the open chairs, his back to the door, and looked from Rsiran to Jessa. One hand slapped down onto the table, the heavy ring he wore thudding against the surface. "You get your arrangements complete?"

Rsiran let out a slow breath. Brusus knew what he'd been doing. Not surprising—he usually did—and Rsiran wondered how much he actually knew. Had he learned about the alloy? Or only that Rsiran worked to fortify the smithy? Either way, Brusus had given him space. For that he should be thankful.

Jessa set her hand on his leg. He appreciated the warmth from it, the comfort she offered. "I just wanted to make sure we'd be safe," Rsiran said.

Brusus met his eyes with a solemn expression. "I'm sorry about what happened, Rsiran. Not sure I ever told you that. I should have brought you in sooner. After all that you did," he lowered his voice, "and the fact that it was your knives I was using to get information, well… I should have told you." He turned to Jessa. "And you. Having Josun take you…"

Jessa shook her head. One hand pulled gently on her hair. It hung loose tonight, flowing over her shoulders. "I'm fine, Brusus. Really."

Rsiran didn't know if Brusus recognized the catch in her voice. Jessa hadn't spoken about what Josun had done to her while she was captured other than to say she was unharmed. Partly he didn't want to know. If he did, would he have simply left Josun trapped within the second mine shaft at Ilphaesn or would he have done something more definitive? The first time he thought he'd killed Josun back in the palace had been hard, but at least then it had been self-defense. Anything he did now would be murder.

Rsiran leaned forward and set both hands on the table. Instinctively, he checked his sense of the knives in his pockets, reassured by the connection. He took a deep breath. He didn't want to confront Brusus, but they needed to understand what Brusus had gotten them into. Only then could they decide if they would help.

"I need to know everything, Brusus. You can't keep us in the dark anymore."

Brusus looked from Jessa to Rsiran as a young serving girl brought a mug of ale over and set it in front of Brusus. She had medium green eyes and long, wavy auburn hair. She flashed a smile at Brusus that he returned.

When she stepped away from them, Brusus turned to Rsiran. "Dangerous topic, even for the Barth," he whispered. "Talk of the Elvraeth, and especially the Forgotten—shouldn't really be having those conversations here. After what happened with Jessa, I realized it was time I understood more."

"*That's* when you realized?" Rsiran asked.

"What can I say? I ignored the risk you both took. We *all* took. But I've been trying to correct that. Tomorrow, I'll come to the smithy, and I'll tell you what I've learned. It's time for you to know everything."

"Just tell us," Jessa said.

Brusus shook his head. "Like I said. It's a dangerous topic."

Rsiran snorted. "Why should we wait? We could go to the smithy tonight. I can assure you it's safe."

Jessa squeezed his leg, and Rsiran immediately regretted pushing Brusus like that. He'd agreed they would spend the night away from the smithy, and now he suggested returning?

Brusus's face hardened. For a moment, his eyes flared a darker green. "That's the problem. Nothing is really safe. Not like I thought. That was my mistake."

Brusus took a long drink from his ale and set it back down onto the table. He started coughing and a hint of blood streaked from the corner of his mouth. His eyes widened briefly, and he looked down at the mug, a curious expression as he stared at it.

"Rsiran—"

He looked over to see what had gotten Jessa's attention. The music in the tavern had fallen silent. None of the serving staff were out on the floor as they usually were. The two men sitting at the table nearest them stood. Rsiran noticed their flint grey eyes first and the swords at their waists next.

Brusus coughed again.

Rsiran glanced down. Brusus's head rested on the table. Blood pooled around his mouth.

"Rsiran!"

He snapped his head around. One of the men had grabbed Jessa. She kicked and jerked away, but he was stronger. The other man's sword unsheathed, and he sliced toward her neck.

Without thinking, Rsiran *pushed* one of his knives toward the man. It sank into his chest. He spun and collapsed. The other man twisted, pulling Jessa in front of him. Rsiran jerked the knife free from the fallen man and sent it flying toward the other's leg. He collapsed with a scream but still held onto Jessa.

She kicked again, stomping on the injured leg, and he let go.

Jessa grabbed his hand.

Rsiran reached for Brusus with his other hand. The only thought in his mind was escape.

Another pair of men separated from the corner table. They had no swords, but the flash of green eyes told Rsiran they were of Elaeavn. Knives appeared in their hands. Slender blades made of steel. Had they been lorcith, he could have used them against the men.

One of the knives spun toward him.

Rsiran Slid.

Taking two people with him was much more difficult than Sliding with only one. The only other time he'd attempted more was when they'd buried Lianna. That had taken him the better part of two days to recover.

He had the sense of movement, slower than usual, and the hot, bitter scent like lorcith. Color blurred past, but not quickly enough.

Something hot and painful stuck into his shoulder.

Rsiran cried out and ripped through the remainder of the Slide.

They emerged in Della's home. Fatigue washed over him, and he nearly collapsed. A small fire crackled quietly in the hearth. Two chairs angled toward the fire. The smells of mint tea and the spicy scent of jarred herbs assaulted him.

"Della?" His voice was weak. His shoulder throbbed and spasmed. Della should have felt the ripples of his Slide. Where was she?

Jessa screamed.

Rsiran spun. Jessa backed toward the wall, arms pinned behind her back by the man who'd thrown the knife at them. She tripped and kicked over a stack of books, but the man held her upright. His green eyes blazed. Rsiran wondered briefly what ability he possessed.

He let go of Brusus, focusing on Jessa. "Let her go." His voice came out hard and angry.

A dark smile twisted the man's face. He had short black hair and a lean face. Heavy embroidery worked along the collar of his dark navy shirt. The forest green pants he wore were simpler, but still embroidered. Expensive clothes, Rsiran knew. Elvraeth clothes.

"That's not the job," the man hissed.

He jerked on Jessa's arms. A knife suddenly appeared and pressed against her neck. A line of blood streaked where the blade touched. Rsiran hoped it wasn't poisoned like Neelish blades.

"What's the job?" he asked.

The man's smile tightened. "You."

Rsiran *pushed* the two knives in his pockets toward the man. As flashed toward him, the man somehow managed to smack them out of the air with his knife, sending them flying across the room, before slipping it back against Jessa's throat.

The man's eyes narrowed. "Come with me, and the girl can live."

Rsiran doubted he'd let her live. His knives were gone. Brusus was down—likely poisoned—and Jessa couldn't move. Blood trickled from her neck.

Without thinking too much—and if he had, he would've hesitated and risked Jessa—he Slid.

He emerged behind the man and grabbed the arm holding the knife against Jessa's throat and twisted. Years working in the smithy—especially the last few months—had built his strength. The man's arm bent and snapped, the knife dropping to the ground. He screamed softly.

Jessa jerked away, and Rsiran felt a moment of satisfaction that she was safe. Then the man twisted, spinning to face Rsiran. His knee came up and connected with Rsiran's stomach. He bent over, the wind knocked from his lungs. Another knee struck his face, sending him backward, sprawling to the ground.

The man knelt on Rsiran's chest. His good hand slipped around Rsiran's throat and squeezed. Rsiran's vision faded, blackness swimming around him.

The man grunted and fell over, the pressure coming off Rsiran's chest.

He looked up. Jessa held the man's knife and had plunged it into his back. Blood slicked the blade. She kicked him for good measure. He grunted again and fell silent.

"Are you…" he started. It hurt to talk and his voice felt rough.

She put her hand to her neck and pulled it away. Blood stained her palm but at least crusted around the wound. "Fine. Just burns a little."

"Brusus?" Rsiran asked, pushing himself to his feet. Everything hurt. His neck, his stomach and face, but most of all his back.

"Still breathing when I checked," Jessa said.

"He won't for long. This poison will work quickly."

Rsiran looked over. Della leaned over Brusus, her hand running across his forehead, pressing down and wiping the sheen of sweat off him. She wore a thick, pale green robe and her grey hair twisted into a bun atop her head. Deep green eyes looked at Rsiran and Jessa before turning to the man lying motionless on the floor.

"Can you help him?" Rsiran asked.

Della stood. Wrinkles around her eyes and mouth deepened. Then she shook her head. "I don't know the poison." She looked down at Brusus. "I'm sorry, Rsiran. There are limits to what I know."

CHAPTER 5

Rsiran sat next to Brusus. They had lifted him onto a cot Della stored in her back room. Since Rsiran had met her, she'd used it frequently, often for him. Dried blood caked along Brusus's mouth. His chest rose slowly, his breathing shallow. Della stood on the other side, hands resting on his exposed chest, eyes wide and blazing a brilliant green.

Their attacker was bound gagged, and shoved into a corner. Every so often, Rsiran resisted the urge to go to him and kick. Della watched him, her face twisted into a concentrated mask.

"All I can do is slow it," she whispered.

Brusus hadn't moved since they'd brought him from the Barth. Jessa had built the fire up in the hearth so it now blazed brightly, pushing out warmth he didn't fully feel. She sat behind Rsiran in the other chair, eyes closed. Her neck had been bandaged. As she'd said, the wound hadn't been deep. And, thankfully, not poisoned. Della promised to Heal her fully later.

Rsiran's shoulder throbbed. Somehow a knife had struck his back as he'd Slid. He didn't think that was possible, but hadn't expected someone could grab hold and Slide with him, either. Della had pulled the knife from his back and Healed his wound. Quick work, not like she would have done had she not had Brusus to worry about, as well, but enough that he wouldn't die from it. His stomach and face still hurt from where the man had kneed him, but there wasn't much to do for that except give it time.

"He grabbed onto the Slide," Rsiran said. He looked at where the man rested. His arms were bound tightly behind him, and his legs were lashed together. Della hadn't attempted to Heal him, but said he'd live.

She nodded. "That can happen if they know you're going to Slide."

"How would they know?"

She frowned. "What has Jessa told you that she sees when you Slide?"

"Most of the time she comes with me."

Della smiled. "When I watch, I see nothing distinct, but there is a pattern. Faint swirls of color. You must know what you're looking for to see it."

Rsiran understood what she implied. "You're saying he's been around another Slider before."

Della glanced at the man. He hadn't moved since they'd tied him. "That's likely how he knew what you were doing. Otherwise, I think you Slide too quickly to catch."

"I didn't realize there was a speed to Sliding."

Della looked at him with concern. "You've grown strong since I've met you. Now all I see are brief flashes. I don't know how he managed to catch you before you Slid."

Rsiran looked at the man's clothing and remembered the deep green eyes. "He's Elvraeth."

"Perhaps he was once."

Rsiran's breath caught. "What are you saying? He's one of the Forgotten?"

Brusus's breathing seemed to quicken, and Della touched his face again, running her hand across his cheeks. His breathing settled back into a steady rhythm.

"All I am saying is he's not of Elaeavn. Whatever else he is, I don't know with certainty."

Rsiran sighed. Elvraeth and Forgotten. A dangerous combination. "Why did he want me?"

She shook her head. "His barriers were too solid. Still are. I cannot Read him."

He looked down to Brusus. If he died, Rsiran would lose any opportunity to understand what he planned, and what he might know about the Forgotten. But it was more than that for him. Brusus was a friend. "Is there anything that can save him?"

Della didn't look up. "As I said, I do not know the poison."

"I could Slide wherever we need—"

"And look for what, exactly? Whatever poison was used on him thins the blood. If we knew what it was, we might be able to help, but I do not. I can slow this, but that is all." She shook her head. "Brusus knew the risks with what he did. Especially lately. I'm sorry, Rsiran."

He swallowed back the lump in his throat. The idea of Brusus dying was too much to take. He'd almost lost him once and had to reveal his ability to save him. Even after what he'd been through—or maybe because of it—he didn't want to risk losing him again.

"And Haern? Can't he help?"

"I can't See where Haern has gone," Della said softly.

Rsiran thought about the lorcith knives he'd made, focusing on them for a moment, but he'd made too many, and there was no guarantee that Haern still carried his. Rsiran could Slide toward each, but what if he came upon a constable? Or worse, one of the Elvraeth? That would be worse for them and would draw attention to Jessa, to him.

But this was Brusus.

His chest felt tight and tears welled in his eyes. He'd been a fool. Letting anger push away his friends—the only people who'd accepted him after everything he'd been through—when he should have been looking for ways to help. Had he done that, maybe he would have realized what Brusus was doing. The stress he was under and the risks he took.

"I see you have come back to us," Della said.

Had Rsiran not known better, he would have suspected she'd Read him. But Jessa read him much the same way, using her Sight to understand the changes in his mood. "I've…" He didn't know what to say. How to explain how stupid he'd been? "I'm sorry, Della."

She laughed, her voice light but strained. "No need to be sorry, Rsiran. We all must work through things in our own way. You have been through more than most in your short time." She met his eyes. An unidentifiable weight settled in her gaze, something that came from years and wisdom. "I can't imagine what it must be like for you. For any of you, really. I suspect the Great Watcher brought you together for a reason. Brusus never saw it like that. Always felt it his responsibility to keep others safe, to protect them from what his mother went through." She lowered her eyes. "Brusus only thought to keep you safe. He didn't know how deep the Forgotten had managed to reach."

He looked over to where Jessa slept. Her breathing seemed easy and steady. Rsiran had panicked when they were attacked, fear nearly overwhelming him at the prospect of losing her again. He wouldn't let that happen.

"I've been doing the same with Jessa. She's been pushing back." It didn't change what he needed to do. For Jessa, he'd do whatever it took.

Della smiled and tottered behind a counter and brought him a mug of mint tea. "I never said it was the right thing to do. Only that was what Brusus chose."

She set her hands atop Brusus. Rsiran hadn't noticed, but in the moments she'd stepped away, color had drained even more from his face. His breathing had slowed. Now that he was aware of it, he heard a steady wheezing. Everything eased as Della touched Brusus's chest.

"You're slowing the poison."

Della nodded.

"And you have to be by him to do it?" He couldn't imagine the strength required to keep sustained use of her abilities.

"I had thought to give him enough time to say his goodbyes." She sighed. The wrinkles around her eyes looked deeper than they'd been. "He won't wake up, but I can hold it at bay longer this way."

"How long?"

She shook her head. Rsiran didn't really need her to answer to know. Already, she faded under the strain. Della was powerful, but not so powerful that she could hold this forever.

"I can make it through the night," Della said. "More than that…" She shook her head again. "More than that, I just don't know."

Rsiran swallowed. The night. How long until morning? Several hours. Maybe he could find Haern in that time. He'd been an assassin, maybe he knew of this poison.

But from Della's face, he doubted she could hold out that long, and that meant that Brusus would die.

CHAPTER 6

Rsiran walked from Della's home. Cool night air gusted at him, and heavy clouds covered the full moon. A cat yowled nearby. Rsiran waited, hoping to hear another, but didn't.

Bad luck, but then again, when had he ever had good luck?

Brusus lay dying. And Rsiran could do nothing about it.

He felt helpless. Surprising, given all he had been through that feeling helpless bothered him so much. But accepting his ability to Slide, and learning he could move lorcith, gave him a measure of comfort most times. Now, neither of his abilities could do anything to assist Brusus.

And then what? Once Brusus was gone, what would happen to him? To Jessa?

They would have to keep themselves safe, but wasn't that what he'd been doing all along?

Rsiran stopped near the end of Della's narrow street and crouched next to a twisted corbal tree. The sharp bark irritated his back, but he ignored it. Tears streamed down his face and he didn't fight them. Whatever Brusus had kept him from with the Elvraeth, Rsiran didn't want him to die because of it.

He buried his face in his hands until the tears stopped. If Brusus were to die, Rsiran would at least learn why. He might not be able to find Haern, but there was some place he could go to find more information.

He made his way along the streets. Lanterns glowed orange with enough light for him to see, but thicker shadows than usual seemed to shift around the street. Rsiran made certain to hang off to the side, not wanting to be seen. He kept his focus on the knives tucked into his pocket, ready to *push* them at the slightest sign of attack. After what happened with Brusus, he didn't want to take any chances.

How had the Barth become unsafe?

A shiver worked through him. The Wretched Barth had become like a home to him since he'd been exiled by his father, the place where he first met with Brusus, where he'd met Jessa and Haern. And Firell. Maybe the Barth had always been unsafe and he hadn't seen it.

He sighed.

Waves crashed along the shore. The smell of salt and fish filled the air, mixing with a hint of coming rain. No gulls circled tonight, their cawing strangely silent.

Near the Barth, he hesitated. Part of him wanted to Slide into the tavern and see what had happened. Doing so would be dangerous. But wasn't Brusus worth the risk?

He glanced up the street to make sure no one watched, and then Slid.

Rsiran had been careful to emerge near a corner along the wall. A defensive position in the Barth, but also one where he might be shadowed enough that others wouldn't notice him at first.

He found the Barth empty.

It was strange seeing no one in the tavern. The smells of baked bread and roasted meats drifted from the kitchen, the food not the same as when Lianna ran the Barth, but still better than nothing. His mouth watered, and he considered grabbing something to eat before remembering how Brusus had been poisoned. He wouldn't touch anything here.

He looked at the table where they'd been sitting. One of the stools had tipped over, but the table looked the same. Dried blood smeared across the surface as if hastily wiped up. The stack of dice Jessa had brought sat untouched. Rsiran slipped those into his pocket.

Nothing else was left, no sign of what happened earlier in the night.

Rsiran turned, thinking to leave, when he heard a soft shuffle from the kitchen.

Was one of their attackers still here?

Against one, Rsiran had a chance. Maybe that would be how he could help Brusus. If he learned what poison was used, Della might be able to save him. Or maybe it wouldn't matter either way. Then he would have revenge for his friend. Didn't Brusus deserve that much?

He Slid toward the hearth on the far wall. There, the door would block anyone from seeing him, giving him some advantage. He grabbed two of his slender knives from this pockets and held them, ready to push on them if needed.

The door swung open slowly. Rsiran readied.

A flash of steel came through the door first, followed by black leather.

Rsiran hesitated. He'd seen that sword before.

The door swung closed. Thom glanced around the tavern, lantern light shifting off his long scar in a strange way. Thom shifted so his back was to the door, spinning quickly to face Rsiran. He held his sword at the ready.

"Why are you here?" Rsiran asked.

Thom flickered his gaze in both directions. He remained tensed, coiled as if to strike. "Same as you, I figure."

Rsiran frowned. Could Thom know about what happened to Brusus? "Why aren't you guarding my father?"

Thom turned away from Rsiran and went to the front door, peeking through the small window. When satisfied, he turned back to Rsiran. "You think I'm the only one hired for the job?"

"How many others did he hire?"

Thom shrugged. "They don't tell me too much. Besides, I'm only helping as a favor. Watching an old man in the woods can be done by anyone."

Brusus wouldn't trust just anyone to watch Rsiran's father. That meant he trusted Thom. Who else did he trust enough to watch his father?

"You know what happened?" Rsiran asked.

Thom shrugged, eyeing him carefully. "For the most part. How'd you learn?"

"I was with him."

Thom glanced at the table with Brusus's blood on it. "You get him out?"

Rsiran nodded.

"Where?"

He considered what to tell Thom. Brusus might trust him, but Rsiran wasn't sure that he did. "He's safe," he said.

Thom sniffed and nodded toward the table. His scar seemed to writhe as he did. "Don't look like he's safe. Where is he?"

"I took him to a healer. She's trying to help him."

"Trying?"

Rsiran nodded. "He was poisoned." He took a shaky breath. "He might not make it. She doesn't know what poison they used."

Thom seemed to consider for a moment. "You see who did it?"

"Not well. They were from Elaeavn, if that's what you're asking."

"You sure?"

Rsiran nodded. "We caught one."

"Just one? He still alive?"

"For now."

A dark smile twisted Thom's face. "You going to murder him if he don't survive? That your plan?"

Rsiran hadn't fully considered what he would do if Brusus didn't survive. But taking out his frustration on the man that had attacked him—and threatened Jessa—seemed as good a plan as any.

"Why do you care?"

"Don't. You just don't strike me as the murdering type."

"You have no idea what 'type' I am."

"No? So you could just walk over to a man," he started, stalking toward Rsiran, his sword raised, "and take your blade and stick it into his gut?"

Almost faster than Rsiran could think, Thom's sword swept toward Rsiran.

He *pushed* the lorcith knives away from him to block the sword. They crossed and slid the sword up and away, deflecting the attack.

Rsiran Slid back a step as he *pushed* the knives along Thom's sword until they reached the hilt, holding the sword away.

Thom dropped his sword. It clattered to the ground. Then he raised his hands up.

"Guess I *do* need to watch out for your blades," he said.

The knives hung in the air in front of Thom. He watched them, a curious expression shining in his eyes. Rsiran *pulled* them back and caught them out of the air.

Thom smiled. "See? You aren't the type."

Rsiran frowned. Had the attack been to prove his point? He glanced at the sword lying on the ground. Definitely one of his. Above the hilt was his mark. "I could have killed you!"

"But you didn't. Me? Someone comes after me with a sword like that, I put them down so they don't try it again." His smile widened. "But like I said, you're not the murdering type. Otherwise, from what I heard, you would have put a knife into your father long ago. Not like you haven't had the opportunity. From what I see, not much slows you."

Rsiran looked away, tucking his knives back into his pocket. He held onto the connection, prepared to *push* them at Thom if he made any movement toward him again.

But Thom simply grabbed his sword off the ground and sheathed it quickly. "Interesting ability you have there. Useful, I should think. Man who can slip anywhere, send his knives at a target... such a man has value."

"Thought you said I wasn't a killer."

Thom laughed. "I said you weren't a murderer. Being a killer is a different thing altogether."

Rsiran shook his head. "You're right. That isn't me."

Thom made his way toward the door. "Too bad. Brusus might have found you useful." He reached the door and twisted the handle.

Rsiran Slid to him and pushed on the door. "What do you mean?"

Thom looked over. "If what I've seen and you've told me is right, Brusus is dying. Were it you, I know what he'd be doing."

"And what is that?"

Thom smiled again. "Brusus would be getting revenge."

Rsiran shook his head. "That's not the Brusus I know. If it were me, he'd be doing everything he could to find a cure."

"You think so? So that's what you're doing, then?"

Rsiran thought of the way Brusus had made sure Rsiran had the healing he needed when they'd first met, the way he hadn't asked anything in return. He'd given him access to a smithy, a place to work and learn to listen to the lorcith, never asking for anything. "I know he would."

"Hmm. Then what are you going to do?"

Rsiran sighed. "He's already with a healer. There's not much more I *can* do."

"But you said your healer isn't sure she can save him."

"I said she didn't know what poison was used. She'll figure it out."

"And if she don't? You think with your abilities, there's nothing you can do to help?"

"I'm no healer."

Thom's smile returned. "Maybe not. But there are places where such things are learned."

Rsiran frowned. "What sorts of things?"

"Poisons. Healing. There might be a price, but if you could help him, wouldn't it be worth it?"

Rsiran considered what Thom said. Wouldn't Della know if there was a place to find a cure? As a Healer—one gifted by the Great Watcher—wouldn't she know if there was something more that could be done? Why would Thom know and not Della?

"Where is this place?"

Thom shook his head. "Not a place I can describe. Got to show you. You can take another along with you when you… travel?" he asked.

"You know the answer to that."

"Ah, that's right. Your girl." His smile had a dark quality to it. "It's a place in Thyr. Not easy to reach, but with your ability…"

"I've never been to Thyr," Rsiran said.

Thom studied him for a moment and then nodded. "Then take me with you, and I'll show you."

Thyr. The last time he'd left Elaeavn—really left the city and Slid to Asador—he'd found his father. Only he hadn't known it was his father at the time. What Thom suggested meant he would need to Slide blindly again. Doing so was difficult work, draining. And taking another would be hard.

But if there was a chance to save Brusus? If Thom knew of a place where a cure could be found, shouldn't Rsiran take it? Thom was wrong about Brusus; Rsiran knew he would do anything if Rsiran or Jessa were in his place.

"What is this place?" Rsiran asked.

"I told you. It's a place you might find an antidote."

"But we don't even know what poison was used."

Thom shrugged. "For some cures, that don't matter."

Rsiran sighed. He already knew what he'd do. What he *had* to do.

"Does this place have a name?"

"Near Thyr. A place called Venass." Thom watched Rsiran as he said it.

Venass. Rsiran had never heard of any place like that, but he wasn't nearly as worldly as Brusus or Haern. He could ask Della, but he suspected she'd tell him not to go. She knew everything Rsiran had been through.

Then there was the issue of what to do about Jessa. When she awoke, she'd be angry if she learned he went without her. Leaving her behind would keep her safe… but bringing her might keep *him* safe. With her Sight, she helped him as often as he helped her.

As much as it might put her in danger, he needed her.

"You will show us Venass? If I Slide us there, you will show us to it?"

"Us?"

Rsiran nodded. Taking both Jessa and Thom might be more than he could manage, especially over great distances. But he had to try. Hopefully all the practice Sliding he'd done recently had strengthened him.

Thom seemed to consider before answering. Then his smile returned. The scar seemed to writhe again as he did. "For you, I think I will."

Rsiran let out a relieved sigh. At least he was doing something that might help Brusus.

CHAPTER 7

T HEY EMERGED IN THE PALE BLUE LIGHT of his smithy. Shadows seemed to slip along the walls. Had he not known better, he would have wondered whether the smithy was empty.

The bitter scent of lorcith assaulted him as soon as they emerged. Jessa released his hand and hurried to the long table and grabbed a pair of long slender steel knives. Rsiran touched her hand and shook his head.

"Lorcith blades."

She frowned.

"They're larger than your charm. I'm more attuned to them."

"What if…"

He knew what she wondered. He'd wondered the same. "I don't think there's another who can use that ability. Certainly not where we're going."

She took one of the long-bladed lorcith knives and tucked it into the waist of her pants. Then she took a steel blade as well. "You don't know that. Better to be safe."

Rsiran laughed as he grabbed ten of his small lorcith blades. He stuffed them into his pockets, wishing he'd thought ahead and fashioned something to hold them. That could come later, if they saved Brusus.

"Ready?" he asked her.

Jessa took a quick look around the smithy. "You don't want the sword?"

Rsiran didn't have to look to know where it was. Tucked beneath a floorboard, he kept it hidden. Something about this sword was different from anything else he'd forged. He felt a connection to it even stronger than what he felt to the knives. "I don't even know how to use a sword. The knives I can *push*."

She took his hand and they Slid, emerging near the wooden hut.

The air smelled different here, cleaner and with less of the bitter odor. The sjihn trees had a distinct smell, a mixture of pine and jasmine that left a perfume on the air the steady wind couldn't quite blow away.

"How do you want to go about this?" Jessa asked. "Did he tell you where to meet?"

Rsiran shook his head. "Only by the cabin, nothing more."

Jessa knelt before the lock, unrolling her lock-pick set. "Maybe I just pick the lock. Keep your strength this way."

"Don't want to just appear inside again?"

Rsiran spun and saw Thom grinning at him, one hand hovering over his sword. Moonlight gleamed off the long scar atop his head just as it had the night before.

"You left him alone?"

Thom shrugged. "He's not going anywhere. That door is as stout as any I've seen. The lock too." He narrowed his eyes. "So you get what you need?"

Jessa tucked her lock-pick set back into her pocket as she approached. "Didn't even have it locked," she whispered.

Thom smiled again. "Like I said, he's not going anywhere."

"Why did you want to meet us here?" Rsiran asked.

"Thought we could move more easily from here. Besides, didn't you want to see him again?" A dark smile pulled on his lips.

"No," Rsiran said. He glanced at the wooden building before turning his attention back to Thom. "Are you ready?"

"I thought you'd be bringing Brusus with you."

"Like I said, he's with a healer. I thought you said you knew a place we could find an antidote."

Thom nodded, slowly, looking through the forest, back toward Elaeavn. "Be easier if he came—"

"He can't," Rsiran said. If he tried to bring Brusus, he would have to leave Jessa behind, and he wasn't willing to do that. Besides, once they found an antidote, he could Slide back to Elaeavn. "And what about him?" Rsiran asked.

Thom's smile returned. "He won't go anywhere. Besides, there are others who know where he is."

"Lock the door," Rsiran said to Jessa. "If everything goes well, we'll return before morning."

Thom eyed him. "You can travel that fast?"

Rsiran nodded. He wouldn't explain to Thom the limitations of Sliding. He didn't need to know that Rsiran had to know where he traveled; otherwise, he risked them during the Slide. Reaching Thyr would take the longest. The return would be easier.

"Hold onto my arm."

Jessa grabbed one hand and Thom watched for a moment before grabbing his other arm. Rsiran considered for a moment before Sliding. He needed to go north, but that was all he knew. Maybe he was making a mistake by trying to Slide all of them there. It would take multiple Slides to reach Thyr, and once they were there, he'd be almost too weakened to do much of anything.

But he would try.

He Slid, emerging as far north as he dared Slide in a single step. The Slide took more effort than he expected, straining him with the transition. The sense of movement was slower—probably from pulling two others with him—and colors streamed passed in swaths of browns and blacks. He'd often wondered whether the colors meant anything. Another question for Della someday.

A wave of fatigue threatened him, but he ignored it.

A cool breeze pulled at his clothes, filled with the scent of grasses and flowers. A wide plain stretched around them. In the distance, now to the south, Ilphaesn rose. The last time Rsiran had Slid this far, he was chasing the sense of the sword Josun had stolen.

Thom gasped. "You've taken us past Ilphaesn in a single step?"

"Which way?" Rsiran asked.

Thom seemed to sense the urgency and looked toward the east. "East. We can reach the Thyrass River and follow it." He pointed. "See that copse of trees over there?"

The moonlight caught them like a smudge of darkness in the distance. Jessa probably saw them clearly. "I see them."

"That way. The Thyrass should be just beyond there."

After making sure they both held onto him, Rsiran Slid toward the trees.

They emerged just at the edge of the trees. Rsiran made certain to keep them out of the shadows, not wanting to plunge too deep into darkness. After his time in the near perfect darkness of the mines, he hated anything that reminded him of it. At least in the mines, he had the sense of lorcith around him. Out here, the only lorcith he sensed was what he brought with him. And the distant pull of Ilphaesn.

Moonlight streamed from overhead, filtering through the upper branches waving in the wind. Shadows stretched across the ground, dancing and flickering. Rsiran felt the same uneasiness he'd felt in the smithy.

Jessa squeezed his hand. He wondered if she saw his unease or whether he'd tensed and she felt it. "See anything you recognize?" she asked Thom.

Thom released Rsiran's arm. He strode toward the trees and into the shadows, moving with a lithe grace that reminded Rsiran of the Neelish sellswords. Rsiran suddenly understood how dangerous Thom would be with his sword.

"Moving this way will take too long," Rsiran said. "Della said we have the night, but I'm not sure we have even that long."

Thom paused and looked back at them. "Della?"

Rsiran nodded. "She's the Healer helping Brusus."

He looked south, toward Elaeavn, and then nodded before turning toward the trees again.

"What do you mean that we might not have the night?" Jessa asked as Thom disappeared into the trees.

He shook his head, looking after Thom. Why was he going into the trees? "I saw the strain on her face after the short time we were there. It's different for you. Sight, I think, works differently. You never get tired from it like I do when I Slide."

"You said it's not as bad since you started practicing."

He nodded. "Not as bad, but not gone. It's worse when I Slide farther distances."

"Or when you bring too many with you?"

He nodded silently. "It's the same for Della with Healing, I think. The more she does, the more she strains. And what she's doing for Brusus is difficult. When she took her hands off him for long enough to grab the book, he started fading again."

"That's why you want to hurry."

"We can't lose them both. I worry about Della. For Brusus, she'll push herself until…"

Jessa squeezed his hand again and leaned into him.

Thom reappeared from the shadows. The moon glimmered off his scar. His mouth tightened into a grim line, and one hand gripped his sword. A finger width of steel reflected the moonlight.

"You said the river is through there?" Rsiran asked.

Thom nodded. "Can't see anything through the trees, but the Thyrass should be just beyond here. Can you move us past here?"

Rsiran looked around, considering where to Slide next. He could see to the northwest or south, but both directions left them farther from Thyr than they were already. Going beyond the forest meant that he would Slide blindly. That was dangerous. "How far do these woods stretch?"

Thom shrugged. "I couldn't tell. Not just a copse of trees, though."

From where they'd come, it hadn't seemed like any sort of forest, but Rsiran didn't know the geography around Elaeavn well. Maybe he should have asked Della for a map. That might have been useful. But could he Slide based on a map or would it not be reliable enough?

Thom shrugged again. "Not like your Aisl. But…"

Rsiran sighed. Everything was taking too long. Time they didn't have. Time Brusus didn't have. And if he couldn't get them to Thyr and back before morning, Brusus would die.

CHAPTER 8

Rsiran considered Sliding them to the north. Doing so might bypass the forest, but would also take more effort on his part. Already, he felt the strain each Slide took. How many more would he be able to make? Taking a detour might require more energy than he could spare, risking not being able to get them back safely. Had he been by himself, he might not have the same issue.

The other option—Sliding blindly—worried him. If they emerged somewhere dangerous, it wasn't just him he risked. It was Jessa and Thom.

The ground was too flat for him to get a good vantage. He glanced to the trees, thinking about whether he could reach one of the upper branches, but decided against it. The branches wouldn't support his weight, and he still wouldn't be able to see where he needed to go.

That left one option that made sense. He didn't like it; doing so meant Jessa would be left alone with Thom. But he had to trust she could handle herself. Wasn't that what she'd been asking him to do?

"Thom—stay with Jessa. I'm going to scout the next spot."

Jessa frowned at him. He could tell from her expression she knew what he planned. "Are you sure that's the right thing to do? Maybe we should stay together—"

"I'll find you." With a soft touch, he pulled on the knife tucked into her waistband.

Thom studied Rsiran's face. "How long?"

"No more than a minute or two."

Thom glanced at Jessa. His face was unreadable. "You're looking for a wide river. When you reach it, go north to Thyr, Venass lies just outside Thyr. Once there…" He shrugged.

Rsiran leaned toward Jessa. "Wait in the trees," he whispered. "I won't be long."

She smiled at him and punched his shoulder. "I'll be fine."

He released her hand and Slid.

Gauging the distance was difficult. From what he'd learned, moving blindly like this left him open to the possibility that he could emerge within a tree or a massive boulder, or buried in a hillside. Sliding required him to be able to move somewhat on his own.

This time, he paid careful attention to the colors blurring as he Slid, trying to mark the distance traveled. Sliding by himself went more quickly, but when he'd traveled what he thought was the same distance as the last Slide, he held his breath as he emerged.

Trees spread around him, one near enough that if he swung his arm he'd hit it. Had he emerged only a step later, he'd have been buried in the tree. His heart thumped loudly and sweat slicked his palms.

No light made it through the dense canopy overhead. All around him were gradients of shadows. Rsiran sucked in a breath, tasting the air. Different from the scent of the sjihn trees, the forest here smelled of earth and decaying leaves. Skin on the back of his neck crawled, and he had the vague sense of something moving behind him.

Rsiran didn't wait and Slid again.

He emerged at the edge of the forest. The darkness of the forest reached behind him, and a wide rolling plain stretched in front of him. A few small trees dotted the plain, but nothing else, and no sign of the river. He glanced behind him, and considered returning, but if he could find the river by himself, they would be that much closer to Thyr… and help for Brusus.

And another Slide, this time crossing the plain. In the distance, the terrain seemed to rise and get rocky.

Another Slide took him to the rocks. The air smelled… wet? He paused. He should return to Jessa, but was that the sound of rushing water he heard?

He Slid again, and this time, he emerged on a rocky slope. Massive stones scattered around him, lit by pale, silver moonlight, looking as if some enormous creature had thrown them around. Below him, a wide river flowed, splashing and burbling loudly in the otherwise silent night. Rsiran hoped this was the Thyrass.

This was as far as he was willing to go. He'd been gone from Jessa for moments, but he didn't like the idea of her left without him, not with a stranger she barely knew. Even if Brusus trusted Thom. And now that he'd been here, he could Slide back fairly easily once he had Jessa and Thom.

He listened for the sense of lorcith, waiting for the pull of Jessa's knife to call to him. For a moment, he couldn't sense it. Something seemed to blanket his sense of lorcith, as if diffusing it. He couldn't get a clear fix on the knife.

Panic rose up in him, similar to what he'd felt when Josun had taken her. He steadied his breathing. Likely a simple answer rather than something sinister. He'd never tested sensing for lorcith on her from a distance, especially now that he'd crafted her a chain out of the heartstone alloy. Perhaps the heartstone blocked him in some ways.

He strained, pushing through the strange fog obfuscating the sense of lorcith he knew was out there. And then, distantly, he sensed it.

Using it as an anchor, as he often did with his forged pieces, Rsiran Slid.

When he emerged, he had two of his blades ready to *push* at whatever might be blocking his sense of the lorcith knife. He stood within the trees again, just past the border of the forest. An owl hooted. Leaves rustled around him.

His panic returned when he couldn't see Jessa. He reached for the charm he knew she'd be wearing and felt it not ten paces from him.

"Jessa?" he whispered.

A shadow materialized. Had he been Sighted, he might have been able to see her before now. She stood, long-bladed knife in hand. When she approached, he noticed a wild and anxious expression in her eyes. Thom wasn't nearby.

"Rsiran?"

"Where's Thom? I think I found the Thyrass River. He said we could follow that to Thyr."

She shook her head. "There's something out here. When you Slid, we heard it moving in the trees. Thom went to look. I haven't seen him since."

Rsiran frowned. He couldn't have been gone more than a few minutes. In that time, they lost Thom. The one person he knew who might be able to help them reach Venass and find a way to reach the antidote.

"Where did you go?" he asked.

"I heard something and thought I could find him." She shook her head. "This place is strange, Rsiran. The trees seem to work against my Sight. Shadows slip around everything."

He frowned, wondering how that was possible. "Let's get out of the forest and give Thom a chance to reach us."

"If he doesn't?"

Rsiran didn't want to think of what they'd need to do if Thom didn't return. He wouldn't give up on helping Brusus—not now—but their chance of success went down without his help.

They Slid back through the trees. When they stepped past the edge of the forest, almost a hard line where the trees ended and the grassy plain began, a knot loosened in his chest that he hadn't known was there.

Rsiran spun, turning to face the trees. A faint sound, almost a rustling of leaves, fluttered but no wind blew across his face. A sense of movement flickered in the forest. He had the vague crawling sensation on the back of his neck again.

Jessa was right. Something was there.

Rsiran readied his knives, but he couldn't do anything if he couldn't *see* anything. And so far, all he had was the sense of another presence.

"What's in there?" he whispered to Jessa.

She stood next to him, one hand gripping the sleeve of his shirt. She knew from experience how quickly he could Slide them to safety. He always felt secure when she was by his side.

But she wasn't always there, was she?

She hadn't been there when his father had first pushed him out, telling him he wasn't welcome… that he was cursed. She hadn't been there with him in the dark of Ilphaesn, nothing but the sound of hammers striking at distant mines, only the call of lorcith for company. She hadn't been there when the shackles held him in place on Firell's ship, preventing him from moving. She hadn't been there when the terrifying fear of failing her had nearly overwhelmed him. And she hadn't been there when he'd had to confront…

Rsiran shook his head. Where had those thoughts come from?

He felt a tug on his arm and turned to see Jessa slowly sinking to the ground. A look of horror came across her face, making her eyes wide. Her mouth worked wordlessly. A light sheen covered her forehead. She stared into the forest, otherwise frozen in place.

Rsiran grabbed her hand to keep her from pulling away from him. What did she see?

What did it matter? He couldn't see anything. Always blind. And Jessa made sure he knew that. Just like everyone else—his sister, his mother, his father, probably even Brusus and the rest of them. Made him wonder why he even bothered coming here, so far from everything he knew, risking his life, exposing him for… what, exactly? When had Brusus *ever* risked himself for Rsiran? Or Jessa…

But Jessa *had* risked herself for him. Why would he think these things?

A cold sweat washed over him as he understood. With an effort, he slammed a barrier in his mind, and then added to it the sense of heartstone. Doing this was different from using a lorcith barrier. With that, the barrier in his mind had always seemed imagined. Using the alloy—adding heartstone—felt like he dragged it from deep within him, an effort that he never had when pulling on lorcith.

Without waiting another moment, he Slid.

They emerged on the rocks near the bank of the river. The air smelled clear and crisp, no longer holding the edge of the forest, the sense of decay from fallen leaves. Now a gentle wind did blow steadily at him, fluttering against his clothes and rustling his hair.

He listened, waiting to see if the terrible thoughts and fears would return. They didn't.

Hesitantly, he lowered the heartstone barrier. Holding that in place was more difficult than simply the lorcith barrier. Working with lorcith nearly daily, sensing it constantly, made it a part of him. He had no idea how he used it to enforce the barrier, only that when he discovered how to add heartstone to his mental barrier, even Della hadn't been able to Read him. With heartstone added, he suspected it acted much like the alloy, preventing even the most powerful Readers from entering his mind. Or more than that.

Jessa blinked slowly, as if awakening from a dream. Her eyes slowly narrowed, and she wiped a hand across her head. She let out a shaky breath and turned to look at him. She didn't let go of his hand. "You're leaving Thom?"

He let out a pent up breath. It came out as a jagged sigh. "Not leaving him. Not yet. But there was someone—or some*thing*—Pushing on us."

Jessa frowned. In the moonlight, he saw her bite her lip as she did. No flower was woven into the charm tonight. She'd taken it out before they left, not wanting the scent to risk giving them away. One hand fingered the hilt of the knife tucked into the band of her pants. "Pushed? Like what you do with lorcith?"

"Not like that. This is different. Like what Brusus does with everyone, but stronger. Darker." A shiver that had nothing to do with the cold worked through him.

Her eyes widened, and he knew she understood. "How do you know?"

He looked back toward the forest. Part of him could sense that darkness back there, as if it still dipped toward his mind, threatening to Push the dark thoughts back into him again. The forest was nothing but a memory from here. He closed his eyes, thinking of the Slide, listening for lorcith. At first, he'd thought maybe Jessa's heartstone chain had diffused his ability to sense it, but now he realized that wasn't it at all.

The strange diffusion of his sense of lorcith was still there, like a mist shrouding everything. He focused, trying to strain and pierce *through* the fog. This time, he had nothing to anchor to and he failed.

Rsiran swallowed. "Didn't you feel it? The pressing fear working through us?"

Jessa's eyes widened slightly, and he knew she'd felt it as well. He wondered what scared Jessa. Not the same as scared him. Did she fear being stranded in the dark, trapped within Ilphaesn with no way to escape, only her Sight keeping her from going mad? Or did she fear Josun's taunts, words meant to frighten? Rsiran had little doubt the man had said plenty to torment her, but Jessa spoke nothing about those experiences. Maybe the fear she'd felt was older, tied to whatever had brought her and Brusus together in the first place.

Whatever she'd felt, the way her face twisted told him she'd felt the same as he had.

"How… how did you know?"

"Those thoughts weren't mine," he answered. Not thoughts of Jessa abandoning him. She would not do that, not after all that they'd been through.

But what had she seen? What left the edge of horror in her eyes?

"We left Thom behind us. In there… with whatever did that to us."

Rsiran hated the idea of leaving Thom there alone. Would he be as susceptible as they had been to whatever Pushed on them or was he left alone?

But worse than that, without Thom, neither of them would know how to reach Thyr in time. Neither of them would be able to find Venass. Certainly not before morning. And Brusus didn't have any more time for them to spare.

Rsiran turned to Jessa, but her face reflected what he felt. Both were already resigned to the fact that they'd failed.

Chapter 9

"I have to go back for him," Rsiran said.

Jessa looked over at him, shaking her head as she did. "You can't go back. What happens if whatever is there…"

He touched her hand and offered a smile. It felt forced, especially not knowing what he would have to face. Something with the ability to Push darkness on his thoughts.

"I can barrier my mind." He spoke more confidently than he felt, but he would have to try.

Jessa shook her head. "No, Rsiran. We can't go back there."

"Not we."

She grabbed onto his hand, as if afraid that he'd Slide from her without warning. "You're not going anywhere without me," she said.

"I can't protect you from this. And we need Thom to find Venass."

"He told you how to find it. We can just—"

"Leave him?" Rsiran finished. "Sacrifice him for Brusus? What would Brusus say if he found out that we did?"

She glanced to the ground. "We wouldn't have to tell him."

Rsiran pulled her to him. "You can wait here. I won't be gone long. I'll Slide, see what I can find, and search for Thom."

Her body tensed and she shivered. "What if you don't—you *can't*—return? What happens to me then?"

Rsiran couldn't leave her here. Not without knowing she would be safe.

He squeezed her hand and Slid, emerging in the heart of the Aisl Forest. The damp earth smelled clean and healthy compared to the forest where they'd lost Thom. A howl erupted, and Jessa jumped, twisting to look around her.

"Why did you bring me here?"

"Wait here. I'll return after I find Thom."

"And if you don't return?"

Rsiran didn't want to think about what would happen if he didn't. It likely meant that whatever darkness existed in the forest had swallowed him as well. He didn't think that he could withstand it if his barrier failed, not without more strength than he possessed.

"If I don't, then you'll go to Della's, and be there for Brusus in the time he has remaining."

He hugged her close and kissed her forehead before releasing her. She let go of his hand slowly. When he Slid, the colors swirling past him, he could almost see the pain on her face.

When he emerged from the Slide, the forest loomed in front of him. He made certain to emerge where the forest started, and stood, watching the steady swaying of the trees for a moment. As soon as he emerged, the darkness started to Push on him, but this time, Rsiran had been ready. He pressed the mental barriers into place, fortifying them with heartstone.

With a Slide, he passed beyond the border of the forest.

Pain shot through his head. Rsiran held onto the barrier, forcing it to remain in place. If it failed, he didn't doubt that he would succumb to the effect of the darkness Pushing on him.

Shadows shifted in the night. Rsiran resisted the urge to Slide away, holding a pair of knives ready for him to *push* away. The sense faded, and he Slid deeper into the trees.

He wasn't certain what he looked for, or what he hoped to find. Had Thom carried one of his lorcith-forged knives, he might have been able to find him more easily, but without the knife, he was searching blindly.

Maybe it didn't matter. Thom had told them how to find Venass. Follow the Thyrass River, make his way north… and then? What would they find?

And if he didn't? What would really change for him? After what Brusus had done, how he'd pulled Jessa and him into his plan to find the Forgotten, could they really forgive him? The Forgotten—at least Josun—knew about what Rsiran could do. Would they come after him, and Jessa? Would they ever really be safe? Maybe it would be best if Brusus *did* die.

Rsiran shivered, recognizing that somehow the Pushed thoughts had made it past his barrier. He focused, pulling on the sense of lorcith, fusing it with that of heartstone, and felt the barrier solidify.

He realized Sliding had changed it. He couldn't Slide and hold the connection to the barrier.

Now that he knew, he would focus as he Slid, make certain that when he emerged, he reinforced the barrier.

But how to find Thom?

Worse, what was out here in the forest?

He needed to work quickly. Not only because he didn't want to remain within the trees any longer than necessary, but also because Brusus depended on him. Regardless of what the thoughts Pushed on him wanted, Rsiran wanted Brusus alive. If the Elvraeth were after them, they would manage that together.

A search. That was what he needed. And he could Slide, moving quickly through the forest. He'd practiced Sliding, so that doing so alone shouldn't be too taxing, but he would need to work quickly so he didn't waste time.

And maybe, if he emerged fast enough, he wouldn't have to focus on his barriers quite as much.

It was worth trying.

Jessa said that Thom had gone deeper into the forest. Rsiran started by Sliding along the edge of the forest, stepping quickly, emerging long enough to search for Thom before Sliding again. Thankfully, enough moonlight trailed through the trees for him to see the forest floor.

He pushed up the barrier again. He had to be careful. Thoughts that were not his drifted in, slipping over his barriers, or around them when they were lowered long enough to Slide.

When he reached the end of the forest, he Slid forward a dozen feet before starting back, Sliding quickly. Each time he emerged from the Slide, he glanced around and then Slid again.

Rsiran lost count of how many times he'd Slid. Occasionally, he caught sight of movement, but it was never there when he Slid toward it. He forced up his mental barriers, and the dark thoughts never fully returned. Maybe he Slid fast enough that it didn't matter.

He was near the center of the forest when he saw a shape lying on the forest floor.

Rsiran *pushed* a pair of knives in front of him, holding them in place. He took a step forward, moving carefully. Another step. Without realizing it, he Slid with each step.

Thom lay on the ground, face down. A pool of blood spilled out around him, staining his shirt. Rsiran couldn't see the injury, but no one could survive that much blood, not without Healing.

Could he take him to Della? The Healer might be able to help… but if he did, Brusus would be left to die. Besides, that much blood… there was nothing that he could do, not for Thom.

The slender steel sword that Thom carried rested on the ground just out of reach.

Rsiran sighed. Now what would he do? Thom was going to lead them to Venass, and guide them toward where to find an antidote, but without him, how would they find it?

Brusus would be lost. He might be able to follow the river toward Thyr, but then what?

He knelt next to Thom. The man had told him to go north to find Venass, but how would they know what they were looking for?

Rsiran reached for Thom's sword when he felt shadows shifting around him.

He stood with a start and *pushed* a pair of knives away from him, out into the darkness of the forest. They whistled through the air, but he didn't hear them hit anything.

As he turned back to Thom, he thought he saw the shadows shift again.

Rsiran didn't have enough knives to waste on darkness.

A howl erupted in the night.

Hating what he did, he Slid away, emerging back in the Aisl.

Jessa paced the small clearing, and relief was plain on her face when she saw him, but it faded when she realized that he'd come alone. "Where's Thom?"

Rsiran shook his head. "I found him…"

"But what?"

"He's gone, Jessa. Something attacked him. I don't know what it was, but there was a lot of blood and I knew we couldn't save him. As I knelt beside him, I saw shadows of it moving in the forest. I couldn't risk staying behind."

She grabbed his wrist and caught his eyes. "We can go back, but after. When it's light. Then we can give him a proper burial."

Rsiran let out a frustrated sigh.

"What now? We go back? Tell Della we failed?"

That didn't seem like any sort of answer. Not one that Rsiran could accept. They still had time. Maybe if they got lucky…if he managed to Slide them to Thyr, they could find Venass on their own. He had seen what he suspected was the Thyrass, so they could follow that, and he could Slide along the shore. With just Jessa, it would be quick work, less straining to him.

But once they reached Thyr? He knew little more than that Venass would be found to the north. And once they reached it, they still had to find the antidote.

There were just too many ways for it to go wrong.

But they didn't know anyone else who could help them find what they needed in Thyr. Della might be able to do so, but Brusus depended on her to keep him alive through the night. Haern might know how to help. In a former life, he'd lived as an assassin and trained in Thyr, but they had no way of finding him quickly. They might spend the entire night just searching for him. Rsiran didn't know anyone else he could trust.

There was someone else who might be able to help, though. Someone he didn't trust… and knew he couldn't trust. But would he help? After everything, it was unlikely, but doing nothing was not an answer, either.

"What is it?" Jessa asked.

He looked at her. As always, he wondered how she saw through him so easily. Even with barriers in place, she always seemed to know a little of what he was thinking. Did she know him so well?

Of course, he knew the answer to that.

"There's someone else we can try who might know how to find Venass, who can help us reach Thyr."

Jessa frowned and then her eyes clouded. She blinked and shook her head. "No, Rsiran. We can't do that. You don't know what he'll do. Besides, he's got no reason to help you!" She trembled again. "We can find Haern. If anyone will know how to reach Thyr and Venass, it will be him. We just have to—"

"Just have to find him. How long will that take? Maybe it's minutes. Maybe hours. If it's the latter, we've lost Brusus."

"You'd risk losing him on the chance that he'd help? He's got no reason to help you."

Rsiran shook his head. "He won't be helping me. But he has plenty of reason to help."

CHAPTER 10

THEY EMERGED IN THE CLEARING OUTSIDE the small wooden hut. It seemed so long ago that he'd been there, but in reality, little time had actually passed. A faint streamer of smoke drifted from the small hole in the roof, the scent mixing with the piney odor of the sjihn trees surrounding them. The wind was still, a sharp change from what it'd been on the banks of the Thyrass River.

Rsiran glanced at Jessa. She nodded. Then they Slid into the hut.

The only light came from glowing embers of the fire. Not enough for him to see well. Jessa wouldn't have the same limitations. He waited as she scanned the room. "I don't know where—"

"You've finally decided to take a stronger hand in tormenting me?"

Rsiran turned. His father sat cross-legged in the corner, as far from the fire and the flat bed pallet as possible. Shadows clung to him.

"I sensed when you came earlier. I knew you'd return."

That was as much an admission of his father sensing lorcith as Rsiran suspected he'd get. But did he share the other ability? Could he push on lorcith like Rsiran? And what about heartstone? Had he mastered that?

"You've been to Thyr." Rsiran didn't ask it as a question. After what happened to Thom, there was no purpose to disguise why he'd come. Brusus didn't have time for him to waste on his father.

Jessa squeezed his hand, keeping him from stalking forward.

For a moment, he didn't know if his father would answer. Then, "I've been to Thyr."

The admission surprised Rsiran. Though Thom claimed he had, hearing his father admit to it was different. "When?"

His father shifted, a sound little more than a rustling of cloth against the wooden walls. "If you came to ask questions of me, then you'll be disappointed. I have nothing to say to you."

Rsiran snorted. "You've never had anything to say to me. Why should this be any different?"

"Rsiran?" Jessa whispered.

"Say your peace and leave me," his father said. "You can't hurt me anymore than they've already tried."

Rsiran swallowed. This was the hard part. "You will take me to Thyr and then onto Venass. There is something I need to find there tonight—"

"I'm not sneaking through the night like a common thief. And I'm not traveling with you as you use your… ability."

Rsiran took a deep breath and held it in. "As I said. I need to reach Venass tonight. You will assist me in this."

His father laughed softly, low in his throat. "There is nothing you can say that will convince me to go with you to Thyr."

Rsiran took a step closer. He wasn't sure he could be convincing in the threat he'd present, but he needed to be for this to work. "If you don't, then I will do to Alyse what you did to me."

He heard his father's soft gasp, and Rsiran knew he'd guessed right. "You wouldn't do that to your sister."

Rsiran took another step forward. His father stood out from the shadows of the wall. He hardened his voice. "Because Alyse was always so helpful to me? I'm sure she didn't care when I was sent off to Ilphaesn. She certainly didn't argue very strongly to keep me at home."

"Leave her out of this. Blame me if you must, but your sister never did anything."

"You just made my point."

His father lunged like a coiled snake, moving faster and with more force than he should have managed with as long as he'd been trapped in the hut.

Rsiran was ready for it.

He twisted to the side and grabbed his father's arm. Then he Slid, emerging just outside the hut, releasing his father as he did. He went sprawling into dry dirt. Moonlight filtered through the trees here, giving enough light for Rsiran to see. A sharpened, slender length of wood dropped from his father's hand. Rsiran Slid to it and kicked it away from his reach.

His father grunted and didn't move.

Jessa came through the door and hurried over to him. She grabbed his hand, as if afraid he would take the opportunity of having his father sprawled across the ground to get revenge. She never seemed to believe that he didn't hold much anger over his exile.

"Like I said," Rsiran said again, "you are going to take me to Thyr and then onto Venass."

His father pushed slowly to his knees and sat. Now that they were out where Rsiran had enough light to see, he realized a deep bruise had bloomed under one eye in the time since he'd seen him last. A dark sneer spread over his face. "And you keep making my point, don't you, Rsiran?"

"And what point might that be?"

"That as much as you claim otherwise, your cursed ability has changed something in you." He wiped his hands on the dirty scraps that were his pants and stood. Rsiran readied to Slide after him if he chose to run. He couldn't risk any more time spent on this. "As I told you it would, it turned you into something worse than a mere thief."

After everything he'd been through, the words still stung. Had he not become the thief his father expected, stealing lorcith from the Ilphaesn mines? Had he not sneaked into the warehouse, repeatedly taking what wasn't his? Worse than that, he'd broken into the alchemist guild house. And now, he'd been brought into a battle between the Elvraeth, both those within the palace and the Forgotten.

His father had always claimed his ability would turn him into a thief, but he *had* become something worse than that. Hadn't he attacked Josun? The first time, he could claim self-defense, the need to protect himself and Jessa, but leaving Josun to suffer and die within the mines was something else entirely.

Rsiran sighed. Everything his father had said about his ability had been true.

That still didn't change what Rsiran needed to do.

"No," Rsiran said. Jessa grabbed his hand and squeezed. "You turned me into that."

He Slid and grabbed his father by the arm, returning to the rocky shore of the Thyrass River.

Chapter 11

The wind had shifted since they'd been on the rocks only minutes before, gusting now out of the west. A hint of the forest hung on the air, that of decay and wet earth, this time mixed with something else, almost a bitter odor. Rsiran dropped his father's arm, letting him slip to the rocks, not concerned if he hurt himself as he slid along the boulders. Jessa tottered atop one of the massive boulders, and Rsiran held her tightly, keeping her from falling.

Fatigue washed over him. He'd have to be careful as they made their way, or he wouldn't have enough strength to get them back. The time in the forest had not only delayed them, it risked him not having the strength needed to Slide them all to Venass and then back home.

"I'm still not sure this was smart," she whispered.

Jessa knew the toll Sliding had on him, and that was just moving the two of them around the city. What he did tonight was harder even than that. "When have I ever done anything smart?"

She punched his shoulder. "You brought me, didn't you?"

"Only because I knew what would happen to me if I didn't."

Jessa laughed, a smile coming to her eyes as she did. "Only because you know what's good for you. Moving around at night looking for something in the dark is what *I'm* good at."

Rsiran smiled. "I think Della would have killed me on your behalf had I left you behind."

As he said it, he noticed his father looking at him, a strange expression on his face.

Rsiran looked down at him. He'd crawled back atop one of the large rocks lining the river and sat staring down at the froth, the same as they had done earlier. "I presume this is the Thyrass River." His father nodded once. "Where from here?"

"If you already found the Thyrass, you should be able to find Thyr without difficulty."

That was the same thing Thom had said. "I told you. I don't need Thyr. I need Venass."

His brow furrowed. "Venass is north of Thyr. More than that I can't really…"

"For Alyse's sake, you'd better come up with a better answer than that."

His father shook his head slightly. "What do you hope to accomplish? You think by finding Thyr, you'll get some kind of reward with me? Or do you plan to steal something else?" He sneered at him. "You're nothing but a thief."

"Careful," Rsiran said. "This thief could leave you wherever he chooses."

His father's eyes narrowed, and he closed his mouth.

Rsiran made sure to hold onto Jessa and stepped down the rocks rather than Sliding. He grabbed his father by the sleeve. The river snaked north in front of them. Behind him, it ran fairly straight south.

Rsiran fixed on the farthest point he could see in the distance. Had he been Sighted, he might have an easier time choosing his targets. What must it have been like for Josun, being Sighted and able to Slide without the limitations Rsiran had?

He Slid, pulling them along the river. Each time, he emerged only long enough to look for another point in the distance. The rock lining the river sloped upward, the river cutting a deeper valley as they went, making it difficult to find a clear vantage. If he could find higher ground, he could fixate on a farther point and Slide a greater distance. Instead, he was forced to travel much more slowly than he would like.

Sliding by himself over great distances was taxing. The time he'd Slid to Asador chasing after his sword, he'd nearly not had the strength to return. Practicing Sliding had increased his comfort with both distances and burden, taking Jessa with him as often as possible, exercising it no differently than he had exercised his arms and chest working the forge. But as much as he'd improved, he still struggled under the burden of transporting three of them.

With each Slide, he sagged under the effort. He didn't want to admit it, but he began to wonder if he'd be able to get them all back to Elaeavn once they found Venass and the antidote. Would he be forced to leave one of them behind? If so, it wouldn't be Jessa. She'd been through too much for him to risk her again. Besides, he needed her Sight.

And then a Slide took them to a ledge overlooking the distant land. Water from the Thyrass cascaded down from the shelf, spilling to a point far below as it ran somewhat east. There, flat ground spread out toward an enormous city in the distance. The river cut through the heart of the city and seemed to keep going, beyond the city, likely all the way to the sea. Rsiran saw no sign of the ocean from where he stood.

Within the city, buildings taller than any in Elaeavn stretched high into the sky, some with bright lights filling the windows. One stood taller than the others, a thick tower made of a pale white stone rose near the edge of the city. A high wall circled the city.

"Is that Thyr?" Jessa whispered.

"That's Thyr," his father said. Rsiran had released him, letting him stand atop the rock next to them. There was no place for him to run. "Home to the Tower of Scholars." He sniffed and looked away. "Great Watcher only knows what else."

"What do you mean by that?" Rsiran stared at the tower that must be the Tower of Scholars rising above the city.

"Scholars claim they can understand anything, even the Great Watcher himself."

Rsiran glanced at Jessa, and she only shrugged. "You never told me you'd ever been to Thyr."

His father looked at him. Once, he'd been a wide man, thick with muscle, and intimidating to Rsiran. The time after Rsiran had been apprenticed with him had taken much from his father, not the least of which was mass from his body, leaving him lean and wasted. No longer did he intimidate Rsiran as he once had. He still managed the same look he'd always given him, one filled with a mixture of condescension and disgust. Rsiran did not turn away from it this time.

"No."

Rsiran shook his head, sniffing out an annoyed laugh. "I could leave you here when we're done, if you like."

"Doesn't matter to me. I'm already dead as it is."

"You think mother would like it if you were dead? Alyse?"

His father stiffened but said nothing.

Jessa touched is arm. "You don't need to keep doing that to him. He's helping you already."

"Doing what?"

She pulled him close and wrapped her arms around him. In the cool of the night, it was the only thing that felt good. She smelled clean, her hair infused with the scent of whatever flowers she'd been picking lately. Nothing like the bitter scent of lorcith he had grown so accustomed to. He hugged her back, resting his chin atop her head.

"How is this any better than what he did to you?" She reached up and touched his face. "You don't need to torture him anymore. You're a better man than he is. I can see that."

The words made Rsiran smile, and he leaned toward her and kissed her on the mouth. She tasted sweet, like a mixture of mint and ale. For a moment, he could forget about everything else, as if the Great Watcher had finally given him everything he needed.

But the moment passed. Rsiran couldn't forget why he'd come. Brusus needed him to succeed. And if Brusus died, Rsiran may never understand what he'd been pulled into. As much as he wanted to help his friend, he wanted answers as well.

He released the embrace and stepped away from Jessa. She stood next to him, holding his hand, as he turned to his father. This time, he softened his voice. "This is where I need your help. Where is Venass from here?"

His father looked as if he might say something, but instead just frowned at him. "What is your business in Venass?"

Rsiran considered lying or simply demanding that his father tell him how to reach it, but decided against it. "A good man will die if I can't reach Venass tonight."

"What kind of good man?"

He met his father's eyes. "The one who saved me when you'd given up on me."

Emotions flickered across his father's face. Rsiran could read none of them. Finally, his mouth tightened. "Do you know what you're looking for?"

"A cure."

His father frowned. "And you think you can find it in one night. In the dark?"

"I don't have any choice. I have to try."

He shook his head and looked away. "Then you're a fool."

There was a note in his voice that gave Rsiran pause. "Can you show me how to find Venass?"

He didn't look over. "Do I have any choice?"

"There's always a choice."

His father turned. "Is there?"

He'd made plenty of choices recently. Not all of them good, and few easy, but he'd always had a choice. "Regardless of what I do, there's always a choice."

"We'll see."

His father stood and took a few steps toward the ledge, beside the waterfall, and leaned forward. Almost too late, Rsiran realized what he was doing and muttered a quiet curse under his breath. If he did nothing, his father would die from the fall. And Brusus would die.

"I'm sorry," he said to Jessa. And let go of her hand as he Slid after his father.

He emerged falling alongside his father.

Wind whistled around him. Rsiran wondered what he'd been thinking. Doing this could mean his death if he was wrong. But it definitely meant Brusus's death if he did nothing.

Above him, Jessa screamed.

He'd never tried to Slide like this before. As far as he knew, it should work the same as taking a step. He prayed to the Great Watcher that it did.

His father was right in front of him. And now the ground loomed before both of them. Another moment, and he'd be too late.

Rsiran grabbed his father by the back of his dirty shirt and Slid again, aiming for the ground. Normally, he had to step into the Slide. This time, he fell.

He emerged rolling onto his side. It didn't lessen the impact, though, and as he hit the ground, his elbow jabbed hard into his side, forcing the air from his lungs. His father rolled next to him and grunted.

Rsiran lay motionless for a moment, feeling to see if anything hurt. His ribcage felt like it might be broken, his arm having pushed into it on landing. It hurt to take a deep breath. His hand ached from gripping his father's shirt. But nothing else.

He stood and resisted the temptation to kick his father. "What were you thinking?" he shouted. "I thought you wanted to see Alyse again!"

His father rolled over. Dirt stained his face and his nose was bloodied, running toward his ear. A dark smile twisted his mouth. "And I said I was already dead. You just haven't seen it yet." He crawled to his knees and looked up the waterfall, shaking his head as he did. "Thought you said I had a choice."

Rsiran grunted. "You did."

His father got to his feet. He stood unsteadily and wiped his hand across his face, smearing the blood that had dripped down his face and brought his hand out to look at it. Then he shook his head again, looking back up to where he'd stood moments ago.

"Then why didn't you let me fall?"

Rsiran grunted again. "You don't get it, do you?"

His father looked back and met his eyes. "Get what?"

"I had a choice too."

Chapter 12

Rsiran left his father standing at the edge of the Thyrass River as he Slid back to the rocks to reach Jessa. As soon as he emerged, she punched him hard on the chest.

"Just what was *that*?" she demanded.

"I couldn't let him fall."

"You risked yourself for him? After everything he did to you?"

He shook his head. "I don't expect you to understand."

She punched him again, this time with a little less force. "You think I don't understand? What I wouldn't give up to see… to see…" She didn't finish. Tears welled in her eyes and she fell into him.

Rsiran pulled her close. He was the reason she cried this time, the reason she hurt. And he'd be the reason she hurt if anything happened to him. Had he really been willing to risk himself for his father?

"I'm sorry."

She pounded on him with closed fists. "You said that already." Her voice sounded muffled as she spoke against him. "Doesn't make it better."

"I know. And I'm sorry." He pushed her back far enough that he could see her face, holding her eyes with his. Hers flared a bright green and she swallowed. "I didn't have time to explain. I don't think I was in any danger... at least no real danger."

"But you didn't know."

He shook his head. "I didn't know," he agreed. "I've never tried Sliding while falling." Now that he had, knowing he could might be helpful, if he could only manage to control the fall at the end. He couldn't end up splayed across the ground each time he Slid, hoping to be unhurt. He'd have to figure out a way to do it more safely. And that meant practicing. Jessa wouldn't care for that, either.

"He's right, you know."

Rsiran frowned. The idea that his father might be right about anything anymore troubled him. "About what?"

"You *are* a fool."

Rsiran laughed softly. "Probably."

He looked over the rocks. His father still stood along the bank of the Thyrass River, staring into the swirling water where it spilled down from the rocks. A thought came to him—if his father *really* wanted to end things, he could simply throw himself into that water. Rsiran doubted he'd be able to Slide into the water and out quickly enough to save them both. He'd never tried water, but it seemed a level of magnitude more difficult than even falling.

"We shouldn't leave him down there by himself too long. I don't know what he might try next," Rsiran said.

Jessa peered over the edge of the rocks, leaning forward more dangerously than Rsiran expected of her, especially after the fall. "I wish we didn't need him for this."

"Me too."

She turned and looked Rsiran in the eyes. "No. I mean it. I don't know what this will do to you. It took you months to get past what he's done to you."

Rsiran smiled sadly. "That's the problem. He's my father. I'll never get past it. Or him."

Jessa bit her lip, and Rsiran wondered if she thought about her father. He knew only a little about him, just that he had been a thief and had been taken away where they had cut off his hand for thieving. Jessa had been saved by Haern, brought back to Elaeavn, but more than that, he didn't know. Eventually she would tell him.

"Don't let him be the reason you get hurt," Jessa said. "Promise me that."

"I promise."

They Slid to the bottom of the waterfall, with water swirling around them, Jessa stalked over to Rsiran's father. She stood nearly a head shorter than him, and her shoulder-length hair fluttered in the breeze. Hands went to her hips, one fingering the hilt of the long knife she tucked into her waist, and she leaned toward him. Rsiran sensed the anger radiating from her.

"If you *ever* do anything to place Rsiran in harm's way again, you won't have to worry about what he'll do to you."

His father glanced from Jessa to Rsiran. A small smile twisted his mouth. Blood had dried around his nose, and he'd wiped most of it away.

"Because I'll be there first." She lowered her voice. Rsiran still heard what she said next. He suspected she wanted him to. "And I won't have the same hesitation to do what's needed to your precious Alyse."

Then she turned and stalked back over to Rsiran. She looked away, staring out toward Thyr. The message was clear to him, and he knew not to press her about what she'd said. Rsiran didn't actually think she'd do anything to Alyse, but the threat unnerved his father.

He glanced from Jessa to Rsiran, his face tense. "Keep the others out of this. I'll get you to Venass."

"I know you will," Rsiran said. Threatening Alyse was all he needed to get his father to comply with them. "Where is Venass from here?"

His father looked north toward Thyr and pointed. "There."

Rsiran frowned. "The Tower of the Scholars?"

He nodded. "The Tower is outside Thyr itself. Separate, the way the scholars imagine themselves. Venass is simply another name for it."

Rsiran looked at the Tower. Thom had intended all along for them to come to the Tower of Scholars? Why not simply tell him?

A chilling thought came to him, and he glanced over at Jessa. Thinking back on how Thom had told them of Venass and how they might find an antidote there, he'd never really been all that forthcoming as to *how* they'd get it. Had Thom intended for Rsiran to break into the Tower? Had he presumed Rsiran could Slide them in? But if he and Jessa weren't invited in, how would they find the antidote? How would they even know what to look for?

Had Thom not been attacked, they could ask him what his plan was. For all Rsiran knew, Thom had a way into the Tower, or a contact that would allow them to find the antidote. But for him to go alone… how would he find a way to save Brusus?

"All I want is an antidote. Thom made no mention of having to break in," Rsiran said to her. The idea of doing so reminded him too much of breaking into the Elvraeth warehouse in Elaeavn. That had not turned out well for him. What would happen were he to break into this? Would he end up with the scholars after him as well? Would Brusus want that?

Jessa looked over. "We have to try or he'll die."

His father sneered at him. "I'm surprised you hesitate. I thought you didn't care what you broke into?"

"Why don't you tell him why you were in Asador?" Jessa said. She made her way over to his father. Her hand had gone back to the hilt of the knife.

His father's brow furrowed. "Asador? I thought this was about Thyr?"

Jessa pulled the knife from her waist. "This is about the same. Why don't you tell him?" He started to turn away, but Jessa grabbed his shoulder and spun him back to face her. "Turn your back to me, and I'll see to it you can't walk again." He tensed and didn't move. "Tell him."

Rsiran looked at Jessa. "What's this about, Jessa? What happened in Asador?"

"He's kept something else from you, Rsiran. I don't know what it is exactly, but I think it's time he starts telling you the truth. You've been so focused on the alloy ever since returning from Asador that you haven't taken the time to find out why your father was there in the first place." She glared at his father. "And I want him to explain."

"What alloy?" his father asked.

Rsiran ignored him and focused on Jessa. "Why he was in Asador doesn't matter to me, does it? It didn't matter until Brusus was injured."

"It matters if *they* are involved," Jessa said, emphasizing "they," like she was talking in code in front of Rsiran's father. "I'd planned to ask Brusus if he'd learned anything before he was poisoned. He's been asking questions, but not too many of the Elvraeth up *there* want to talk, at least, not about *them*. It's probably the reason he was poisoned."

"What alloy?" his father asked again.

With what little they knew about Venass and the Forgotten, maybe Jessa was right. He should have taken the time to ask more before dragging his father with him to Thyr. For all he knew, he actually did what the Forgotten wanted. "Why were you in Asador?" he asked his father.

He'd opened his mouth to say something—probably to ask about the alloy again—and promptly closed it.

Rsiran stepped toward him. "And don't think you can divide Jessa and me with your words. She wasn't the one to send me to the mines to work without any intention of bringing me back. She's the one who helped me, who saw through the lies you'd been feeding me trying to make me think what I could do was a curse. There is no one in this world I care about more than her." Rsiran practically trembled as he said those words. "So I ask you again. Why were you in Asador?"

His father looked at Jessa with a troubled expression. "They needed a smith. I'm a smith."

The way he said it told Rsiran he left something out. "That's not the only reason."

"Do you need to know more? Do you really think it will help you save your friend?"

It wouldn't. Precious time was wasted as they stood on the bank of the Thyrass River, but Rsiran suddenly wanted to know. After what happened with Shael, the demand that he'd made of Rsiran, and the exiled Elvraeth… he *needed* to know why they would want a smith.

"Why would they need a smith?"

His father looked up and met his eyes. "You don't know?" His voice made it clear he didn't believe what Rsiran said.

Rsiran shook his head.

"Then why were *you* in Asador? Why did you take me away?"

"I went for Jessa. Someone had taken her, and I wanted her back."

His father looked from Jessa to Rsiran. "That's the only reason?"

Rsiran had no intention of telling his father about the sword he'd made, the one Josun had stolen from his smithy. And if he didn't bring it up, maybe it meant his father didn't know about it.

"The only one that matters."

His father staggered to a nearby rock. The fall still affected him, and he wobbled on his feet, unbalanced. He dropped onto a rock and held his head in his hands, rubbing the first two fingers of his hands along his temples. "You really didn't know," he whispered.

Rsiran looked over to Jessa. "Why did they want a smith?" When his father said nothing, he stepped toward him, not Sliding so as not to use energy he might need, and stood in front of him. "What was this about?"

His father looked up. "I don't know whether to believe you're too stupid to know or whether you're just lying to me."

"That makes two of us," Rsiran said. "Doesn't change that you're going to tell me what you know."

His father looked past Rsiran and up at Jessa. "I serve the Elvraeth, no different from you."

Rsiran shook his head. "I don't serve the Elvraeth."

"Then you're more a fool than I realized if you think you can oppose them."

"Oppose them? Is that what you think?"

"Why else would you take me from them?"

Rsiran hesitated. His father thought he'd been working for the Elvraeth in Asador. Coming from Elaeavn, of course he would. He'd never had any reason to question their judgment. But Rsiran had seen what the Elvraeth were willing to do. Not just Josun Elvraeth, but the warehouse filled with crates sent from around the world, some of which contained riches Rsiran once would have been unable to imagine that were kept from the rest of Elaeavn, told him all he needed to know about the Elvraeth.

And then there were the Forgotten. Men and women exiled from the city for crimes against the Elvraeth. Families and lives destroyed. What would Brusus have been had his mother not been one of the

Forgotten? If the others of the Forgotten were like Josun, Rsiran would have a hard time sympathizing with them.

"Whatever else you might think, the masters you served in Asador were not Elvraeth."

"You've proven yourself ignorant about everything else, why should I believe you about this?" His father paused and met Rsiran's eyes. "What alloy were you working with?"

Something about the way he asked the question told Rsiran that he already knew. Did it matter if his father knew he worked with heartstone? Rsiran had never seen him working it when he was still apprenticed in the smithy, but that didn't mean his father didn't know how. There was enough of the alloy present in the Floating Palace; *someone* still knew how to mix it.

"A lorcith alloy," Rsiran answered. He watched his father carefully as he did, but his face didn't give anything away. He wouldn't mention heartstone by name.

His father frowned. "Lorcith can't be mixed into an alloy. I thought you learned the basics from me, but perhaps you really are too foolish to—"

Jessa cut him off by kicking him in the knee. "Watch how you speak to him."

His father looked up, a flat expression on his face. He looked past Jessa and over to Rsiran. "Are you just wasting what you've stolen then?"

Rsiran shook his head. He wouldn't argue with his father about this. Doing so would do nothing to convince him. "I didn't steal your lorcith."

"I saw you come into my shop. Enough of my ore had been taken that I felt the need to watch for it. Who else can pass through doors as if they aren't there?"

"One of your precious Elvraeth," Rsiran answered. "Someone who nearly killed me. Nearly killed Jessa. All for lorcith. He was the reason I was in Asador." He leaned closer to his father. "You think I'm the only one with the ability to Slide? With the ability you claim curse by the Great Watcher? The Elvraeth can as well." He paused, letting the words hit home. His father's face remained unchanged. "But I still don't know why they wanted a smith. What did they want you to do?"

He didn't know if his father would answer. He sat, staring toward Thyr. Moments passed, time—Rsiran realized—that he should be spending searching for the antidote to save Brusus. Standing and arguing the merits of the Elvraeth would not save him. Each moment he wasted meant less time to search.

"They wanted me to make weapons."

"What kind of weapons?"

Rsiran thought he already knew the answer. After what Josun had been after, he thought he knew, but he wanted to hear his father say it.

"Lorcith-forged weapons. Dark weapons." He looked over, his eyes hot and angry. "I studied knives they brought me. It didn't take long to recognize the mark."

Rsiran stared at him. He'd marked everything he ever made with his distinct mark. He'd done it from the beginning. The lorcith had practically demanded that he do it, and the forgings never felt complete until they had his mark on them. That also made them easier to track.

"They wanted knives?"

"Some. But what they really wanted were swords."

Rsiran glanced at Jessa. "Why swords?"

There was a reason he hadn't discovered. What was it about the lorcith-forged weapons the Forgotten wanted? Steel swords were plentiful, but that wasn't what Josun had wanted. He'd wanted the sword

Rsiran had made of lorcith… but more than that, he wanted a heart-stone alloy sword. But why?

His father shook his head. "I don't question the Elvraeth."

Rsiran didn't push on that point. Nothing he said would convince his father he hadn't been taken by the Elvraeth. "Did you make them any swords?"

His father met his eyes. "You said you've listened to the lorcith. That you let it guide your forgings."

Rsiran nodded.

"Then you know lorcith will not easily make swords. Doing so requires the smith to have a dark heart. That is what the lorcith calls to." He hesitated. "My attempts wasted precious lorcith. I disappointed the Elvraeth because I couldn't do what they wanted.

A dark heart. Rsiran considered how he'd been feeling when he forged the sword. He'd been angry, upset with how his father had banished him to Ilphaesn, but grateful for the smithy Brusus had given him. And the sword came into being, the lorcith guiding his hand.

That hadn't even been the first time he'd forged a sword. Before his father had exiled him, he'd nearly forged a lorcith sword.

Was it him? Did he have the darkness inside him his father claimed he needed?

Jessa touched his arm. It was a subtle gesture, not enough for his father to notice, but Rsiran appreciated the reassurance.

"That's all they wanted from you? To make swords?" Jessa asked.

He shrugged. "I wasn't the only smith in Asador."

"You didn't wonder why?" Rsiran asked. "Weren't you the one who always warned me against making weapons out of lorcith?"

His father sneered. "*You* would lecture me on this?" He shook his head. "No. I didn't think to question. When the Elvraeth ask something of you, you do it."

"Even when it's wrong?"

His father looked away. "I wouldn't expect you to understand. You have no sense of duty. Of responsibility. Why should you recognize the Elvraeth authority?"

Rsiran sighed. Arguing simply wasted time. They needed to move on to Venass, to find an antidote, and then return to Brusus if there was still time. "Anyone can abuse authority given to them. The Elvraeth… they don't see the effect of their rule. They rarely leave the palace. They simply sit looking down from the Floating Palace, passing judgment on others forced to make hard decisions." He looked at Jessa. "They are no more fit to rule than I am."

CHAPTER 13

RSIRAN HELD ONTO JESSA'S HAND. The sound of the water spilling over the edge of the rocks swirled loudly behind him. Darkness still covered the sky in a thick blanket, but the night passed quickly. A few stars twinkled overhead, no different from the stars of Elaeavn. Would the Great Watcher look after him even here?

"We need to go," he said. The time spent speaking with his father had given him a chance to recover some of his strength. Sliding from here would still tax him, but not as much as it would have if he'd gone immediately.

His father stood. Rsiran was thankful for that. Dragging him through the Slide required more energy than if he'd stepped lightly. He wouldn't tell his father that; likely, he'd drop to his knees so as to avoid aiding him.

Without another word, he focused on the Tower. Atop the rocks, standing above the waterfall, the Tower had appeared to stretch high into the sky. Down here, close to the Thyrass River, it reached impossibly high.

They Slid, emerging still outside of Thyr, but near enough that the air changed. The stink of the city assaulted his nose, a mixture of dung and sweat and filth so different from Elaeavn. No breeze moved through, and the still air tasted thick and sticky. The wall he'd seen surrounding the city blocked most of his view; only the highest buildings were now visible. And still the Tower.

This close, he saw how the Tower was separate from the city. Near enough that it overlooked Thyr, but outside the walls, as if to keep separate. How had he not seen that from the higher vantage?

"The Tower?" he asked.

His father nodded once.

Rsiran prepared to Slide again, trying to pick a place. He needed to get closer to the Tower, and then he could figure out how he was going to get in.

"You might find it more difficult to reach than others. The scholars are almost as protective of their secrets as the alchemists."

Rsiran wondered what his father would say if he learned how Rsiran had Slid into the alchemist guild house. "I don't want their secrets. Only an antidote."

They Slid.

This time, it was different. Something about the Slide reminded him of pushing through the heartstone alloy barrier. There was the sense of slow movement, almost an oozing, and terrible effort. Rsiran pressed forward. The resistance built and built, different than he experienced with the alloy, until he didn't think he'd be able to pass through. For a moment, he felt the same as when he'd first tried Sliding into the palace, before he'd learned he could overcome the alloy. But this was different in a way he couldn't completely explain.

Then they were through.

They emerged from the Slide standing in a wide field in the shadows of the Tower. The ground around them was barren dirt. Nothing grew. The air smelled hot and bitter, different from the lorcith he'd grown familiar with from his time in the mines and in the smithy. This scent burned his nose, and he held his breath, afraid to take in air. A faint sense tingled along his spine, leaving the hairs on the back of his neck standing on end.

"What is this?" Jessa whispered. She coughed softly, covering her mouth to keep from making noise.

His father looked at her. "I told you."

Jessa looked to Rsiran. "There's something wrong here."

Something about this place felt wrong in a way he couldn't completely explain. He stared at the landscape around the Tower, looking for anything. He saw no signs of plants—nothing at all seemed to grow in the area around the Tower of Scholars.

"Do you see anything?" he whispered.

Jessa did the same as he'd done and twisted around. "Nothing. There's nothing. No plants. Nothing moves. Just that Tower, and I feel…" She shook her head. "I feel like something's crawling in my head."

Since the forest where they'd lost Thom, Rsiran had tried to keep his heartstone-infused barriers in place. Because of that, he felt nothing. Jessa would have powerful barriers of her own; she'd lived in Elaeavn long enough, working through the underworld of Lower Town in most of it, that she'd have needed to barrier her mind from Readers.

He looked at his father. He showed no sign of discomfort. His father was Sighted. Not as powerful as Jessa, but a useful skill for a smith. But he also heard the call of lorcith. Could he reinforce his barriers the way Rsiran had learned to do, using lorcith to fortify them?

"This isn't what we needed," Rsiran said, turning to his father.

He looked back at him and shrugged. His once broad shoulders looked frail and weak as he did. "It has been a great many years since I was in Thyr. And I've never been to Venass, only heard it spoken of."

"You said you knew of it."

"And I did. I do. Venass is the Tower." He nodded toward it. "If a cure is what you seek, then the scholars will have one but there will be a price. There is always a price."

The sensation Rsiran felt when he'd first emerged pulsed stronger. He knew then what it was. Lorcith. Nothing else pulled at him like that.

It seemed to come from all around, but different from anything he'd ever experienced. Not a steady pulling at him, like unshaped lorcith ore, and not the strong connection he felt after he'd forged it. This was a pulsing, erratic and irregular.

Dizziness swept over him and he staggered, falling to his knees.

"Rsiran?"

Jessa's voice came from far away, softer than it should have been.

Pain shot through his head, mixing with the dizziness.

Above everything came the irregular pulsing.

He grabbed his head, pushing on his temples, trying to force up his barriers. Nothing changed. Heartstone already infused his barriers.

"Rsiran?"

He sensed her kneeling next to him from the lorcith knife tucked into her waist. Then her hands touched his arms, his face, his head, smoothing through his hair.

"What is it?" she asked.

He swallowed against the agonizing pain in his head as he tried to answer. "My... head. Lorcith."

"But your father..." Her hand fell away from his forehead as she trailed off.

"What about my... father?" he asked.

He tried sitting up, but the dizziness kept him from managing it. Instead, he preferred to remain motionless. They needed to get away. Whatever was happening made it impossible. The pain shooting through his skull seemed to move him, as if sliding him across the ground. He had a sense of being drawn forward. With dawning horror, he realized he was pulled toward the Tower.

"Jessa!" he said.

Rsiran tried opening his eyes but couldn't. He was left in the dark, the only sense that of movement and the pulsing lorcith. It felt too much like when he'd been stuck in the mines.

Jessa didn't answer. Rsiran tried calling out for her again but didn't know if his mouth worked.

Then he felt a drawing sense. If Jessa grabbed at him, he didn't feel it. Everything spun around him, colors swirling violently.

Understanding swept over him, breaking through the nausea and dizziness long enough for him to cry out in fear. He was Sliding, but he wasn't in control of it.

CHAPTER 14

THE MOVEMENT STOPPED.

After a while, Rsiran dared open his eyes. Pale light came from somewhere overhead. He was in a small room resting on smooth, cool stone. Markings were etched into the stone of the room, writing he didn't recognize. The air smelled different. Sharp, almost spicy, but foul as well. When he looked down at himself, he understood why. Vomit covered his legs, pooling on the floor next to him.

At least his head no longer hurt as it had.

It still throbbed, but it had faded, softened somewhat. Memories of the nausea and dizziness almost made him retch again.

How much time had passed? By his measure, too much of the night had already passed when they'd Slid to Thyr. Spending time trapped… he looked around, seeing nothing but stone walls stretching to a ceiling high overhead… somewhere did nothing to help Brusus.

All this effort to save him would be wasted. He should have stayed in Elaeavn. At least then, Jessa would have been safe.

But for how much longer? If Josun worked with the Forgotten, would they come searching for him? Would *he* be drawn into that battle?

Rsiran considered lying back down and resting his head but decided against it. Instead, he studied the room.

A narrow door split one wall. Made of a dull grey metal, it looked much like lorcith, only he hadn't thought lorcith existed is such quantities outside of Ilphaesn. Nothing else was in the room with him.

How had he gotten here?

The last time he'd been captured, he'd Slid onto Firell's ship. Shael possessed some sort of Elvraeth chains that blocked him from Sliding and also prevented him from sensing lorcith. Tentatively, he reached for the sense of lorcith knives in his pockets. The sense was there, but distant, different than it should be. Almost as if shielded.

He tried pushing on the knives but felt no movement.

A moment of panic worked through him, but he pushed it away.

He suspected he had been drawn into the Tower of Scholars, but how? The pulsing sense of lorcith? He'd felt as if he'd Slid… but nothing like he normally felt. He'd had no control and his head had pounded.

What then?

Rsiran pushed himself to his feet. Sitting here would get him nowhere. If he could Slide out of the Tower, he could return… where? To Thyr? The Thyrass River? Where would he go to look for Jessa?

She was lost. And it was his fault.

Rsiran closed his eyes, focusing on her flower charm, but felt nothing. He tried searching for the knife he'd asked her to carry, but he couldn't find it, either.

Lorcith was not shut off for him, just reduced. But how?

He made his way to the door, but there was no handle and no way to open it. If he was to escape, he'd have to Slide past it. At least Sliding didn't require access to lorcith. It only helped when he needed an anchor; otherwise, it wasn't something he required.

Yet, as he focused on trying to Slide, he found he couldn't.

Just like he'd been on Firell's ship, he was trapped. Only this time, he had no idea who captured him or why. And this time, Brusus would die if he couldn't escape. All because of him.

* * * * *

Rsiran sat cross-legged on the cool stone. His eyes were shut, and he simply listened for the lorcith, but terrible thoughts kept creeping in, reminders of his failings. He forced a focus on the lorcith, trying to hear its song. He'd done this before, but only when in the smithy and needing to learn what shape the ore needed to take. This time, he simply tried to connect to his knives.

He'd spread them across the stone in a semicircle, the tips pointing toward the walls. Lorcith was there, but just at the edge of his senses. Had he not known what he felt, he might not even realize it was lorcith.

Rsiran focused on his breathing. Each breath moved slowly, in and out of his lungs. His chest hurt from when he'd fallen with his father, and taking deep breaths aggravated it, but he forced thoughts of that away, choosing to ignore them. Once his breathing felt regular, he worked on clearing his head. His mind raced with fears of Jessa and Brusus, worry about what would happen to him, to his friends, with his capture. Those fears mixed with the knowledge that they would suffer because of his failings, because of the darkness that existed within him.

His father was right. Lorcith had changed him.

For a moment, he forced those thoughts away, letting his mind go blank.

Time passed. Rsiran didn't know how much time. Enough that he got lost in his breathing, in the blankness of his mind. After a while, he became aware of a soft humming, distant, as if through the stone. He could not feel it otherwise.

The humming became greater. Pressure built in his head, but not like it had outside.

Though he tried to ignore it, the sound persisted, like a bee buzzing in his ear. If he could, he would have swatted it away. That would do nothing but destroy his sense of calm.

And then he heard the lorcith.

He didn't know how much time had passed before he reached the point where he heard it again. Minutes or hours. Time became meaningless as he focused. Distantly, he knew he needed to feel urgency or Brusus would fade, but even that thought had been pushed away.

He felt the knives first.

The awareness was different from what he usually felt. Rather than a comfortable drawing sensation, this felt raw, as if the lorcith scraped against exposed nerves. Rsiran didn't try pushing it. Something deep within him warned against that. Rather, he listened.

As he did, he heard other lorcith around him, more than he expected. It filled the walls, as if buried in the mortar. The door sang to him, telling him how it had once been shaped out of a massive nugget of lorcith. Had he wanted to, Rsiran suspected he could get the story of where it came from, how it had been shaped. And he would, but later.

Beyond his room, lorcith permeated everything.

That realization almost made him lose focus. Why would there be so much lorcith? Had he been drawn somewhere in the Floating Palace and not into Venass like he thought?

Rsiran focused on his breathing. Had he not experienced isolation from lorcith before, he might have panicked. But this isolation was different from before. Whereas the chains he'd worn served to cut off his access to lorcith, this time, everything around him seemed to serve as a barrier to it.

Slowly, he regained his connection to the metal. He traced it in his mind, using it to guide him through the halls as he'd once guided himself through the Ilphaesn mines in the dark. He sensed a void in the lorcith and Rsiran followed it, moving up. Stairs, he decided. The void worked up and up until it stopped. He followed it down the hall, tracing to a point near him, seemingly just above him. There was a door there, similar to the one closing him in the cell.

Struggling to maintain his calm, Rsiran pressed past the door. Walls infused with lorcith surrounded him, but there was something else. Something familiar.

He'd hoped for the lorcith knife he'd made Jessa or the charm she wore around her neck. He felt neither of those.

For a moment, he lost hope. He thought by following the lorcith, he could reach Jessa. But what if she weren't trapped as he was? What if she still stood out on that strange barren land, the hot air burning at her nose and throat, thinking he'd Slid away from her? Worse, what if she didn't want him to find her, didn't care what happened to him, simply thanking the Great Watcher he'd finally been taken from her…

Rsiran realized what was happening. Similar to what happened in the forest, he was being Pushed. This was subtler than before and even that had been an exquisite touch. Had he not been reaching, questing with the lorcith, he might not have realized what was happening.

How long had he been subjected to the Pushing? From the beginning?

But he didn't dare push up his barriers. Doing so might block him from following the lorcith. So he struggled to ignore the dark thoughts working against him, slowly seeping into his mind, mixing with his thoughts, until Rsiran no longer knew which were his and which were being Pushed.

He returned his attention to the distant room. Lorcith filled the walls, the floor, the door. Everything. But there was more. Inside the room was something else, not just the walls and floor. There he felt slender rods bound close together. Had he not made them himself, he wouldn't have any idea what he felt. A lock pick made especially for Jessa.

His breath caught. Could she be there?

Without her, he wouldn't go anywhere.

He listened for other lorcith. The knife she carried. The charm, but found nothing.

What if she'd been taken somewhere else? What if it wasn't even her?

Rsiran wished he shared Brusus's abilities, especially now. If he were a Reader, would he be able to tell what Jessa was thinking? Could he somehow send her reassurances that he was unharmed?

He couldn't let himself think like that. He needed to reach her. But he'd already learned he couldn't Slide. The lorcith infused into everything blocked him somehow.

But that had been before he had something to anchor to. Could he anchor to the lock pick or would that not be strong enough?

Rsiran scooped his knives back into his pockets—he might need them if this worked—and steadied his breathing and held onto the sense of the lock pick in his mind. Always before, when he anchored, he used the anchor more as a way to guide his Slide, but that failed when he tried.

He didn't move. The sense of the lock pick filled his mind until that was the only thing he knew. Then he *pulled* on it, attempting to Slide at the same time.

Pain split his head and he nearly screamed.

Had he not been enveloped in the sense of the lorcith, he might not have managed to withstand it. As it was, he nearly lost his concentration and with it, the connection to the lorcith.

Rsiran steadied his breathing, *pulling* and Sliding at the same time.

The pain persisted, a shooting sensation that worked through his mind. Taking shallow breaths, he *pulled* and Slid.

It was nothing like any he'd ever done. He moved slowly, dragged by his connection to the lorcith he anchored. No colors flashed past him, and there was no sense of wind or movement. The only sense he had was darkness and the bitter scent of lorcith.

And then he emerged.

Rsiran let go of the Slide. Pain receded from his mind but did not leave entirely. The awareness of lorcith remained, unchanged and everywhere around him.

He blinked his eyes open.

Resting on the stone was the lock-pick set he'd made for Jessa rolled in black leather. But otherwise, the room was empty. His heart hammered, beating in time to the still fading throbbing in his head.

He pocketed the lock-pick set. He'd traded one cell for another.

Chapter 15

Rsiran didn't move at first. He listened to the lorcith, breathing slow and steady.

A mixture of emotions built within him. Irritation with Brusus. Had he not involved them in his plots, they would never have been put in the position to need to help him. Anger at his father. Rsiran suspected he kept something from him, but after everything they'd been through together, he no longer blamed him for that. He could not change his father any more than he could change the Great Watcher. Maybe part of his anger was with himself for thinking he needed to reach out to him in the first place. What had his father ever done to deserve compassion from him? He'd certainly never shown it to Rsiran.

More than anything, he had a building sense of failure. He wouldn't find Jessa. Whatever else happened, he had failed her.

He stretched out with his sense of lorcith again and moved past the walls surrounding him, past the floor infused with lorcith, and reached the door. There, he hesitated, listening. Like the last door, this door was made entirely of lorcith. A massive nugget must have been used to forge the door, a size he'd never seen before. Where had it come from?

So he listened. The door told him of its forging. A master smith ages ago listened to the lorcith but guided it as well. Different from how Rsiran usually worked with lorcith, letting it guide him. But Rsiran sensed from the door how the master smith and the lorcith had worked together.

He traced the lorcith farther, deeper into its past. The lorcith was willing to share with him its story. Pulled from the rocks by dozens of miners, there was rejoicing when the ore was found.

How was it that he could get so much from the lorcith? Was if from his connection or the way he listened? Or did it simply have to do with the massive amount used? He'd never seen a find that size. What would happen in Ilphaesn if the miners came across a find like that? Would there be rejoicing and celebration like he sensed happened when this nugget had been found, or would the miners argue over who found it, using it as their way to purchase freedom?

Reluctantly, he pushed past the door. Had he more time, he would be interested in listening to the lorcith. No longer did it seem strange to him that he understood the ore had a story. Maybe everything did if only there was someone attuned to listen.

Outside in the hall, he followed the walls again. He came to an opening, but it led down, back toward where he'd been jailed before. He moved his questing away, sensing for other places to follow. But there were none. Just this hall and the one below him. Both were completely infused with lorcith in a way that he couldn't move past.

Rsiran blinked open his eyes, letting go of his probing of the lorcith. He was truly trapped.

* * * * *

More time passed. Time Brusus didn't have.

Rsiran did nothing but focus on his breathing and listen to lorcith. At first, it was just the lorcith in the walls and floor, the knives he'd brought with him, and Jessa's lock pick.

He hesitated. *Why* had her lock pick been here? If it was here, then so was she.

Rsiran tried again to listen for the knife she carried with her, the one he'd suggested she bring. If he could find that, he might be able to use it to reach her. He steadied his breathing, thinking of the knife, letting the memory of its forging fill his mind. For a moment, he thought he felt it, but it slipped away. The lorcith in the walls overpowered it.

If he couldn't sense the knife, he wouldn't be able to sense the charm he'd made her. Much smaller than the knife, he hadn't been able to sense it when Josun had trapped her in the Ilphaesn mines.

But could he sense the heartstone alloy chain?

He'd never tried before, but after his time on Firell's ship, he knew he could sense heartstone. Rsiran worked to steady his breathing again. Thinking about reaching Jessa had sent his heart fluttering, and he had to suppress it before he could listen for the heartstone alloy.

When finally ready, he sent out his awareness.

The awareness was different than with lorcith, but could he anchor to it as well? Rsiran didn't really understand how he did it. If he survived, it would be another question for Della. By now, she'd grown used to them. He ignored the lorcith, ignored what he sensed in the walls and the floor. He ignored the sudden flare of lorcith he felt trying to suppress him. It took every ounce of focus he could muster, and even, then it almost wasn't enough.

And then he heard it.

The alloy sounded different than the lorcith did. Lorcith was always eager for him to hear it. Once, he'd heard it described as a song. Rsiran suspected that was true; there was a certain musicality to the way it called to him. The alloy felt harder. More distant.

He didn't know what he sensed. But the fact that he felt anything gave him reason to believe he could anchor to it.

As before, he held onto the sense of the alloy, *pulling* rather than stepping into the Slide. Pain again split his head, but softer. He had the sense of slow movement, a hint of colors, and the bittersweet scent of the alloy.

And then he emerged from the Slide an open room. Blue light bloomed around him, coming from sconces set into walls, so similar to the Elvraeth lantern he had in his smithy but had never managed to replicate. It took a moment for his eyes to adjust, but when they did, he saw Jessa sitting on a plush, dark leather chair.

One hand twisted a finger through her hair. The other fingered the charm around her neck. Rsiran realized he sensed the lorcith in the charm again, as if passing through the lorcith-infused stone walls freed him from the barrier that had been in place.

Worry twisted her face, but she looked otherwise well. She didn't seem to notice him at first.

Rsiran stepped toward her. The movement startled her and she blinked, lunging from the chair and grabbing him in an embrace. Somehow, she still smelled sweet, a mixture of whatever flower she'd been wearing earlier in the day and her spiced soap.

"Are you hurt? Did they…" She didn't finish. Her hands ran along his face, touching his cheeks, his lips, his neck, before working down his arms.

Having her touch him again filled him with relief.

"I'm fine, I think. Are you okay?"

Jessa hugged him in answer, gripping his shirt and clinging to it as if not wanting to let go.

He looked around. Walls made of a chalky white stone were bare, only the sconces marring them. Other than the chair, nothing else cluttered the room. Smooth, black marble tiles set along the floor, the color contrasting with the walls.

"Where are we?"

She took a slow breath and finally let go, stepping away from him. She looked around, eyes flickering to the sconces and then the floor. "The Tower of Scholars."

"How did we get here?" He thought he knew but wanted to know for sure. The strange pulsing of lorcith had *pulled* him, forcing him to Slide. But if Jessa was here, had they pulled her into a Slide the same way they had with him, or had she come here in a more traditional way?

"You don't know?"

Rsiran shook his head.

Worry lined Jessa's face. "You... you couldn't stand. Something happened and you screamed. And then we all were here."

"All?" Had he done that? Was it *his* fault Jessa had been captured this time? If he couldn't even protect her when he was with her, how could he hope to keep her safe when they were apart?

And where was his father?

She nodded. "But they said you wouldn't be able to escape. That they had... done something... that kept you from using your abilities. That you would die if you couldn't get free." Her wide eyes told him that she'd learned more than that, but she didn't say anything more.

Rsiran swallowed. "Lorcith infused the walls. The floor. Everything where I was."

"I don't understand. Then how were you able to reach me?"

"I found your lock pick."

Jessa frowned and shook her head. One hand slipped to her pocket. "Lock pick?"

Before he could answer, Rsiran felt a flash of lorcith and spun, putting Jessa behind him.

A man in a flowing tunic of white, embroidery running down the collar, and inky black trousers stood in front of him. He had dark skin, nearly black, with patches of white on the surface of each hand. His head was shaved completely, including his eyebrows. Metal pierced his ears, his brow, and his lips. His mouth parted in a smile.

"He should not have been able to. Interesting. Perhaps you don't have to die, Mr. Lareth."

Chapter 16

With Jessa pushed behind him, Rsiran prepared to Slide. Now that he could sense lorcith again, he felt the distant awareness of the lorcith sword in his smithy burning like a star in the night in his mind. If he anchored to it, he could have them back to Elaeavn.

But he still wouldn't have what they came for. If this was one of the scholars, Rsiran could ask for an antidote. That was why they had come, wasn't it?

More than that, he suspected the scholars weren't trying to harm him. Had they wanted to do so, they would have killed him while he was incapacitated. Leaving the lock pick in the other room had not been an accident. That meant…

"A test?" he whispered.

The scholar's mouth tightened.

"You pulled me here for a test?" Rsiran grabbed Jessa's hand in case they needed to Slide away. At the same time, he made certain his connection to the lorcith-forged knives he carried would let him *push* them were that needed. He wouldn't be caught unprepared again.

"You brought yourself here, Mr. Lareth. You chose to come." A strange accent lilted his words, making them harsh and difficult to understand.

Rsiran watched the scholar's face. The piercings through his brow and lip were made of lorcith. As were piercings Rsiran couldn't see. Small bars of lorcith penetrated his stomach, his chest, even his fingers.

"Why test me?" Rsiran felt his anger building and pushed it away. With what had happened to them already, he felt as helpless as he'd felt the first time he'd faced Josun Elvraeth. But unlike that time, he didn't intend to be used.

"It was no test," the scholar answered. He stood at ease, only the way he pressed his lips together showing any sign of tension. "Either you escaped or you did not."

Rsiran's mind raced, trying to understand what was happening. Like in Elaeavn, so much seemed hidden from him. At least in the city, he knew some way to keep himself safe. Here… here he had no way of knowing if he *could* be safe.

But for the scholars to know that he might escape, it meant they knew he could Slide. "Who told you?"

"Told me?" the man asked.

"About my ability. Who told you?"

The tension in his face softened, his lips parting. "No one had to *tell* me, Mr. Lareth. We can sense when one with your particular ability nears. If we could not, no secret would ever really be safe."

"How can you sense it?" Della could sense the ripple of his Sliding, but he'd thought that a gift from the Great Watcher. Did the scholars have someone with that kind of ability? Or was this different, something they had discovered?

He knew nothing about the scholars. What if they could access the same abilities as those from Elaeavn? The Great Watcher didn't *have* to gift only the Elvraeth.

The scholar's eyes narrowed. "Just know that we can."

"What are you?"

The question came out more bluntly than intended. The scholar spread his hands wide and tipped his head slightly. "You came to the Tower of Scholars and ask what I am?" His eyes narrowed.

As they did, Rsiran thought he saw a flash of green, but it faded and was gone. He pushed up his mental barriers anyway, fortifying them with heartstone alloy rather than lorcith. It would take more energy to maintain but would be stouter.

He watched the scholar's face as he did. Had his expression changed?

"I didn't come to the Tower seeking the scholars."

"Then how will you find the antidote you seek?"

Rsiran glanced back at Jessa briefly. Had she told the scholars what they searched for, or had they somehow Read him? Jessa stared past him, not taking her eyes off the scholar. From the way her jaw clenched and her brow furrowed, she seemed to be trying to see something about him.

He turned back to the scholar. "Yes. I was told I could find it in Venass."

The scholar's lip curled slightly. "Venass and not the Tower?" He frowned. "That is why you came?"

Rsiran nodded. "If you know why I am here, why are you surprised I would seek Venass?"

"Who told you of Venass?"

With the question, Rsiran felt relief that the scholar had to ask. He hadn't Read him. But he was certain someone had tried Pushing him while he was trapped in the cell. It was the same sense he'd had in the forest when they'd lost Thom. That meant another with abilities.

Unless another answer existed. Could the scholars have a way to recreate abilities given by the Great Watcher? Had that been how they'd been *pulled* into the Tower?

Rsiran frowned. This place looked nothing like what he expected, and he didn't think he would find the antidote Brusus needed. And without it, his friend would surely die.

"I don't understand."

The scholar smiled. The piercings made his face grotesque with the expression. "Then you have come to the right place."

* * * * *

The scholar led them down a long hall. His slippered feet made no sound on the tile. Jessa moved softly behind Rsiran, still gripping his hand, unwilling to release him. As they followed the scholar, Rsiran tried Sliding them a step, wanting to know if he could. He succeeded, but had a sense of something else pressing on him as he did. Would he be able to Slide them from the Tower if needed, or had the scholars learned some way of preventing him from Sliding away from them?

The sense of the sword reassured him. He could anchor to it if needed.

"What of the other who was with us?"

The scholar tipped his head slightly. "Your father? He is unharmed."

They knew about his father. Did they know how little he mattered to Rsiran? "Can I see him?"

The scholar glanced back at him. "Do you want to?"

Rsiran watched the walls as they made their way through the Tower. Like the room, the walls were bare. Sconces like those in the room burned with blue light. Rsiran trailed a hand along the stone and found it cool, almost damp. The air had a chill to it and something else, a hint of an odor he couldn't quite place. With each step, he was aware of how much time they spent. Time Brusus didn't have.

"I need help for a friend and was told I could find it in Venass."

They turned a corner and started up a wide flight of stairs. "Interesting that you use that term. It is an ancient term and known only to a few," the scholar said. "I should like to know how you have learned it."

Rsiran looked over to Jessa. "I heard it in Elaeavn."

The scholar tapped his lip piercings together. As he did, Rsiran felt a soft surge of lorcith and smelled a hint of the bitter metal. "Elaeavn." His eyes narrowed. "Few outside the Tower know of Venass. And none in Elaeavn."

Rsiran wondered if he should reveal that Thom shared the name with him, but decided against it. "Someone does."

The scholar frowned and then continued up the stairs.

Rsiran looked over at Jessa, feeling a hint of worry. If the scholars had Readers, he might be able to fortify his mind with the alloy to prevent access, but would Jessa? What would happen if the scholars learned it was Thom who told them of Venass? What did Rsiran even know of Thom?

But… why had Thom not told him that Venass and the Tower of Scholars were one in the same? What purpose would he have for hiding that from them? It risked delaying them from finding help for Brusus, and without that help, he would die.

The stairs opened onto a wide landing. Here, a massive hall stretched before them, much wider than on the floor below. At the end of the hall, a set of double doors made of thick lorcith arched high overhead. The doors were larger even than the one in his cell. What size nugget must have been found to forge doors of such size? How much would they weigh?

Shelves lined the walls, as did a few boxes that reminded him of the strange crate that Brusus had shown him on his first visit to the warehouse; the wood seemed to have been peeled away in layers to be opened. Rsiran tried to slow to get a better look, but Jessa pulled him along with her.

As they reached the doors, the scholar paused. He looked as if he would say something, then the tips of the lorcith rods piercing his lips touching softly, but shook his head and pushed open the doors.

Rsiran realized after they swung open that he hadn't actually touched them.

He pressed against his awareness of the lorcith, wondering if he could influence the doors. The massive doors responded to his touch, swinging softly with his gentle *push*. The scholar glanced over at him and frowned.

"Where are you taking us?" Rsiran asked.

Jessa had been silent since they'd left the room in which Rsiran had found her. Now she tensed, her hand in his palm slicking with sweat. Rsiran looked around, wondering if she'd seen anything. He saw only more of the pale white walls they'd seen elsewhere. No sconces hung on these walls but moonlight streamed through a window high overhead. At least it was still night, but which night?

"What is this place?" he asked again. His voice carried across the room, bouncing from the tile floor to the walls before finally fading.

"Rsiran…"

He looked over to Jessa. Her eyes were wide and darted from side to side.

"What is it? What do you see?"

"That's just it. I don't know."

The scholar chuckled softly, sounding almost like a growl. "You will pardon the darkness. This is a room of solitude," he said as if in answer.

Rsiran thought he understood what troubled Jessa. Like he'd been trapped in the cell without the ability to Slide, Jessa couldn't see into the darkness any better than he could.

How could the scholars counter their abilities?

And why would they need to? "Why did you bring us here?"

"As I've said, you brought yourself here, Mr. Lareth. You sought our aid."

Rsiran shook his head, studying the walls around him, but unable for his eyes to pierce the shadows. "I didn't come seeking aid. Only an antidote."

"Is that not aid?"

Rsiran didn't like what that implied. Would he owe something to the scholars if he accepted the antidote?

"And you have something that will help?"

A smile twisted the scholar's lips, pulling on the lorcith piercing in a way that left his face twisted and grotesque. Something about the smile reminded him of the way Thom had smiled at him.

"There is always something that can help. You must be willing to pay the price."

Next to him, Jessa squinted, trying to peer into the darkness. Shadows slipped around the strange room, shifting with the clouds rolling over the moon, changing the moonlight in ways that looked almost unnatural.

"What price?"

"You have only been brought this far because you can travel. Others will wish to study, to learn how you managed to leave that room. That is the price."

Jessa squeezed his hand hard. He looked over and saw her shaking her head.

"Don't do it, Rsiran. You don't know what they will do to you."

"Do? We wish to understand, that is all. He will be unharmed."

Rsiran studied the scholar and then turned to Jessa. "Isn't this what we came for?" he asked. "If we find an antidote, Brusus will be healed."

"But what of you? What price will you pay for him?"

"Wouldn't Brusus do the same for us?" he whispered.

"Would he? What happened when I was captured?" she whispered. "How hard did Brusus look? Where was his sacrifice then?" She looked around. "I think you should take us from this place, Rsiran. See if…" She lowered her voice. "See if he's been healed."

Rsiran considered how much time had been spent just reaching the Tower of Scholars, the strain he'd placed on himself Sliding here. Were they to return to Elaeavn to see if Della had managed to Heal Brusus, Rsiran doubted he would have the strength needed to return here, especially considering how difficult it had been to escape from the room in which he'd been held.

And would they even *allow* him to return? Something told him that he and Jessa had only been granted access. He might find the Tower blocked to him, as he'd once found the Floating Palace.

"If I don't accept this offer now, it won't be offered again, will it?"

The scholar's mouth twisted. "You are insightful, Mr. Lareth."

He looked back to Jessa. "For Brusus… we have to accept the exchange. It might be his only chance."

She leaned into him, and he felt her trembling softly against him. "I don't want to lose you." She whispered softly so that he would be the only one who could hear. "When they said you were kept in a room and all you had to do was escape, I… I…" She shook her head. "There wasn't anything I could do but wait. I don't think I can stand waiting again."

Rsiran would do anything to keep Jessa safe. But he owed Brusus. And this was something he could do. If all they wanted was to study him, then Rsiran would have to risk it.

"For Brusus," he whispered to Jessa. Then, he turned to the scholar. "I accept."

The scholar walked away from them, disappearing into the shadows. There was a sound like that of whispering, though it seemed mixed with a strange scratching. Then the scholar returned, clutching a dark bottle made of wood against his robes. When he reached them, he held it out.

Rsiran hesitantly took it. As his hand curled around the bottle, the scholar's mouth twisted in a dark smile. Rsiran shivered, wondering what, exactly, he'd just agreed to.

CHAPTER 17

THE SCHOLAR WALKED THEM DOWN DIFFERENT STAIRS that slowly widened, opening into a grand staircase as it descended from the strange room. Rsiran carried the heavy wooden bottle capped with wax. A dark rune had been burned into the surface. He traced his finger around the rune as they walked.

Jessa walked next to him in silence.

Rsiran couldn't help but think he'd made a mistake. What if Della managed to Heal Brusus? Then everything he'd done would've been unnecessary. But if she hadn't and Rsiran managed to bring an antidote to her… would it have been worth it?

Only time would divulge that answer. Time, and learning exactly what the scholars wanted from him.

The scholar said nothing more until they reached the landing at the bottom of the stairs. Another set of wide, lorcith-forged doors stood closed in front of them. In the light of the pale blue sconces hanging along the walls, he saw markings on the door, shapes and characters he suspected had meaning.

He squeezed Jessa's hand and motioned softly toward the door, hoping her Sight would allow her to draw the shapes again. She frowned at him, briefly startled, then stared at the door. Rsiran couldn't tell whether she saw anything of use.

"You are free to leave, Mr. Lareth. You will receive a summons for the study. You would do well to answer."

Rsiran clutched the wooden bottle tightly against him. "And if I don't?"

The scholar tapped the lorcith piercing his lips together again, and Rsiran felt a soft surge of lorcith. The doors swung open without the scholar touching them.

Rsiran looked at him, wondering if the piercings gave him control over the lorcith. He hadn't seen any other scholars to know if others had similar piercings or if they were particular to this one scholar. The man watched him and said nothing.

"What of my father?" Rsiran asked. He didn't feel strongly about helping his father, but he'd brought them to Venass. Rsiran would work out later how his father knew of it.

"For now, your father will remain as our guest."

"That wasn't the agreement," Rsiran said. He didn't want to leave the scholars with anything they might use against him. Already, he began to feel uncomfortable with what had happened. How much had he sacrificed to help Brusus?

"No. There is no agreement for Neran Lareth."

Rsiran turned to face the scholar, knives ready to *push* at him. As he did, he wondered if they would even work against him. If he could control lorcith the same as Rsiran, would the knives find their target or would he be able to deflect them?

The scholar studied him, an almost amused expression flickering across his eyes. He stood at ease, arms clasped behind his back.

"You will not harm him."

He tapped the piercings together again. "Have you come to care about him?"

Jessa leaned toward Rsiran. He resisted the urge to look over, unwilling to look away from the scholar.

Rsiran leaned forward again. "Don't push me on this."

"Or what, Mr. Lareth? What do you think you will do? You will return to Venass?" He almost smiled. "And then what? How will that turn out any differently than this time?"

Rsiran felt anger rising within him. Was this another test? They'd already helped him, giving him an antidote that might save Brusus. Why would he argue with them before leaving?

"Your traps did not hold me," he reminded. "Remember that if you think to harm him."

The scholar tipped his head forward, only the slightest bow. "We do not forget, Mr. Lareth. That is why you were granted passage."

Rsiran watched him for another moment and then pulled Jessa with him and stepped through the doors. As he did, he had a sensation of movement, a swirl of colors, and smelled a hint of bitterness. Rsiran turned, and the Tower was now far behind him, the doors closed. Thyr stretched behind it.

They'd Slid away from the Tower.

Rsiran shivered, realizing what had just happened. Had they forced him into a Slide, using his ability to carry them away from the Tower? Or far stranger, did the scholars have the ability to Slide, and now wanted to know how he could Slide past heartstone alloy? Either way, he realized he might have underestimated them.

Jessa stared at the Tower. She chewed at her lip and one hand gripped the charm around her neck. "What will happen when they decide to study you?"

"I don't have to return." But he was no longer certain that was true.

Jessa shook her head. "This was a mistake. Brusus wouldn't want you to do this."

"Brusus will want to live."

Jessa sighed. "At what cost?" She turned to him and took both of his hands in hers. "We've been upset at Brusus for pulling us into the Elvraeth plot without asking, but what have we just done?"

Rsiran realized she was right. What had he done? Agreed to assist the scholars in exchange for the antidote, but what did he really know about them?

He sighed. If all they wanted was the opportunity to study his abilities, what could that hurt? But if that was all, why did he have the feeling he'd been duped into an agreement that had implications he hadn't considered and could not foresee?

Rsiran looked at the slowly lightening sky. Much longer, and it would be morning. Della would have spent most of the night working on Brusus. In that time, she would have expended much energy, possibly more than she could sustain. After everything they'd been through, it was time to return.

Jessa watched him, her eyes narrowed with concern. "Rsiran…"

The way she said his name told him she'd seen enough on his face to practically Read him. If only he could do the same with her. "You're right," he said simply. "I don't know what I've done. We should have spoken to Della before running off with Thom, but I thought—"

"You thought you could help. I know that's all you ever want to do."

Rsiran sniffed. "Maybe I'm more like Brusus than I realize."

Jessa laughed. After the night they'd had, the sound lightened his mood, stealing away some of the tension that had begun seeping through him.

"You're damn near as stubborn as he is."

"I'm sorry."

Jessa kissed his cheek. "Don't be. Stubborn is good. If you hadn't been so stubborn and determined, I don't know that I would have gotten away from Josun Elvraeth." She shivered. "Being stuck in the mine… waiting… not knowing…" She swallowed.

Rsiran pulled her into him. She hadn't said much about her time captured by Josun. And he hadn't pressed her on it, knowing Jessa would tell him when she was ready. "I know. I've been there too."

She shook her head and started to push away. "That's just it. You *don't* know. I might be Sighted, but that doesn't help when you're trapped someplace like that, always wondering if Josun would return, never knowing if he'd bring food or water or if something worse would come. There wasn't a lock I could pick. Nothing but bars and rock. And the water crashing far below."

He hadn't realized how hard it had been for her, but of course it would have been difficult. Jessa was used to being in control, knowing that—especially in Elaeavn—there wasn't anyplace she couldn't sneak. Josun had taken that control away from her, made her dependent on him for her safety and well-being.

"I'm sorry, Jessa." And her capture had been his fault. Josun wanted to hurt him. By going after Jessa, he knew he would get Rsiran's attention. "I know how awful Ilphaesn can be." The darkness, the smell of lorcith and sweat all around, the steady tapping as the ore was mined. Those thoughts still kept him awake at times.

"At least when you went to Ilphaesn, you weren't trapped. You could always Slide away." She lowered her head onto his chest. "The whole time I was there, I prayed to the Great Watcher that he would give me your gift, just long enough to escape. And when you came… when you appeared with Josun… I thought…" She coughed and wiped away the tears welling in her eyes. "I thought he'd captured you too."

Rsiran held her, rocking in place as he did. "But he hadn't. I got you to safety, Jessa."

"Did you?" she asked. She moved away from him and looked back at the Tower. "Is that what we've found? Safety?"

"We'll get through this. I'll Slide us back to Elaeavn. Make sure Brusus is well. Then we can talk to Della and find out what she knows of the Tower and the scholars."

"That's just it, Rsiran. If it's not the scholars, it's someone else. The Elvraeth. The Forgotten. Damn, you even have the alchemist guild after you."

He'd almost forgotten about that. Considering everyone he'd encountered as he tried to determine what Brusus was planning and what had happened to Jessa, the alchemist guild seemed the least important. Yet, in Elaeavn, they were nearly as dangerous as the Elvraeth.

"You think to keep us safe by barricading us into the smithy, building walls that others can't get through. But that's no way for us to be."

Rsiran sighed. The heartstone bars had been meant to keep them safe, at least in the smithy, but now he wondered if they ever could do that. They might keep someone from Sliding in, but there were other ways to get to them. What had happened to Brusus showed him that.

"I wanted to keep you safe."

"That's not safe, Rsiran. I'm not sure we can *ever* be safe, not like we once were."

"What do you suggest? We go find a place to hide? Tuck ourselves into the Aisl and live like our ancestors did?"

Jessa pulled herself toward him again. "Would that be so bad?" Then she laughed. "But no, that's not what I'm suggesting." She shook her head. "I don't even know *what* I'm suggesting. We can't keep ourselves apart like this anymore. We have to trust our friends to help. When we stay separate is when others get hurt. First Lianna. Now Brusus."

She didn't say it, but he knew she feared Haern was next. Or Della. More than any of them, if something happened to Della, it would devastate Rsiran most of all. She had always been the one with the answers.

"You're right. Too much has gone on for us to stay away from our friends."

He looked back at the Tower rising above Thyr. The white stone looked bleaker in the fading night. What would it look like in the daylight? A few slatted windows dotted the sides of the Tower. Could he simply return the antidote if Brusus was already gone?

"We'll return. Tell Della what happened. She'll know what we should do next."

The relief on Jessa's face was clear.

Rsiran took one more look at Thyr and then Slid them to Della's home.

CHAPTER 18

A FIRE STILL CRACKLED IN THE HEARTH of Della's home when they emerged from the Slide, filling the room with heat and the scent of her mint tea. The cot in front of the fire was empty. Blood soaked sheets were crumpled near the end.

Rsiran's breath caught. "We're too late," he said.

Jessa let go of his hand and hurried over to the cot. She lifted the sheets, as if Brusus were simply hiding rather than missing. She looked back at Rsiran, her eyes wide. Her gaze flicked past him, and he spun to see what she looked at.

Haern sat staring at them. The long scar across his face, running from his ear down his cheek, caught the firelight. At least it didn't seem to writhe like Thom's scar had. "It's late." He sat atop a tall stool, feet kicked up on a shelf. His eyes were half-closed, as if sleeping.

"Where's Brusus?" Jessa asked.

Haern frowned. "Della took care of him. Spent most of the night trying to get him well. He kept bleeding and bleeding." He nodded toward the pile of sheets atop the cot. "Mostly from his mouth and nose. Damn nasty toxin they used, but one I'd seen before." Haern looked from Jessa to Rsiran. "Hear we have you to thank for him making it to Della?"

Was Haern saying Brusus was dead or still alive? "We were with him in the Barth when the attack came," Rsiran said.

"Attack? I thought it was poison."

"That's what took Brusus. Someone put something in his ale. But there were others. Men with swords. Looked like Elvraeth."

Haern frowned. "Elvraeth in the Barth? I've never seen any venture far into Lower Town, let alone into one of the taverns. How sure are you?"

Rsiran sighed. "I don't think they were *our* Elvraeth." He paused, looking around Della's home. "Is Brusus…" He couldn't finish the question.

And Haern didn't offer an answer. Instead, changing the subject. "So you know."

Rsiran frowned. "I know?"

Haern tilted his head toward the door and Rsiran understood. The palace. The Elvraeth.

"When did you learn of the Forgotten?" Haern shifted on his chair, swinging his legs down.

"After the alchemist guild, when Jessa was taken," Rsiran said, looking back at her, but she was silent. She stared at the sheets on the cot as if Brusus might reappear. "Did you hear what happened to me?"

"I heard. Hoped it wasn't true," Haern answered. "You know I can't See you like I can the others."

"Then you know what Firell did. What Shael had him do," Rsiran said.

Haern rubbed a hand across his face and shook his head. "Still can't believe Firell would do that to you. To Brusus, really. That man owes him more than most."

Rsiran leaned over the cot, running his hand across the surface. How long ago had it been that he'd been the one lying atop the cot depending on Della's skill to Heal him? Now, with Brusus gone…

"I'm not sure Firell had a choice," he said absently.

"Always have a choice," Haern said. "It's what you do with it that matters."

Rsiran looked up. "I think Josun had someone Firell cared about."

"Probably Lena. She's the only one he would have done that for."

Rsiran spun. Brusus stood in the doorway to Della's back room. Normally faded green eyes shone with a bright intensity. He looked weakened and pale, but *alive*.

"Brusus?" Jessa said his name and took a step toward him before catching herself.

Brusus smiled and brought a hand to his mouth as he coughed. Bloody phlegm splattered in his palm. "The same," he said. His voice sounded different. Hoarse, as if he'd been yelling for hours.

"How are you?" she said.

"Same as any of us. Della Healed me."

"I thought she didn't know what poison had been used on you," Rsiran said. That was the reason he'd gone with Thom, the reason they'd Slid all the way to Thyr for the *chance* they might find an antidote.

Rsiran held the wooden bottle, finger running along the charred edges. What had he sacrificed unnecessarily? Had he only listened to Della, he might have learned she could Heal Brusus. Instead, Thom was lost. His father now trapped in the Tower. And Rsiran owed the scholars… something.

Jessa looked over at him. The look on her face told him she shared his thoughts.

"I'm not sure that always matters for Della," Brusus said. He took a few unsteady steps into the room. Rsiran hurried forward to put an arm around him and guided him toward a chair in front of the fire. Brusus smiled at him weakly. "Where have you two been? When I came around, Della said you were the reason I was alive." He laughed. "Again. I've got to stop getting into situations like this, Rsiran. Can't keep owing you my life. Hard to repay that debt."

"Who is Lena?" Rsiran asked.

Brusus ran a hand through his hair. "Lena is Firell's daughter."

"Daughter?"

Brusus nodded. "Mother is Ylish. A woman Firell met while smuggling. She sailed with him for a while, but when she became pregnant, she returned to Yl. He doesn't talk about her much. I think he regrets that he can't be with her, but Firell doesn't know anything other than his ship. Asking him to give up the sea would be like asking Jessa to give up sneaking. Or you to give up your smithy."

Rsiran thought of how hard that would be. Would he be willing to do it? Would he really give up working with lorcith?

He looked over at Jessa. For her, he would. He would give up everything to be with her.

Is that what she had done to be with him? Had she given up what she was?

The idea made his heart sink.

"But if you know of her, why wouldn't he have come to you for help?" Jessa asked.

"That's not Firell. He takes care of his own business." Brusus shrugged. "If Josun was threatening harm to Lena, then I can't blame him for doing what he needed to save her."

Rsiran tried to imagine his father doing something similar for him but failed. For Alyse, he likely would do anything. But for Rsiran?

Now that Josun was out of the way, trapped in the mines, what would happen to Lena? What would Firell do now?

"You haven't told me where you were," Brusus said.

Rsiran looked over to Jessa. She shook her head.

Brusus frowned. The brightness to his eyes faded the longer he was with them. "What don't you two want to say?"

Rsiran turned to face Brusus. He clutched the bottle of the antidote in his hand. "We thought you were dying."

Brusus leaned forward. The green to his eyes surged briefly. "What did you do?"

"I thought I could help you. Della said she couldn't help you. You needed an antidote or you wouldn't survive."

"An antidote? How did you expect to find an antidote?"

"We went to Thyr. There is a place where poisons and their antidotes are studied. I thought if we could find something…"

"Thyr?" Haern asked, puzzled. "Why would you go to Thyr? There are other places… safer places… than Thyr."

Rsiran glanced at Jessa again before turning back to Brusus. "Thom suggested we go to Thyr. Other than Asador, I haven't been anywhere." Brusus wore a look of confusion. "I didn't know what else to do, Brusus. I couldn't just wait for you to die."

Brusus blinked. As he did, his face relaxed, and Rsiran could tell how much the poisoning had taken from him. Where he'd once worn his age well, the wrinkles around his eyes giving him a dignified air, he now looked beaten. His dark hair streaked with silver stood on end, making him seem wild. More fitting for someone of Lower Town than Upper Town where Brusus always pretended to live.

"I don't understand," Brusus said. "Who's Thom?"

CHAPTER 19

Rsiran waited for Brusus to laugh, but it didn't come. "What do you mean?"

Brusus shook his head. "Who's Thom?" he repeated.

Rsiran looked to Jessa, but she frowned. "Thom. Man from Thyr you hired to watch my father."

Brusus turned to Haern. "You weren't watching him?"

Haern stood and walked toward the fire. His jaw clenched. He'd slipped a coin from his pocket and worked it along his fingers, making it dance from one finger to the next. "I'd been watching. I had." He flicked his eyes to Rsiran. "Keln watching with me. You couldn't expect me to be there all the time."

Brusus sighed. "You seen Keln recently?"

Haern's eyes lost focus and he looked as if he stared past Brusus. His face flattened into an unreadable mask. Moments passed and then he blinked, shaking his head. "I can't See him."

"What does that mean?" Brusus asked.

Haern gave Brusus a look. "It means I can't See him." He shook his head. "It's not like with Rsiran. This is different."

"Dead?" Brusus asked.

Haern pursed his lips and his brow furrowed, pulling on his scar. "Maybe dead. Maybe not. Like I said, I can't See him."

"Then what?" Brusus pushed.

"I don't know."

Brusus studied Haern, but he didn't elaborate.

"Shielded?" Rsiran asked.

They turned to Rsiran. Haern frowned and asked, "Shielded, how?"

"Like how the alloy prevents me from Sliding," Rsiran started, not explaining that it no longer did. "Or how we can barricade our minds to keep from being Read."

Haern frowned. "It is possible. Always before, I could See Keln. Now... now I simply can't. Perhaps that is it."

His tone told Rsiran that he thought it unlikely.

Rsiran looked at Brusus. "You don't know Thom?"

Brusus watched Haern for a moment more before turning back to Rsiran. His head wobbled as he moved, swaying as if he'd had too much ale. "No. And from Haern's expression, he's not someone he hired."

Rsiran thought about what Thom had said. Hadn't he mentioned Brusus? Or had Rsiran been the one to bring him up? He couldn't re-member. Now, it didn't matter. Thom had died in the forest.

But why would Thom make up a story and then agree to take them toward Thyr? Unless there was something he needed, something only Rsiran could do?

Like Sliding him there.

"Tell me about Thom," Brusus suggested.

Rsiran sighed and grabbed a stool from along the wall and sat. Jes-sa came and leaned against him, choosing to stand. One hand gripped the charm on her necklace. The other rested on his shoulder. "Not sure what there is to tell, now."

Brusus grunted. "You thought he knew me?"

"He said you did a job together in Thyr." Rsiran watched Brusus, looking for a hint of reaction. When Brusus's eyes widened briefly, Rsiran frowned. "You know him, don't you?"

"What did he look like?"

"Dressed in black leathers. Carried a sword—one of mine, I think. Not scared when I Slid around him. Had a long scar across the top of his head."

Brusus leaned back and closed his eyes, sighing. "I know him," he agreed. "But not by Thom."

"Who is he?" Rsiran asked.

Brusus shook his head. "Name doesn't really matter, not with him."

"Is he really from Thyr?"

"Ahh, who knows with him?"

"Why?"

Brusus leaned forward. "He's a powerful Reader, but more than that. He can Compel too. Not many with that set of abilities."

"A Reader? But he's from Thyr! I saw his eyes—"

Brusus smiled. "Like mine?" he asked. His eyes suddenly appeared a deep brown, the shade nearly identical to Thom's, before fading back to the pale green they'd been when Rsiran first met him. Brusus shook his head. "Like I said, he's powerful. More skilled than me in that area."

"Why would he say he's from Thyr?" Jessa asked.

"For all I know, Thyr might be his home. I don't know if he was Forgotten or the child of a Forgotten. Either way, he's not of Elaeavn."

Rsiran leaned back, trying to think of everything Thom had told him. Had everything been some sort of plan to get him out of the city? Had he known what would happen in Venass? Did he expect Rsiran to get stuck, unable to Slide away?

"If you went with him, where is he now?"

Rsiran shook his head. "Dead," he started, thinking of how they became separated in the forest. Had that been Thom's plan as well? Not the dying, but separating from them? "I can't Slide someplace I've never been, at least not all at once. Traveling to Thyr took lots of smaller Slides. One of them let out near a small forest. I went ahead, looking for the way to Thyr, but we lost him in the forest."

"Lost?"

Jessa's face darkened and she answered. "There was a presence there. Something Pushing dark thoughts onto us." She shook her head. "I've never experienced anything like it before."

Brusus's eyes narrowed. He coughed again, a bit of dark blood coming from his mouth. "He got lost in the forest because of this presence?"

"I went back and found him," Rsiran said. "I don't know what happened, only that whatever else was in the forest got him." He'd intended to go back to bury him, but maybe he needed to go back to investigate what strange presence might be in the forest.

"Do you know what he wanted with you?" Brusus asked.

Rsiran shook his head. "He was taking me to Thyr, to a place called Venass."

"Venass?" Brusus said.

Haern sucked in a breath. "He told you of Venass?"

Brusus turned to Haern. "You know of this place?"

"You know what I did before." He said it as a statement rather than a question.

"Yes, but what does that have to do with this place?"

Mystery seemed to surround Haern, and his past, so the idea that he might know of Venass shouldn't come as a surprise to anyone in the group. And though Rsiran hadn't known it when he first met the man, he later learned of Haern's previous occupation as an assassin before returning to Elaeavn with Jessa. He'd learned of Haern's attachment to Jessa one night when Haern thought Rsiran had been putting Jessa in danger. The man had grabbed Rsiran and prevented him from Sliding. It was during that scuffle, a knife had been drawn and Rsiran learned about his other ability: he could *push* on lorcith. Because of Haern's "attack," Rsiran had learned to *push* and *pull* on his knives, which was how he got Jessa away from Josun that night in the palace.

Haern had a dark expression on his face and had yet to answered the question, so Brusus asked again. "Haern, what do you know of this place?"

"Venass is a dangerous place. Different from what you'll find in Asador. There, the university is prized, a part of the city." He shook his head. "Venass stands apart from Thyr. Even I never managed to reach its doors."

Rsiran turned to Haern, but Jessa spoke first. "Why would you try to reach the scholars?" she asked.

A cynical expression slipped across his face. "Scholars? Is that what you think they are?"

Rsiran shook his head. He had no idea what took place in Venass. The only scholar they'd seen had lorcith piercing through his skin that Rsiran suspected gave him power over the ore. And they nearly trapped him in a room, the lorcith-infused stone all around him nearly too much for him to escape. "The antidote we needed to help Brusus was supposed to be found in Venass. That was why Thom wanted me to go there." Except, if Thom didn't really know Brusus, then there had been another reason he wanted Rsiran to take him there.

He looked over at Brusus, at how weakened he was. Thom had supposedly gone looking for him after the attack. Had he known about the poisoning? If that was the case, maybe he wanted to draw Rsiran away from Brusus and eliminate one threat.

Haern leaned toward him. "Tell me you didn't reach Venass." He studied Rsiran's face and then turned to look at Jessa. His eyes took on the faraway expression he wore when using his ability. He blinked. "You did, didn't you?" he whispered.

Rsiran held out the wooden bottle as an answer. He set in on a small wooden table. After everything they'd been through to get it, having it out of his hands was both a relief and distressing.

"Did what, Haern?" Brusus asked.

Haern leaned back and sighed. His eyes drifted closed again. He'd palmed the coin in his hand while asking about Venass, but now brought it back out and made it slip from finger to finger. "Fools. All of you. You're damn lucky to be alive."

"They didn't want to hurt us," Rsiran said.

Haern snorted. "No. You're no good to them dead."

Brusus looked from Haern to Rsiran. "You're going to have to explain what this Venass is, Haern. Why was it a problem that Rsiran went there?"

Haern breathed heavily but didn't answer.

"Venass. More commonly known as the Tower of Scholars," Della said.

Rsiran looked over at the door. The old Healer had slipped silently among them at some point. She stood behind her row of shelves that held medicines and spices, sprouts of her grey hair visible above the top of the shelf. She tottered toward them, leaning on a long cane. Rsiran had never seen her use a cane before. Her usually bright eyes had a rheumy look to them. She sighed softly.

"And they are scholars, but of an arcane sort," she continued. "They are men with some power who chase the abilities others were given by the Great Watcher."

"You know of this place too?" Brusus asked.

The scholar had seemed surprised that anyone in Elaeavn would know it by the name Venass, but both Haern and Della knew. What did that mean?

"Know of it? Yes, I know of Venass," she said slowly. "But I hadn't suspected them being behind the attack at the Barth, and by the time I learned, Rsiran was already gone." She looked at Rsiran, her weary eyes briefly regaining a hint of their previous vigor. "Had you only asked… had you only said something about where it was you planned on going, what you planned to do." Her voice held sadness. And disappointment. It was the disappointment that hurt Rsiran the most.

"I had to do something," he said softly. "Brusus was dying."

Della nodded. Both hands cupped over the top of the silvery cane. "Then it is my fault as much as yours."

He shook his head. "It was my choice."

Della smiled sadly. "As it was mine not to share with you what you needed to know. And for that, I'm sorry."

Brusus tried to stand and failed. "What is this, Della? What are you and Haern not sharing about this place?"

Della watched Rsiran as she answered Brusus. "Venass is a place of study, but unlike the people of Asador, they care little for histories or the stars or philosophy." She sighed. "They are men and women once of Elaeavn who study power. They use what they learn to twist the abilities the Great Watcher granted us. And Rsiran, I suspect, interested them greatly."

With Thom and what he'd seen of his ability, Rsiran should have known they had a connection to Elaeavn. Which meant they must be Forgotten as well. "That was the price of the antidote." He pointed toward the wooden bottle on the table.

Della looked at it, frowning, and picked it up. She pulled the stopper from it and raised it to her nose, inhaling slowly. "An antidote," she repeated.

Rsiran nodded. "Thom told me I could find an antidote in Venass. Isn't that what it is?" If they hadn't given him a real antidote, would he really feel obligated to return for them to study him?

But Della nodded. "It is. And it would have worked, I suspect." She paused, looking to Brusus. "Strange they would know which antidote to provide for Brusus."

Brusus's eyes narrowed, and then he flashed a look at Haern who only nodded. Brusus sighed. "Damn," he whispered.

"What?" Rsiran asked.

"This wasn't about me."

"How could it not be about you? You were poisoned!" And, he suspected, the one that Thom wanted in the end.

Brusus laughed until it turned into a cough. When it cleared, he shook his head. "I remember. And I thought this was about what Rsiran did in Asador, revealing his ability to Slide as he chased Josun looking for Jessa." He looked at Della. "It's about that, but it's more than that, isn't it?"

"It seems that way."

Jessa squeezed Rsiran's shoulder. "Brusus…"

"This was never about me. The poisoning, the attack in the Barth. None of it." He leaned forward, and a pained look came to his face as he looked at Rsiran. "This was about *you*."

Della rested a hand on Rsiran as she moved past him. A wave of relaxation swept through him, and some of the fatigue faded. Then she tottered toward the cot, clearing the bloody sheets away so they piled on the floor before she sat.

No one said anything until she was settled.

"Why would they want me?" Rsiran asked. But even as he did, he understood. They wanted to learn how he could Slide. Possibly more than that now. He'd shown them he could escape their cells.

Did they know he could use the heartstone alloy to Slide?

"I don't think they know the full extent of your secrets, Rsiran," Della said.

She'd Read him. There was no other explanation for her knowing what he'd been thinking.

He pushed up his barriers, testing to ensure they were fortified with the alloy. Satisfied they were, he let himself relax.

"What secrets?" Haern asked.

"Those are for Rsiran to share," Della said. "We all have things we prefer to keep quiet."

"Not if it places the others in danger," Brusus said.

"Like how you shared with Rsiran the story behind the Forgotten?" Jessa said. She stood facing Haern, anger flashing across her face. "Or how you made clear to Rsiran what you planned when you threatened him outside the Barth?"

Rsiran touched her arm, wanting her to relax. Getting angry didn't help any of them. And she was tired. They both were. They needed sleep—him especially so he could Slide again if needed—but now wasn't the time for that.

"No, Rsiran. If Haern's going to spout off about secrets, then he should share too."

"Like you have?" Haern whispered.

Jessa glared at him. "Rsiran knows about my past."

Haern snorted. "I'm sure he does."

Della tapped her cane on the ground. It snapped loudly, cutting off conversation. Everyone turned to look at her. "Do you think this makes us stronger or weaker? Rsiran needs our support, and arguing about what we hide—often from ourselves—does nothing. Already, he has many powerful enemies. Should he have new ones from among us?"

Rsiran looked at Jessa. Her eyes scrunched as they did when she was worried. One hand slipped to his leg, holding him. Rsiran looked at Della and saw the weariness on her face. How much longer could she hold out as she was? Like the rest of them, she needed sleep. And Brusus—injured and poisoned, barely able to sit in the chair—he seemed more concerned for Rsiran than himself. How had Rsiran ever doubted him?

Last, he turned to Haern. Always difficult to know what went on behind his eyes. He watched Rsiran, the dronr flipping from finger to finger.

Rsiran needed to explain to his friends. If he didn't, how were his actions any different the way Brusus had hidden things from them?

"There is a lorcith alloy. Mixed with heartstone," Rsiran began. He stared at Haern as he said it. Why shouldn't he share with them? Besides, everyone other than Haern knew already.

"You told me of this alloy," Haern said.

"And how it can prevent Sliding?" Rsiran asked.

Haern nodded. "I've learned much about the alloy since you told me of it."

Rsiran frowned. "What does that mean?"

Haern shrugged. "That parchment you took from the alchemists?" Rsiran nodded. "I managed to have it translated."

Brusus looked at Haern. "You didn't tell me this."

Haern watched Rsiran and shrugged.

"What did you learn?" Rsiran asked.

"Blocking one from Sliding is not its only purpose. But an important one. There are other uses, ones that Venass would be most interested in learning."

"It doesn't block me."

Haern blinked slowly. "At the palace. You said you couldn't reach Josun at first. That you had to use the sword he'd stolen from you."

Rsiran nodded.

"Now you no longer have to have something you've made?"

"I think of them as anchors. And no, I don't."

"What of your other ability?" Brusus asked.

In answer, Rsiran focused on the chain hanging around Jessa's neck. As he did, he felt the hard presence of the alloy, so different from pure lorcith. He pulled on it, lifting it gently, careful to leave the lorcith charm alone.

Haern watched Rsiran, but when he saw what he did with the necklace, he shook his head. "That shouldn't be possible."

"Now you see why they would think Rsiran dangerous," Della said.

"With Venass involved, this has become about more than just the Forgotten," Haern said to Della. "I had not thought that Josun was with them, but what if that was wrong?"

She tapped her cane softly. "I'm beginning to think this has always been about more than the exiled Elvraeth."

Chapter 20

Rsiran stood before his forge dressed again in the grey clothing from the mines, letting the flames lick the coals, the hot fire slowly building. Sweat slicked his brow and dripped into his eyes. He wiped it away and stood there for another moment. This close to the forge, the air smelled hot and bitter, like the lorcith itself.

The fires of the forge welcomed him. He'd always found it relaxing to stand in front of the coals as they heated the metal, but real peace was only found when hammering the heated metal into shape. What he needed now was that peace.

He felt rested, even though he'd only slept for a few hours. Fitful dreams called to him, threatening to pull him back into the cell in the Tower of Scholars. Each time he settled into sleep, he thought he sensed lorcith growing around him, drawing him toward it. And this time, he didn't think he'd be able to escape.

Part of him suspected that if he returned to the Tower, there would be no getting out. At least, not easily. The last time it had taken him sensing his lock pick and then Jessa to escape. He no longer even felt safe Sliding. What would happen if the scholars somehow *pulled* him as he Slid? Della had demonstrated how Sliding could be influenced. And if they could influence his Sliding—as evidenced by how they'd drawn him into the Tower in the first place, and *pushed* him out when he left—would he be in danger every time he tried Sliding? Would he simply appear in the Tower unintentionally?

And then what would happen to Jessa?

Rsiran sighed. What would happen to Jessa if he reneged on his agreement with the scholar and never returned? Would they manage to get to her, take her to their tower? Getting her out of there would be harder than saving her from Josun. At least with Josun, he thought he understood his abilities. Rsiran had no idea how the scholars manipulated lorcith as he did.

He reached into the bin and took out a small lump of lorcith, not bothering to look as he selected it. As he pulled it out, he saw that it was a perfect size for one of his knives. With what he planned, he might need them. Rsiran regarded the lorcith and debated whether he would ask it to accept the alloy, then decided against it. Nothing could be gained by mixing heartstone into the lorcith.

He looked around the smithy. In spite of all the heartstone alloy around him, all the effort he'd gone to in order to keep himself and Jessa safe, it seemed that he would be unable to do so. Would they ever be able to stop running? Would he and Jessa ever find peace?

Once the lorcith reached a soft orange glow, he lifted it from the coals and set it on his anvil. Then he took the hammer he'd long ago borrowed from his father's shop and began working the metal.

With each swing of the hammer, he felt his mind clearing. He hammered, flattening one side and then lifting with the tongs and twisting the lump. Another swing of the hammer. It rang out loudly in the confined space, but he'd given up fearing the constables would discover his unauthorized forge. They never came through this part of Lower Town. The only people living along this street were squatters like him, men and women with no right to the buildings they occupied. They would no more go to the constables to complain than he would.

The hammer swung again. His mind had emptied. There was nothing but the pull of the lorcith, and he let it draw him, guiding his hand. Each time, twisting and turning, slowly folding the hot metal into shape. When the lorcith cooled, he brought it back to the forge, heating it until it was workable again. If he waited too long, the metal would no longer take on the heat, instead becoming brittle, but Rsiran was a skilled smith, especially with lorcith, and knew just when to bring it back to the coals.

He switched to a smaller hammer, this one a remnant of his time in the Ilphaesn mines. Of all the tools he used forging lorcith, for some reason, this one always helped the most. He made smaller swings now, and no longer did the hammer ring out loudly in the smithy. Now it sounded muted. Each stroke became more deliberate now.

Rsiran glanced at what he was making. Not a knife as he expected. Instead, the lorcith folded out flat, becoming a rounded sheet. Had he wanted a knife from it, the lorcith would have agreed. Somehow, he knew that much. But he hadn't insisted. Because of that, the lorcith pulled itself into its own shape.

He almost hesitated, wondering what he might be making. Then he swung the hammer again, pushing away any questions. He'd already given himself to what the lorcith wanted from him.

Rsiran kept hammering. A shape continued to emerge from the metal as the lorcith changed from a flat sheet of metal into a curving shape, like one half of a ball. Again, Rsiran nearly hesitated, but pushed forward.

And then it was done.

He set the hammer down and wiped the sweat from his forehead. As the metal cooled, he studied what he had made. It was unlike anything he'd ever done before. In spite of that, it was no less exquisite. From the way the metal appeared to run, he could tell he'd folded it several times. Distantly, he remembered doing it, but the memory came as if through a fog. The metal had been folded back on itself several times and then flattened again. Each time, he'd folded it at a slightly different angle. This created a strange dimpling to the finish that had nothing to do with how he'd hammered it.

As he looked at it, he realized it was incomplete. The half he looked at was just that—half. He would need to make the other half. One of the lumps of lorcith in the bin next to the forge called to him, like a twin of the one he'd just worked. Without touching it, he knew it would make a similar shape. But then what? What was this for?

Rsiran carried it to his bench and set it next to the other shapings he'd made. He could study it later and try to learn why the lorcith had wanted to make *this* shape.

"Something troubles you?"

Rsiran turned. Jessa stood at the other end of the bench, watching him. He hadn't heard her come in. He sighed. "It's just that…" He shook his head. "If Della is right about me, you're not safe. Not here and not with me."

Jessa looked at the forging he'd made and slipped around the table until she reached it. She ran her hand over the surface, as if feeling the dimples the folding had made, and then lifted it, twisting it to study it. "You can't see what you did here," she said, ignoring his comment.

Rsiran shook his head. "You know I can't. I go by feel. The way the metal folds. The way the lorcith tells me to change it." He smiled. "Had I your Sight, maybe I'd be a better smith."

She pushed her fist into the curve. It fit snuggly. "I'm not so sure. If you had my Sight, you might not use the connection to the lorcith in the same way. This way, you're forced to listen to it and not get distracted." She set it back on the table. "Where's the other half?"

He pointed to the lump he'd pulled from the bin.

"You already know?"

He shrugged.

"Is it always like that?"

"Not usually. I'm not sure why the lorcith wanted me to shape it like this."

"Why not make a knife?" She lifted one of the smaller knives off the table and spun it briefly in her hand. Then she slipped it into her waist.

"I was too tired to make a knife."

Jessa laughed. "You realize you sound crazy?"

"Why?"

She tapped the bowl with her knuckles. It rang with a muted sound. "What you've made here is much harder than the knives you make."

He shook his head. "Not really. Knives," he began, trying to think of how to describe what is was like when he made knives, "are like suggesting something to the lorcith. It's an effort of will. I push a little, they push a little."

"Like a negotiation."

Rsiran frowned. "Not like that, I don't think. That's more how it feels when I work with the alloy. With lorcith, I have to continue to suggest what I'd like to see it become."

"And if you don't?"

He ran his hand over the recent shaping. "Then I make things like this. Or the charm on your necklace."

Jessa lifted the charm and looked at it. The charm had a spiraling shape, but the bottom flattened out, widening into something that looked almost like a leaf. She had once described the striations she could see in the charm, because Rsiran couldn't see them. He could feel them, if he listened. He wondered if that was the same thing.

"Listening and letting lorcith guide me is easier. And sometimes I need it to help me clear my head."

"I understand. You think it dangerous when I sneak around through Elaeavn, but it's relaxing to me. Sometimes, I simply sit and look over the city, watching the night move around me. When I do that, I feel like I can find peace."

Rsiran hadn't known that before. "I think it's the same when I work at the forge."

Jessa walked over and put her arms around him, looking up into his eyes. "Did you find answers this time?"

He sighed. Would Jessa understand what he needed to do or would she disagree and argue? "Not the kind that I need. I don't know when Venass might summon me. They were willing to attack Brusus to get to me." He closed his eyes. Could they really only have wanted *him*? "Maybe this is just about me and my abilities, but why? What do they want from me?" He opened his eyes and looked to her. "What if it's not only about Sliding and there's something else that we're missing? I can't risk another attack on my friends. I can't risk something else happening to you."

"You're going to Ilphaesn to see Josun, aren't you?" She pushed away from him. "You don't think I know how you've been keeping him alive?"

Rsiran hesitated. "I should have told you. It's just—"

"You didn't think I'd understand?"

"After what he did to you?"

Jessa looked up and smiled at him. "He didn't do anything that hasn't been done before. At least this time, I knew you wouldn't rest until you found me. That wasn't always the case before I met you."

"I'm sorry. I should've told you."

"Yes. You should have." She leaned toward the flower in the charm and inhaled. "What do you think he even knows?"

Rsiran sighed. "Maybe nothing. Maybe where to find the Forgotten. Or what they're after. I don't know, but I'm tired of *not* knowing."

"And Venass?"

"Venass and the Forgotten are together. I need to find one to understand the other. And I'm not risking going back to the Tower."

"You think the Forgotten are any safer?"

"We have one of them trapped."

Jessa touched his hand. "What you're doing might be crueler than you realize."

"Asking him what he knows about the Forgotten?"

She shook her head. "Keeping him alive."

Rsiran turned to the table stacked with his forgings and picked up one of the small knives. He *pushed* on it, and it spun in his hand softly. "I can't just kill him."

Jessa smiled. "I know. You're like a babe."

"I thought that was because I couldn't see in the dark."

She shrugged. "Partly. Keeping him trapped in the mines is no better than what he did to me."

"What do you suggest, then?"

"I don't know. I'd say to ask Brusus, but I know how he'd answer."

Rsiran nodded. Brusus would take the practical approach, especially after everything Josun had done to them. "If I let him go, then we have to fear him coming for us. There's nothing else to do with him."

"Like I said, it would be better if you let him die."

He set the knife back down and looked over at Jessa. "That's not me."

"I know. That's part of what makes you unique. Even after everything that's happened to you, somehow you still find a way to feel compassion for those who've harmed you."

"Compassion? I practically forced my father to come with us to Thyr. Then I left him there with the scholars." Only the Great Watcher knows what the scholars would do with his father—or to him, if Rsiran didn't return as he'd promised.

"And saved him when he jumped along the way. And made a point to tell him about your sister." She shook her head, her hair swishing across her face. "You're a regular ass, aren't you?"

Rsiran laughed and turned to look at his forge. "It doesn't feel like I'm compassionate."

"Probably not. But you aren't a killer, either. With what they did to you—Josun especially—no one would fault you if you simply…"

When she trailed off, Rsiran turned. "Simply what?"

She shrugged. "Stopped taking him sacks of supplies. Or Slid him to the top of Ilphaesn and dropped him. Either way, no one would fault you."

Rsiran watched Jessa for a moment before shaking his head. "You would."

Jessa smiled. "Maybe. But I'd understand too."

She walked to the table and grabbed a pair of slender knives, tucking them into her pockets. She waited for Rsiran to do the same. He picked out the smaller lorcith blades, narrow bladed but balanced so they flew straight, and slipped them into his pockets.

Then she took his hand and looked up at him. "I'm ready when you are."

CHAPTER 21

RSIRAN GRIPPED JESSA'S HAND TIGHTLY, worried how she would react. The last time she had been to the Ilphaesn mines had been when Josun Elvraeth trapped her there, preventing Rsiran from sensing the lorcith charm she still wore.

They emerged in the mine, just inside the entrance, the bitter lorcith all around them. Rather than clearing it from his mind to sense for the heartstone alloy chains, he relied on Jessa to see if Josun approached. Had he brought a lantern, he wouldn't even have needed that.

Here, close to the entrance, light from the crescent moon filtered through the thick slats of heartstone alloy. With the chains Josun wore, the bars might as well have been iron. But they served a purpose in keeping out anyone else who might Slide. He didn't know who else might come for Josun, especially considering that Della had sensed other ripples from Sliding, so the bars were his only way to ensure that Josun remained trapped.

Waves crashed along the rocks far below them. Rsiran remembered the time he discovered the opening for this cave, how he'd attempted to Slide here with Jessa, but the alloy had blocked him, nearly tossing them into the sea. At least now, he might be able to save them if that happened. After what he'd discovered in Venass, how he'd managed to Slide without moving, he thought he might be able to escape anything. It would be a useful skill.

"Where is he?" Rsiran asked.

"I don't see him."

Rsiran followed his sense of lorcith down into the mines. With Jessa next to him, he had the advantage that her Sight would protect them. And by keeping his connection to the lorcith, he could use his knives if needed.

Jessa held his hand, squeezing it tightly as they made their way into the darkness.

Lorcith all around him guided his steps.

"Up ahead," she whispered.

She pulled on his hand and slowed him. Rsiran waited, knowing Josun would come to them once he saw they were here. As he waited, he pushed away all sense of lorcith, clearing it from his mind. The more often he attempted to clear his mind like that, the easier it became. Each time, he managed to push the soft call of the lorcith more quickly than before. Now he managed it within a few short breaths.

Then, free of the lorcith, the alloy called to him.

Rsiran felt it moving toward him. Still chained to prevent him from Sliding, Josun walked toward him. With Jessa along, Rsiran considered *pushing* on the chains to keep Josun from getting too close, but decided against it and wasn't certain that he even could.

He needn't have worried.

Jessa let go of his hand, leaving him standing alone in the dark and unable to see her.

Then he heard a low grunt. The chains dropped toward the floor, rattling against the stone in the strange, muted way they had.

Jessa grabbed his hand again. Tension working through him eased as she did.

Josun laughed. Rsiran felt it as the chains moved, rising from the ground as he stood. "I deserved that. And that's more than Rsiran ever did to me."

Rsiran felt Jessa stiffen and wished he'd brought his own lantern so that he didn't have to depend on Josun lighting it.

With the thought, the orange glow flickered into view. Rsiran slammed his barriers into place, fortifying them with the heartstone alloy, remembering all too well how easily Josun managed to Read him.

Josun laughed again. "So predictable," he said. He stepped back against the wall of the cave, the lantern sending dark shadows flickering up and down the cavern. Josun moved the lantern so it rested between them. "But then… not." His eyes narrowed, and the shadows filled the hollows below them. "No bag of supplies. And you brought her." He frowned. "Why are you here?"

"Answers," Rsiran said. "That's why I'm here."

Josun smiled. "You've always wanted answers, Lareth, but you've never asked the right questions."

"Are you from Elaeavn?" Rsiran asked.

The smile on Josun's face faltered for a moment. "You came to me in the palace. You know I am Elvraeth."

"But not of Elaeavn," Rsiran repeated. "You're one of the Forgotten?"

Josun's hands twitched, twisting the chain between them, as if he hoped to pull it off. The smile turned into a sneer. "If I had been exiled, would I have been allowed in the palace?"

No, Rsiran realized. He wouldn't. "But you support the Forgotten." He waited and Josun didn't deny it. "Someone you care about. Who?"

"You say that word as if you understand what it means. Can you truly understand what it's like to be exiled from your home, from everything you've ever known? Can you understand what it's like to be suddenly *less* that what you are?"

"Yes."

Josun studied him. Then he laughed again, a harsh and angry sound. "You think your exile is the same? You were sent to the mines by your father to work, but you were never really in any danger, were you? With your gifts, you could always escape and return. The exile you ask me about is different. There is no return."

"You weren't exiled," Jessa said. "You have no idea what it's really like, either. You made a choice to leave the city."

Josun leveled his gaze on her, studying her. Then he rattled his chains violently at her.

Jessa didn't move.

"Why did you help them?" Rsiran asked.

As Josun leaned against the wall, wild hair resting against the stone of the mountain, Rsiran didn't think Josun would answer. His fingers drummed over the top of the cuffs, slipping up to the chains. "You get used to them after a while. Is that how it was for you?"

Rsiran frowned. "What?" he began, but realized what Josun asked. His eyes drifted down to the chain stretched between the cuffs on his hands. The dull metal had a muted gleam in the soft orange lantern light. "I never got used to them."

And he never wanted to. Thankfully, he hadn't worn them for long. After Shael had captured him and put the ancient chains on him, Rsiran had learned how to release himself, enough that he hadn't been tormented by losing his ability to Slide for nearly as long as Josun had suffered with it.

Losing the ability to Slide had been only a part of what the chains suppressed. He wondered if Josun learned about their other impact, but decided he probably hadn't. Josun couldn't hear the soft call of the lorcith, and would have no idea how it pulled on him. To have it suddenly silenced wouldn't bother him nearly as much as it had Rsiran.

Josun sneered at him. "That's right. You managed to escape. How was it you accomplished what no Elvraeth has ever managed? How was it that a *smith*"—the title dripped derisively from his tongue—"managed to escape the ancient heartstone chains?"

Rsiran thought about answering, but Josun would never understand: Rsiran had listened to the call of the lorcith and surrendered to it. "Tell me why you returned to Elaeavn. Why did you want the lorcith? Where were you sending it?"

Josun shook the chain again, looking from Rsiran to Jessa for reaction. "You already know, it seems."

"Know what?"

He turned, leaning his head against the wall. As he did, he looked smaller, broken somehow. Rsiran felt a pang of guilt for leaving him locked in the tunnels as he was. There had to be another way, a different place. With the Elvraeth chains, he couldn't Slide anywhere. Could he return Josun to the city and entrust his care to Brusus?

Not until after he determined what the exiled Elvraeth wanted from him. What the scholars wanted from him. Only then would he consider an alternative for Josun.

Josun looked over, a dark gleam to his eyes. "You know about the exiles, but you will never understand what they desire. The son of a smith could never understand. And you can never understand why I would want to help, or how I could help." He laughed in a dangerous and deranged way.

Rsiran kept his expression neutral, not wanting to give Josun any insight about what he needed from him. "What did you want in the palace? Did the scholars send you back?"

Josun grunted. "There were many reasons for me being in the palace."

"Why the lorcith sword?"

Rsiran hadn't worked out why Josun wanted the sword, but there must be some reason. And having learned that his father had been abducted and taken to Asador to study Rsiran's forgings meant there was more to that than what he had learned.

"The sword…" Josun looked as if he tried looking past them. "I still can't believe you made that. An apprentice, and not even Elvraeth born. But you don't even know what it is, do you?" Josun blinked and turned to look at Rsiran. "You don't realize what that blade could be, what it symbolizes?" He watched Rsiran, tilting his head strangely as he did, twisting as if trying to understand a puzzle. "No. I see you do not." Josun laughed again and slapped a hand against the stone. "And I thought you did. I thought that was the reason you chased *it* instead of *her*." He pointed to Jessa. "But you didn't chase the sword at all. Not at all." He frowned. "Then what is it? How did you learn how to make a blade like that?" He asked the question aloud but seemed to speak mostly to himself.

Rsiran glanced at Jessa. "This was a mistake," he whispered.

Josun darted forward, tipping the lantern over as he did.

In a flash, Rsiran *pushed* three knives from his pocket so they suspended in the air, pressing toward Josun, pushing him back toward the wall of the cavern.

Josun put his hands up, the heartstone alloy chain linking the cuffs clinking across his head. "Ah… I forget about that particular ability of yours. So useful. So useful. Only, I know you won't do it, Lareth. Haven't I told you that you're not a killer? You don't have that in you."

Rsiran gritted his teeth and glared at Josun. With the lantern tipped, the shadows in the cavern looked different, stretching long toward the mouth of the cave. "Try me."

He *pushed* the blade forward slightly, surging it toward Josun's neck. His deep green eyes followed the trail of the knives unflinchingly. As they neared, Josun leaned forward, pressing his bared throat against the tips of the blades.

"All I have to do is push. Or fall. And then you'll see what you could be. You would be surprised at the freedom, Lareth, when you no longer fear taking a life."

Josun smiled and twisted as if to slice his neck against the knives Rsiran held in the air.

With a sigh, he *pulled* them back to him and caught them, stuffing them back into his pockets. "I won't give you that satisfaction."

"You've already given me much satisfaction. Now leave me. Unless you've brought more food and water." He looked and saw their empty hands and shook his head. "Oh, right. That's not why you came. You thought I'd share the plans of the Forgotten. Why else would you have come, and without supplies for me, I might add. Well, even if I knew I wouldn't share their secrets, or their location. Yes, I of course know of their interest in you, but that's all I know. You see, I haven't been Forgotten, so they do not even claim me." He laughed bitterly.

"After all that you've done for them?" Rsiran asked.

"Why do you think I went after the council? Why do you think I harvested the metal? And I might have succeeded had you not…"

He looked at his leg, where Rsiran had stabbed Josun with the poisoned blade when still learning to control his ability to *push* on his forgings.

Whistle dust. Meant to poison the council, but not enough to kill. It would've just made them sick. Rsiran thought that Josun had a darker reason, but could it have simply been to gain favor with the Forgotten?

"How do you think to find out their secrets, Lareth? You're nothing more than a smith." He paused and studied him. "And not even that any longer. Run away. Return to the city and the foolish belief that the Elvraeth protect you."

"You might have been more skilled than I was once, but no longer," Rsiran said. "I will find out what they want with me."

Josun looked at him then turned and looked down at his arms, at the chains preventing him from Sliding. "Perhaps I'm not as strong as you," he said softly. "But I still doubt you'll find them. And certainly not before they find you. They've been in the shadows for too long, they know how to wait. And when they come for you…" He cackled and rattled the chains.

Rsiran jumped and immediately pushed back the annoyance he felt. "What does that mean?"

Josun snorted. "It means… it means that you are nothing more than a smith, and not even of the guild. If they want something of you, you would do well to provide it or…"

"Or what?" Rsiran demanded.

Josun shrugged. "Or suffer." He shook his chains again. "And I can see that you've suffered already." He laughed again as he backed against the wall of the caves.

Worry wrinkled the corners of Jessa's eyes, different from the concern she'd had about him coming here in the first place. She glanced over at Josun, biting her lip as she frowned.

They Slid from the mines—leaving Josun leaning against the wall, staring down at his chains—with no more understanding than when they'd arrived.

CHAPTER 22

RSIRAN LEANED ON THE TABLE IN THE SMITHY. Behind him, the forge heated, coals glowing a deep red and orange. He didn't know what he'd make, but needed to clear his head again. The scent of lorcith hung more strongly in the air as it always did with a heated forge.

Jessa was gone, searching for Hearn and checking on Brusus, while he couldn't shake that he was missing something. The Forgotten had attacked Brusus, and Thom had used that attack to get Rsiran to the Tower of Scholars. From what he could tell, Venass had sent the Forgotten after him because of his abilities. Or maybe it was the other way around. Either way, he was convinced they worked together.

Then there was what Josun had wanted from him. Why the sword? What about it was important? Would it have somehow helped Josun find the Forgotten? And he still didn't understand why Josun had been shipping lorcith. That was tied into it all somehow. Could he have been getting the lorcith to Venass? Was that how they had such massive amounts throughout the Tower?

Rsiran hated the idea that he would always have to fear the next at-tack, and always have to worry about what would happen next. They'd attacked Brusus, and Josun had already gone after Jessa. What would happen next?

Could Rsiran use his sword to find them?

But… not his sword. This wasn't the sword Josun had wanted. What he had *really* wanted was a sword made of the heartstone alloy.

Why?

The man he'd seen in Venass had been able to use lorcith, and had *pierced* himself with lorcith. That was important somehow, Rsiran was certain of that. Was it the alloy that Venass wanted? Did they think to control it as they controlled lorcith?

He didn't know enough.

He thought of everything stored in the warehouse. Items of wealth and culture kept from the rest of Elaeavn, but for what reason? The palace Elvraeth wanted the same thing as those exiled. As the scholars in Venass. Everyone wanted power. From what he'd seen, none used it well.

He picked up the sword, holding it with a loose grip as he swung it from side to side. The lorcith blade practically hummed, pulling on him. Had that sense grown stronger in the time since he'd forged it? More than any of his other creations, he felt attuned to the sword.

What was it about the sword that Josun wanted? Why would he also want a sword made of the heartstone alloy? Without knowing, he didn't think he would fully understand what was going on. After what he'd been through, not understanding put those he cared about in danger.

Rsiran set the sword back atop the table and made his way to the bin of lorcith. He stood in front of it, eyes closed, as he listened.

At first, he felt it as nothing more than the distant sound he always heard with lorcith. Each piece called out to him in its own way, as if begging for attention. When he felt a strong enough connection, he sent out his request, framing it as an image in his mind.

Rsiran had never done anything like this before and wasn't completely certain it would work, but he listened.

As he did, one of the lumps of lorcith called back to him, responding to his request. Rsiran kept his eyes closed and reached for it within the bin.

When he pulled it out, the lump of lorcith was larger than many. And heavy. He held it, debating whether he was making the right decision, before setting it on the hot coals of the forge.

The lorcith slowly began to warm, building to a hot glow. As it did, he turned to the smaller bin nearer his table. There, kept in a covered box, he had the last of the heartstone he'd managed to collect from where it had been hidden within the warehouse. Rsiran popped open the lid and looked inside. Only a few small squares remained. After they were gone, Rsiran didn't know where to find more. Heartstone was not mined in Ilphaesn like lorcith was. He wondered if he could use his ability to find more, but worried he would not be able to.

In the middle of the box was a larger square. For what he planned to forge, he needed a larger piece. But did he dare use it?

Without thinking on it more, Rsiran grabbed the square and took it to the forge. Learning to work with heartstone had been difficult. Already soft, it didn't take much heat to melt. And melting wasn't really what he needed anyway.

Mixing lorcith with heartstone was more a melding of the two. When both glowed steadily, he moved them to his anvil and set the heartstone atop the lorcith. Then he began folding them together.

He worked slowly, heating it as needed, until he *felt* the alloy form. It changed something of the lorcith, taking away its quiet call, the soft music he'd once heard throughout the mines of Ilphaesn, and made it harder and harsher.

Then the real work began.

As the alloy, Rsiran no longer could allow the metal to guide his forging. Not as he could with lorcith. The alloy did not sing, but it *did* have a call. He could use that, and listen to it, but focusing required losing himself in the forging. In that way, it was no different from forging lorcith, only he'd begun to learn to control the connection to lorcith, to no longer lose himself quite as completely.

He hammered, focusing on the image of the shape he wanted the metal to take. Each blow of the hammer took extra effort, as if requiring a part of himself, more than what lorcith required when he worked with it.

Rsiran lost himself in the forging. Heat. Hammer. Fold. Over and over until the shape of his forging began to emerge from the metal.

After a while, Rsiran switched to a small hammer, making delicate adjustments. Whatever his father thought about letting lorcith guide him, had Rsiran not listened to the lorcith as he worked with it, he never would have learned some of these more subtle lessons. Each time he worked with lorcith, he learned something new. Even the half bowl he'd made, he'd learned how to hammer the metal perfectly flat before curving it again. This forging required everything he'd ever learned.

And then it was done.

Rsiran set the hammer down and looked at the forging lying on his anvil.

A long blade, shaped into a sword, nearly the twin of the one lying on his table. Only this sword was made from the heartstone alloy.

As it cooled, Rsiran lifted it and brought it to the table to rest next to the other sword. Unlike the lorcith sword, the metal from the alloy was muted and dull. Still, the small work with the hammer had led to the metal seeming to flow from the tip to where it would attach to the hilt.

And, strangely, just like with the lorcith sword, he felt an affinity to this forging.

Rsiran frowned. The sense was different from what he felt from the bars he'd made to protect the smithy. Those he felt if he focused on them, but they didn't call to him like the new sword did.

All it needed was an edge and a hilt, and the sword would be complete.

He turned at the sound of the door opening, expecting Jessa. How would he explain what he'd made? Would she understand?

Rather than Jessa, Brusus came through the door alone.

He looked weak though still stronger than when Rsiran had left him. His eyes shone with a pale green, and he walked with a slight limp. The deep indigo shirt he wore had heavy embroidery around the collar and strips of black running along the sides that matched simple black pants.

Brusus closed the door and clicked the lock before turning back to Rsiran. He swept his eyes over the smithy, lingering on the forge. "You've been working."

Rsiran nodded. Did he tell Brusus about the sword? "I needed to think."

Brusus nodded. He looked at Rsiran, something about his expression hesitant. "I wanted to thank you for what you did. Without you there…"

Rsiran shook his head. "You don't need to thank me, Brusus. You needed help. I was there."

"But I do. I don't like getting into the habit of owing others. Now with you, I feel I'm so deeply indebted that I'll never repay what you've given me."

"There's no debt to repay. You'd do the same for me."

A wide smile split his face, bringing back some of the joy Rsiran was accustomed to seeing. Since Lianna had died, Brusus hadn't been the same. Not that Rsiran could blame him. He didn't want to think of what would happen were the same to happen to Jessa.

"That I would. Probably not as well. That's not my gift." Brusus stayed near the door, as if unwilling to come too close. "Jessa told me what you did to get us out of the Barth. I'm not sure I fully understand what happened."

"They wanted *me*, Brusus," Rsiran reminded.

Brusus sighed. "Perhaps. There's more that I don't know," he said softly. "I wish that I could understand… but it's beyond me." He cast his gaze around the smithy before settling on Rsiran. "I wanted to talk to you about what you've planned."

"To find the rest of the Forgotten? So far, I haven't come up with a plan. Before I decide anything—including whether I return to Venass to repay my debt—I need to know what they all want of me. I know the scholar spoke of learning how I can Slide past heartstone. And I've learned that there are Forgotten who can Slide…" Rsiran sighed in frustration.

"And *I* know you think I've kept things from you." He raised his hands, stopping Rsiran from saying anything. "You don't have to deny it. I *have* kept things from you. Dangerous things. But I didn't do it to keep you from knowing, I did it because I thought you knowing would be more dangerous." He inhaled deeply. "I wanted to protect you. All of you." He turned and looked around the smithy again. "Damn great job I did of that, it seems."

Rsiran laughed. "You could have done better."

"I thought being Elvraeth born would let me protect the people I cared about. Even that isn't always enough."

"You've done what you could," Rsiran said. And it was true. Since he'd met Brusus, everything he'd done had really been to position them better. Had it not been for Josun, they would still be sitting in the Barth, sipping at ale and dicing. Safe.

Brusus sighed again. "He's always played me well. Too well. I think he knew that my mother was one of the Forgotten—and Elvraeth—long before we learned enough about him to know he sided with the exiles."

Rsiran didn't know how to phrase the question that had bothered him since learning of the exiled Elvraeth. But he needed to know.

Brusus smiled, but it seemed a sad smile. "Ask it, Rsiran."

"And your mother? Is she a part of them?"

The corners of Brusus's eyes tensed. In that moment, Rsiran wondered if Brusus would answer him honestly.

"I don't know. You know as much about me as nearly anyone. More than I'm comfortable sharing." He looked up, and deep green flashed in his eyes. "I know you'd never do anything with that knowledge, but having it out there in the world…" He shook his head. "It's not easy for me."

"I understand," Rsiran said quietly.

Brusus nodded. "That's why I trust you'll do what's right. Why I've always trusted you to do what's right. More than anyone I trust—including Haern—you understand."

"Della knows. She understands," Rsiran said.

He tipped his head in agreement. "She knows. There's not much she doesn't know about me." He took a few steps into the room and turned. "My mother brought me to Della after I was born. I… I don't know much about her other than what Della told me. She left me in Elaeavn, thinking I would have a better life than I would had I grown up in exile."

"Why?"

Brusus shook his head. "The other cities tolerate our kind, Rsiran, but they do not love us. We are gifted by the Great Watcher and they are not." He made a motion around him, sweeping his hands. "You have your own gifts, valuable ones, clearly. And think of how you feel about the Elvraeth, about the abilities they possess. Now think of how a person with no gifts would feel about even the weakest person in Elaeavn."

Rsiran had never thought of it like that before, but it made sense after hearing Brusus say it. Hadn't he always wished he had the abilities of the Elvraeth? Sliding was useful—now that he no longer feared what he could do and had embraced his ability—but hadn't he often wished for the ability of Sight or even to Read? What must those living in Asador or Cort or Eban feel about the people of Elvraeth, knowing what they could do?

Was that the reason the scholars wanted to study him? Della had said they are men and women once of Elaeavn who study power. They seem to be working with the Forgotten already. But ability with the heartstone alloy is something they would all want to learn about.

"I hadn't considered it like that before."

Brusus chuckled. "Most don't. Unless they leave Elaeavn, few think about it. That's why my mother didn't want me growing up in a city where my ability was rare and misunderstood, where what we could do was viewed as dangerous. Something to be feared rather than appreciated."

"Like Sliding?"

Brusus nodded. "Like Sliding. You know what it's like growing up like that. How hard it was for you when you discovered your ability, only to learn that your father considered it dangerous."

"He thinks it's more than that."

"Does that matter?" Brusus asked. "Has it ever mattered? The Great Watcher doesn't give us abilities we aren't meant to use. It's *how* we use the gifts we've been given that defines us." He fixed Rsiran with eyes that were suddenly deep green. "You've never shaken your concern for what your father thinks of what you can do, but what do *you* think? How many people have you been able to help because of your ability? How many times have you saved those you care about?"

Rsiran laughed. "You don't have to convince me, Brusus. I'm not ashamed of my ability anymore."

Brusus's brow furrowed as he frowned. "I hope not."

He said it in a way that sounded unconvinced. So much like Jessa in that. And hadn't Rsiran gone to see his father in the hut in the Aisl? Maybe Jessa was right—maybe he still sought his father's approval.

Rsiran realized the reason Brusus would want to reach out to the exiled Elvraeth. "Is that what this has been about for you? Trying to find your mother?"

Brusus sighed again and swallowed. The tension around his eyes returned. There was more to his story than he shared, Rsiran realized.

"Partly," he admitted. "That's why I needed your knives. Oh, they helped get information in the city, but I've never really needed lorcith blades to get that. What I needed was a way in. Once exiled, the Forgotten disappear. For years, I thought they might be hidden in one of the great cities. Asador or Cort or—"

"Or Thyr?" Could the exiled Elvraeth be there as well? Were they with the scholars?

Brusus nodded. "Or Thyr. But Haern says there are no exiled Elvraeth among Venass. Only others of the Forgotten. I searched each city, looking for any sign of them. It's as if they never existed."

"You didn't believe that."

"No. And Della suspects they gathered somewhere, only even she doesn't know where they might hide. After trying for years and failing, when I met you and saw those knives…" He shook his head. "No one had made weapons like that in over a century. At first, I thought maybe the exiles had made them." He smiled. "Better I found you, I think. Only later did I think that the Forgotten would want them. Since the Ilphaesn mines are completely controlled by the guild, the Forgotten have no access to lorcith on their own." He blinked. "At least, I hadn't thought they had." His face darkened. "Josun proved otherwise."

"So you just wanted to reach the exiled Elvraeth?"

Brusus crossed the distance between them and rested his hand on Rsiran's arm. "That's not why I wanted to help, Rsiran. I saw in you much of myself. The uncertainty. The anger at having to hide who—and what—you are."

Rsiran swallowed. If all Brusus wanted were knives, he wouldn't have pulled Rsiran in as a friend, introducing him to the others. To Jessa. And wouldn't he have done anything to help Brusus had he known what he needed?

"Do you think reaching the exiles might help you find your mother?" Rsiran asked.

Brusus rubbed a hand across his face. "I don't know. She could have gone and hidden in some small village somewhere for all I know. Or maybe she went to one of the greater cities where the other Forgotten can be found and I just didn't see her."

"You don't think she did."

"I don't think she did." Brusus shook his head. "Every time I've tried getting close to them, someone has gotten hurt." He sighed. "After Jessa was taken, I realized everything I did put us all in more danger."

"You didn't think that after what Josun did to Lianna?" From the hurt look on Brusus's face, Rsiran immediately wished he hadn't said it. "I'm sorry. That didn't come out how I meant it."

Brusus sniffed. "What Josun did to Lianna was done as a message to me. What he did with Jessa involved you. There's a difference to me."

Rsiran frowned. "Not to me. He killed one of us. And tried to take another. Sometimes I think I should let him die trapped in the mines."

Brusus's head snapped up. "Josun lives?"

Rsiran nodded.

"After what he did to Jessa… the way you said you found her, hidden within Ilphaesn… you let him live?"

"I should have told you," Rsiran said. "I didn't know how, and honestly, I hadn't decided what I was going to do with him."

"He can't escape?"

"Not while wearing the Elvraeth chains."

A dark smile slipped across Brusus's mouth. "He could be useful to us. And not just to me. He might be able to—"

"I've already gone to him to ask what he might know."

"And?"

Rsiran shook his head. "He says he's not privy to where the Forgotten are, because they do not claim him as one of them. If he is to be believed, he seems his attempt to poison the council was simply to gain favor with them. Maybe sending the lorcith too." Rsiran was less certain about that part.

Brusus sighed. "Just as well. Knowing Josun, he'd stab me in the back as soon as he had the chance."

"Don't give him the chance."

Brusus picked up the forging of the half-formed ball and twisted it in his hands. "If Josun can't find them, I don't think we will have any better luck."

"And he wasn't any help regarding Venass, either."

"He's Elvraeth born, Rsiran. He probably doesn't even know about the Forgotten Venass claimed and the Tower of Scholars." Brusus set the forging down and clasped his hands together. "We'll keep you safe."

"That gets harder now, doesn't it? The Forgotten and Venass are not the only ones after me. The guild. The palace Elvraeth. It would seem I'm quite popular."

Brusus surprised him by laughing. "Yeah, you've got yourself into some trouble, haven't you? And you thought living with your father was bad!" He clasped Rsiran on the shoulder. "Don't worry. We'll find a way to protect you."

Rsiran wasn't certain that Brusus could, even though he would want to. Rsiran recalled how difficult it had been to escape Venass. He'd very nearly been trapped by the guild. And if the Elvraeth came for him… Though his abilities were growing stronger, he feared there was nothing that he could do to keep himself safe, let alone Jessa, when the next attack came. And with what Josun had said, he was certain the Forgotten—either exiled Forgotten or Venass—would come after him again.

Chapter 23

RSIRAN SAT ALONG THE DOCKS IN LOWER TOWN, staring out over the water. The sun shone brightly overhead, the first time he'd seen it in several days. The air carried the scent of the sea, that of salt mixed with fish coming off ships, as well as an undercurrent of rot that seemed to permeate everything in Lower Town. Still, Rsiran felt comfortable here.

Wind whipped in from the north carrying a hint of lorcith from Ilphaesn. He suspected he was the only one who would notice it. As usual, he felt drawn toward Ilphaesn.

Behind him came the sounds of the streets. At this time of day, Lower Town was awash with people. Many came down from Upper Town to trade at the docks or pick up the fresh catch. The rich— and those living within the palace—sent carters to the docks so they wouldn't have to come to this part of the city. Even when he'd lived with his parents in the middle of the city, Rsiran had never understood the reluctance.

A few ships moved in the distance. Massive sails swelled with the wind, pushing them onward. A sleek, twin-masted ship with a hull painted crimson sailed out of the bay, slowly making its way north. Another ship, this smaller and with a single mast, worked toward the shore. Rsiran didn't know enough about markings to know where either ship came from. Neither looked anything like Firell's ship. Since he'd escaped, Rsiran had wondered what happened with Firell. Likely, he'd taken his store of lorcith to Asador as he'd said. And from there? Firell could be anywhere. At least he wouldn't have to worry about Josun anymore.

"Might be others to worry about."

Rsiran jumped, realizing his mental barriers were down and slammed them into place. Brusus stood behind him, dressed in a navy tunic and dark brown trousers. A matching cloak hung off one shoulder. Dressed as he was, Brusus could fit in Upper Town. Down in Lower Town, he seemed out of place.

"Brusus."

He tilted his head. "You need to be careful with your thoughts. You can be… loud… sometimes."

Rsiran frowned. "Loud?"

Brusus shrugged. "I don't know how to explain it any better than that. Some people's thoughts are like that. Yours were never quiet, but over the last few months, they've gotten louder. Most of the time, you're shrouded, like nothing is there, but when you forget to shroud your thoughts…" Brusus shook his head. "It's like you're screaming."

"Can everyone hear them?" The idea horrified him and made him realize he needed to be more careful.

Brusus shrugged again. "I don't know. I've got some skill with Reading, you know. Perhaps it's just me." He took a seat on the narrow bench overlooking the dock and stared out at the water. "You worry about Firell?"

Rsiran stood, making certain his barriers were in place as he considered how to answer. With what had happened, anything he said might not make much sense. "We know that Firell and Josun worked with the Forgotten, probably shipping lorcith to them. When he captured me, I got the sense that Firell only did what he had to do."

Brusus nodded. "That would be Firell. Practical like that. Ship captain has to be, I suspect." He sighed. "And I'm sorry about Shael. Were it not for me, he'd never have met you. He always did seem too eager to know what you were forging, always trying to suggest things for you to make. I thought he just wanted coin."

"He worked for Josun and wanted something made. A forge of sorts, only one that would force heartstone into lorcith. It's probably a good thing I wasn't able to make it."

Brusus gave him a strange look. "You sound disappointed."

"Not disappointed. There is so much I could have learned had…"

"Your father?" Brusus asked.

"I'll never learn from a master smith. Not what I need to know."

Brusus laughed softly. "You sell yourself short. I'm not sure I've seen metalworking skill such as yours before."

Rsiran didn't deny that he'd gained skill. Lorcith had taught him how to be a smith. But there were parts of being a smith he still didn't know. And now, never would.

"You still wish you could learn from him."

"He is—was—one of the finest smiths in Elaeavn." And now Venass held him. Rsiran knew he should care more about that, but it was hard for him to find it within himself. "But that's the only reason I would help him now."

"Jessa told me how you Slid after him when he jumped toward the Thyrass River."

"We needed him."

Brusus frowned. "Is that the only reason?"

Rsiran grunted. "The only one that matters. I thought I was finding an antidote for you. Had I known what I was getting into…"

"Had you told Della what you planned, it wouldn't have been necessary."

"I had to make a decision. If I hadn't and Della hadn't Healed you, you would have been lost."

Brusus smiled at him. "You'd do it again?"

"If it meant saving you."

"Even knowing what you know now?"

"That's just it. What do I really know now? That the scholars in Venass are something to be feared, and probably Forgotten. I already feared the exiled Elvraeth, what's another group chasing me?" he said bitterly.

As he said it, he realized it was true. He'd wanted to do everything he could to keep Jessa and the others safe, but he couldn't prevent everything from happening to them. Hadn't what had happened with Lianna taught him that?

"I don't think I can just sit around and wait for the next time someone comes after me," he told Brusus.

"I still have some connections in the city," Brusus said.

"Including the palace?" Rsiran asked.

"Some."

Hopefully Brusus's connections in the palace would give him warning if they had recognized Rsiran. "Then there's the guild…"

"They've been silent. No word on a break-in."

That didn't mean they didn't know about Rsiran, though. "We'll have to cross that bridge eventually," he said. "But for now, I think keeping aware of them is the most important thing. But the Forgotten… we don't know anything about their connection to Venass, other than our conjecture that the Forgotten who attacked in the Barth were sent by Venass."

"You think to find more information, but how will that change anything?" Brusus asked. "Other than you once again heading toward danger?"

"It probably won't change anything for me. From what I can tell, the Forgotten Josun sought already know about my abilities and want to use me. Whether as a smith or for my ability to Slide." He still didn't know if any other than Josun knew of his ability to *push* on lorcith. Had he been smarter, he might have hid that ability better. "And now Venass wants to study me, probably for the same reasons. They're connected, Brusus. We have to know how. And I can't wait for them to find me."

Learning more might even keep him safe. If he could learn what they wanted, he might be able to use it to keep them from attacking him or his friends.

"I'm not so certain of that, Rsiran. Anything you do only draws more attention to you. There are certainly others—some worse than Josun—who can hurt you."

"They've already come after us once. What happens when they do it again? How many attacks can we survive?" That had been the only thing he'd learned from his conversation with Josun—that they would, indeed, come. Rsiran turned toward the water, steadfast in his resolve. "I think it's time we know more about them."

"And then what? You think to request a meeting with the Forgotten *and* Venass? Tell them both to please leave you alone? Maybe you think you can convince them to stop seeking to regain power, because from I can tell, that's what they ultimately want. And if they have indeed joined forces, it's possible we won't be able to stop them."

Rsiran started up the street, walking along the shoreline. Not far in the distance, the row of warehouses began. In there was the warehouse where everything really began for him. Where he'd exposed his ability to Slide to Brusus. Where he'd first met Josun. Where he'd seen the excess the Elvraeth possessed and did nothing but collect. Other than what Brusus had taken from there to sell, most of it still sat in the warehouse collecting dust.

Without meaning to, he started toward the warehouse. Brusus followed after him, waiting for Rsiran to respond. "They've been after something else," he said, realizing a connection between the Forgotten and Venass that he hadn't made before. "And not only lorcith."

"What?"

The warehouse. Josun had been there the night he and Jessa had gone to look at that crate—a crate with wood much like what he'd seen in Venass. There was something in the warehouse the Forgotten wanted that was tied to Venass, but what?

Rsiran stopped in the middle of the street. A carter walking behind them had to swing wide around them so he didn't collide with them. What was in the warehouse that they would have wanted? They hadn't moved anything from the warehouse that was of any real use, nothing… but the strange box full of the cylinders.

"What did you do with the cylinders?" he asked Brusus.

Brusus frowned. "What?" He shook his head, realization dawning on his face as he glanced in the direction of the warehouse. "Why are you asking about them?"

"Do you still have them?"

Brusus shrugged. "Most of them. Some were sold. The metal too valuable to simply leave useless like that."

Rsiran shook his head, starting toward the warehouse. "What if they're not useless?"

"We don't even know what they were for. They were shipped here years ago. Likely some sort of gift for the Elvraeth. Rsiran?"

He paused and looked back. Brusus stood at the edge of an intersection in the street, looking at him with worried eyes. He flicked his gaze past him, looking down the row of warehouses and toward the shadows stretching there. Rsiran turned and followed his gaze. A sellsword slipped into the shadows, disappearing. Brusus knew firsthand what could happen were they to get too close to the sellsword.

Rsiran turned away from the street, but not before seeing the sellsword slipping along the edge of the buildings, slowly oozing toward them. Only when he was back on the Bay Road did the sellsword stop following him. Even then, he stood at the edge of the shadows, staring toward him. Had he recognized them?

Brusus said nothing as they made their way up the street, toward his smithy. Rsiran could have Slid into the warehouse—and likely would when Jessa was with him—but not yet.

"What were you thinking?"

Brusus glanced around and pitched his voice low as they made their way along the street. One of the ships settled against the dock as they walked, and nearly a dozen dock workers scurried into action, catching lines and tying them off or hoisting a plank to unload the day's catch. Carters lined up along the dock, waiting to purchase fish fresh off the ship.

"If you wanted to go to the warehouse, just Slide there."

Rsiran glanced over his shoulder. He had the creeping sensation that the sellsword still watched him, though he couldn't see him anywhere. If he had Sight like Jessa, he might be able to. "Why would the Forgotten suddenly come out of hiding after all these years?"

"You think it's the warehouse?"

"Not the warehouse. At least, not entirely. We've found heartstone there, but we've also found those strange cylinders. That's what helped me make the connection. Venass and the exiled Elvraeth. There's got to be more to them than we know."

Brusus flicked his gaze toward the warehouse. "We could gather the cylinders…"

They started up the slope, working their way toward the smithy. Once they reached an alley, Rsiran would Slide them the rest of the way. "That still won't answer how they're connected. And Josun doesn't seem to know where to find the exiled Elvraeth, but there's one who does. And maybe if I find him, we can get a step ahead. Figure out why Venass would be interested in me." And find a way to avoid their summons. Maybe even figure out a way to get his father back.

Brusus watched him, understanding settling in his faded green eyes. "It's a terrible idea."

"You're not going to try and talk me out of it?"

"Would it make any difference? You're still going to try and find him anyway."

"Who?" When they'd turned off the street and onto the alley leading toward the smithy, Rsiran felt Jessa approach by the charm she wore. "Who is Rsiran going to try and find?"

"Shael. Damn idiot wants to find Shael."

CHAPTER 24

Rsiran hunched over a scrap of oiled wood, staring at the markings etched along the slick surface. He worked a fingernail into the layers of wood, peeling it back. Jessa sat next to him, studying him in the flickering light of the hearth flame. She hadn't said anything since they returned from the warehouse.

"These are the same markings I saw in Venass," Rsiran said, breaking the silence. "Same wood too. I'm sure of it."

Jessa leaned over the scrap and frowned. "Are you certain? I don't remember seeing anything like them."

He closed his eyes, visualizing the way the symbols had been etched into the lorcith-infused stone. At the time, he hadn't known what they meant. Still didn't, but he began to realize they were the same language.

"They were on the wall in the room I was in. I remember seeing them, but not what they meant."

"They could mean anything. Or nothing at all."

The same thoughts had crossed his mind. "What if they're connected? What if these crates came from Venass?"

"Why would Venass send crates to the Elvraeth?"

Rsiran didn't know. "And why would the Forgotten be interested in them?"

Her hand slipped onto his leg and she leaned toward him. She smelled of the fading lilac she wore today. "There's probably nothing to any of it. These crates are hundreds of years old."

Rsiran nodded. "Probably."

"But you think the Forgotten and Venass are working together. And if that's the case, then I don't think we should be trying to find anything that Venass might want. We've already seen that the scholars can do *things* they shouldn't be able to do. What if this device lets them do something like that? Why get in their way?"

Rsiran laughed, though an edge of nervousness flowed through him. "What do you think the cylinders will do? Let them Slide to Elaeavn? If they could do that, there's nothing stopping them anyway."

Jessa sighed and looked back at the scrap of wood. "I remember how excited I was when we first found those cylinders. The different metals, some gold, some silver, all with the same shape and designed to fit together. Now…"

"I know. Now you wish we never would have found them."

"At least they've been kept from the Elvraeth. At least Brusus didn't sell them."

Rsiran still didn't know why.

The door to the smithy clicked open, and they both turned. Rsiran readied a pair of knives to *push* if needed, but Brusus came through the door, closing it quickly behind him. A sheen of sweat coated his face, and a smudge of dirt or oil worked along his chin. He carried a couple of small boxes, similar to the one Rsiran had recently helped Jessa steal.

"You could help, you know?" he said. "Maybe could even Slide these here, rather than making me carry them. Some get heavy. Don't know why. They're all the same shape."

Rsiran pushed to his feet and laughed. "I've told you how different metals have different weights." He looked at the boxes. "Which ones did you bring?"

Brusus frowned. "What do you mean by that? I told you I'd bring all of them."

Rsiran shook his head as he glanced at Jessa. "That's not all of them. There were dozens of different cylinders in that crate."

"I already told you. I sold some. I kept some."

He grabbed the nearest box and carried it toward his table before setting it down. He didn't feel the pull of lorcith or the alloy from within the box and wondered what metals these would be made from. Rsiran worked one of his knives under the edge of the box, prying it open. A cylinder of dull iron rested inside. He opened the next. This was grindl, a semi-valuable metal. Rsiran looked up at Brusus.

"You sold the gold one?"

He nodded. "I got nearly fifty guildens for it."

"And the silver?"

Brusus shrugged. "Only ten."

"Who bought them?"

Brusus turned to look around the smithy. His eyes hesitated when he caught on the bars of the alloy pressing through the floor and stretching toward the patched ceiling overhead. "Shael bought a few of them. I thought your plan was to find him anyway?"

Shael again. How tightly tied to all of this was he? "I think I need to. We need to know what he wanted. What this device can do."

"Now you think you're going to recover all the parts too?"

"I don't know. One thing at a time."

"Better blame Della for what we don't have," Brusus said.

"Della?"

He shrugged. "She wanted me to get rid of the Elvraeth property. Thought it dangerous I had it lying around or something." He grinned and shook his head. "She knows me better than that. I don't keep things just lying around."

Brusus started toward the hearth and stumbled, staggering to one knee. Rsiran Slid to him quickly and put his arm around Brusus's waist, catching him before he could fall. Another Slide took them to the hearth where he lowered Brusus to the ground.

"Are you…"

Brusus nodded. "I'm fine. Still get weak from time to time. Della helped, but the poison they used…" He shook his head and forced a smile. "Nothing to worry about. I need more rest, is all."

Rsiran glanced back at Jessa. He read the worry on her face. It matched what he felt. "You won't be able to come with us for this, Brusus."

"You're not keeping me out of this, Rsiran. If you find the Forgotten—"

"Then I come and bring you to them. Until then, you can stay in Elaeavn and rest."

Brusus looked past him to Jessa. "Tell him I'm fine."

Jessa knelt alongside Brusus and looked from Rsiran to Brusus. "I'm with Rsiran on this, Brusus."

"Figures."

She went on as if he said nothing. "It's safer if you stay here."

Brusus sighed. "At least take Haern. With what he knows, you might need him."

Rsiran had considered Haern but shook his head. "It's easiest with two," he started. It was easiest with him going by himself, but he didn't tell Jessa that. She wouldn't let him go without her anyway. And he might need her Sight. "And when I find Shael, I'll need to be able to bring him with me. Can't do that when I'm Sliding more than Jessa. Just be ready for us to return. We'll need your particular gifts to know what he might be hiding." Even three stretched his abilities farther than he felt comfortable. When they'd gone to Venass, it had taken nearly all of his strength to reach it. Returning would have been difficult if they'd still had his father with them. He wouldn't risk that again, not with someone he cared about.

"You know I could help." Brusus didn't speak with the same force as he usually did.

"You know you can't," Rsiran countered. "I will find Shael. Then we'll find the Forgotten."

Brusus nodded toward the collection of cylinders on the table. "And that? What do you plan to do with that?"

"One thing at a time. First we'll find out what Shael knows." And then the Forgotten. Along the way, somehow, he'd have to find a way to avoid returning to Venass. Rsiran doubted that he would find it as easy to escape the next time.

* * * * *

Rsiran held Jessa's hand as they emerged from the Slide atop Krali Rock. She looked at him, a question in her eyes. Wind whipped around them, carrying the expected scents of the docks and the sea, but other scents as well, that of smoke and wood and the distant fragrance of the Aisl. The moon stood out full and fat as it hung over the bay, silver light streaming toward the shore. Dark shadows swooped overhead, gulls circling and landing. Occasionally, one cawed, splitting the silence of the night. Other sounds, most coming from the Aisl, were too low to hear well. Rsiran wasn't certain he wanted to know what made those sounds anyway.

He always liked using Krali Rock as a starting point for his Slides, especially when he didn't really know where he was going. There was something about the height, the way he could see and feel everything around him as if he sat with the Great Watcher, that he found connected him to the world. Closer to the ground, he had no sense of the same. There, he felt confined by the city, trapped in his own smithy, though by his choice. Anywhere else didn't offer the same promise of safety.

"How do you think you'll find him?" Della held tightly to his hand. She wore a long jacket, woven of thick wool Brusus had procured for them, dyed a deep brown meant to blend in anywhere they might go. Rsiran wore a similar jacket.

"He was with Firell the last time I saw him."

"That was weeks ago."

Rsiran couldn't believe it had been that long. Weeks since Jessa had been taken from him. Weeks since he determined to do what was needed to rescue her. And weeks since Josun had been captured, left in chains in the hidden mines of Ilphaesn.

"Firell will know where he went. Probably took him there by ship."

"And if he doesn't? Or if we find the Forgotten? Are you ready for that?"

They would have to find the Forgotten eventually, but he wasn't sure what would happen if they found the Forgotten but not Shael. What he wanted was answers, not another attack.

Standing here, looking out over Aylianne Bay, he wondered if he could find Firell's ship and then Slide to it. When he'd been able to see the ship, it had been a risky Slide. The last time he'd Slid there, he'd known Firell carried some of his forgings and used those to anchor him. What if those forgings weren't there? What if Firell had moved them off his ship?

Rsiran didn't think he had.

It was a risk, but one he needed to take. If he was wrong, he had faith in his ability to get them to safety again. They wouldn't get trapped like they had with the scholars again.

Rsiran cleared his head, pushing away the sense of lorcith pressing on him from the city all around him. This was more difficult than usual. The swords in his smithy sounded most loudly against his sensing, one asking him to take it with him while the other—the one he'd made of the heartstone alloy—practically demanded Rsiran return and take the sword with him. He would worry later why it felt so insistent.

When the sense of those forgings moved to the back of his mind, he pushed away the other forgings of his in Elaeavn. After all the time he'd spent working at the smithy, many items he'd made were in use throughout the city. Easiest to ignore was the unforged lorcith, most of which he kept in his smithy. There were a few other collections, one he suspected in the alchemist guild house, that he pushed to the back of his mind. Then he felt Ilphaesn.

The massive mountain worked with lorcith suddenly blazed against his senses. Rsiran could practically see it, as if the ore glowed with his awareness. Tunnels wove through the wide mountain, mineshafts worked throughout where lorcith had been taken out of the mountain for centuries. And still there remained massive amounts of the ore.

All of this Rsiran pushed to the back of his mind as well.

And then he sensed less lorcith.

There were other collections around him, some distantly that seemed to have nearly as much as Ilphaesn. Rsiran nearly lost his focus with the realization. Wasn't Ilphaesn the only source of lorcith? If there was another source, wouldn't the Elvraeth want to control that as well?

"What's wrong?" Jessa squeezed his arm as she asked. She didn't like standing too long atop Krali with the wind blowing, threatening to toss them from the top of the rock.

He shook his head, straining to keep his focus. He would have to think about the other lorcith he sensed later.

Rsiran pushed away the sense of the other lorcith. All unshaped lorcith disappeared, pushed into the back of his mind. All that was left were pinpricks of his forgings.

Which one would be Firell?

He listened. He didn't know how long he stood atop Krali, focused on the lorcith. It could have been moment or hours. Eventually, he felt one of the forgings that seemed more familiar than the rest, one he'd held more than once.

Reaching for it, he held it as an anchor, hoping it was one Firell carried. If it wasn't, Rsiran had no idea where he Slid. He could Slide alone, leaving Jessa here, but she would be angry if he even suggested it.

After squeezing her hand, he Slid.

Chapter 25

THE SLIDE FELT NO DIFFERENT FROM ANY OTHER. Colors swirled past him, almost creating a pattern. The swirling colors had a contour to them, a depth. Rsiran suspected this implied the distance they traveled. The air tasted stale and bitter, in a way, reminding him of mined lorcith. Jessa trailed along with him, a silent shadow he couldn't see well while Sliding. He felt her presence and held tightly to her. He did not want to learn what would happen if they lost the connection while Sliding. Rsiran held onto the faint sense of his forging, anchoring to it as it drew ever closer, the sense of lorcith growing stronger.

Then they emerged. Movement stopped. They were here.

Darkness surrounded him. He welcomed back his sense of lorcith and felt a few items nearby, only one he'd forged himself. Others were shaped, not mined ore, but not his work. The air was musty and damp, though he didn't sense any of the salt from the sea. Had he missed his mark? Was this *not* Firell's ship?

"What do you see?" he whispered.

Jessa held onto his hand. "Not much. Walls. Part of a knife on a table, probably yours. A small box…"

She let go of his hand as she trailed off.

Rsiran latched onto his sense of the charm as she did. If something happened, he wouldn't lose her as he had the last time. There came the sound of nails squealing and Jessa grunted.

"What is it?"

She started back toward him. "Nothing. Box was empty—"

Light bloomed around them, a bright orange light. The suddenness burned into the back of Rsiran's eyes, but he knew the color made it even harder for Jessa to see, nothing like the blue heartstone lanterns.

"Thought you might return."

Rsiran spun to the sound of the voice. He readied a pair of knives, prepared to *push* them if needed, but at what? He couldn't see anything until his eyes adjusted.

"Firell?"

The light dimmed slightly as the lantern was set down. A figure stepped forward, past the light. Firell looked different than he had the last time he'd seen him. Haggard and worn. A bandage wrapped around one arm.

"Aye."

"Where are we? Your ship?"

Firell grunted and shook his head. "My ship? You been on my ship, Rsiran. You think this anything like it?"

Jessa stood next to Rsiran and took his hand. Not for reassurance. She knew to be close in case they needed to Slide to safety. "If not your ship, then where?"

"You don't know?" He turned and dimmed the lantern before facing them again. "Thought that was how you found me."

Rsiran shook his head. "I followed my forging."

Firell looked to the knife resting on the table. "That? I don't know much about that ability of yours, but you must have been pretty close to notice that."

Rsiran didn't argue with him. It didn't do any good for Firell to know how far he could sense his forgings. "Where, then?"

"They took my ship. Got into port, and the Forgotten put one of your knives to my throat as they walked me off. Claimed I did something to Josun." He spat the name bitterly. "Not that I wouldn't have. Just that I didn't. Don't know what happened to the Elvraeth. Haven't seen him since you came on my ship."

Rsiran felt himself relaxing and forced himself to be more vigilant. Firell had turned on them once already. How did he know he wouldn't do it again? Could he trust anything Firell said?

"You the one who managed to take him?" Firell asked.

"He doesn't even know how to reach the exiled Elvraeth."

Firell laughed until he coughed. "He tell you that?" Rsiran nodded. "And you believed it?"

Rsiran glanced to Jessa. "Who took your ship? Where's Shael?"

"Shael?" Firell shook his head. "Don't know about Shael. They walked him off, too, but not the same way. He didn't have to worry about a new smile like I did."

They'd found Firell, but not Shael. But maybe whoever had taken Firell would know where to find Shael.

Rsiran's eyes had finally adjusted to the orange light. The soft glow reminded him so much of his time spent in the mines. He didn't know it at the time, but the orange light made it hard for Sighted to see well, putting everyone on equal footing. He wondered if Jessa saw nothing more than he did.

They stood in a small room. She had been right. There wasn't anything other than a table with the knife resting on it and the box, now with its top peeled away. How had Firell hidden from Jessa's Sight?

Something about the knife wasn't quite right. Rsiran moved toward it and *pulled* it to him. It flipped through the air awkwardly, and he caught it.

Not a full knife. Most of the blade was gone, leaving only the tang where it entered the handle. From the mark and the way the metal folded together, Rsiran knew it was one of his earliest forgings, made shortly after Brusus had found him the smithy.

"What happened to the blade?" Lorcith was strong, but with enough force became brittle. This had broken, leaving only the handle.

Firell frowned at him. "You happened to the blade. When you came to my ship and did… whatever it is you can do."

Rsiran didn't remember any knives breaking as he'd Slid through the ship, but once Shael captured him in the Elvraeth chains, everything after that had been a blur. "This is all that's left?" Firell nodded. "Why keep it?"

"Thought that…" He shook his head and took a deep breath. When he looked at Rsiran again, his eyes looked hollow. The bright, playfulness he'd always had before was gone. "They didn't see it as a threat and let me keep it."

"And you thought I might come looking again."

Firell shrugged. "I thought there was a chance."

Jessa pulled on his arm. "We should go, Rsiran. Something about this place makes me uncomfortable."

Rsiran nodded. He wouldn't make her stay here. It was too much like what Josun had done to her. "Where did they take Shael?"

Firell shook his head. "Didn't see where they took him. Too busy trying not to bleed."

"Why would the Forgotten imprison you?"

"Still haven't learned much, have you, Rsiran? You think I did what that Elvraeth wanted by choice? You think I would have betrayed Brusus had I any other options?"

"There's always a choice."

"Not when he's got your daughter." Firell's voice caught. "Don't know how he found out about her. In my line of work, need to keep certain things secret. Safer that way."

"He Read you, Firell," Rsiran said softly. He remembered how Josun had practically crawled through his mind trying to Read him. Only by using lorcith to fortify his thoughts had he managed to block Josun from Reading him.

But Firell? He might be able to create a mental barrier, but would it be stout enough to block a powerful Reader?

"Why are they keeping you here?"

"Waiting for him to return. Thought he'd have come by now. Usually doesn't stay away from Asador too long."

Asador. At least now Rsiran knew where he and Jessa were. But why Asador again? It was where he'd found the sword Josun had stolen from him. And where he'd recovered his father.

"He's not coming," Rsiran said.

Firell leaned forward. "You killed him?"

There was more than surprise to the question. Fear and worry mixed in as well. Firell didn't care about what happened to Josun, but he might not be able to find his daughter again if Josun were truly dead.

"I did the same thing to him that he did to Jessa."

Firell looked over. Relief swept across his eyes. "Where is he?"

"Someplace he won't be found."

"How? He's like you, Rsiran. And we weren't able to trap you for long."

Rsiran shifted, turning to face Firell. "He's nothing like me."

Firell held up his hands. Blood soaked the bandage on one arm. Dirt stained the other, caked under his nails as if Firell had been trying to scratch his way to freedom. "I meant nothing by that. Just that you both have the same ability. The chains he gave us didn't work on you. What makes you think they'll work on him?"

"They hold him."

But for how long? Josun was Elvraeth, which meant he possessed some degree of each ability. What if Josun had some of the same ability as Rsiran? What if he could hear the lorcith? Would he be able to use that and *push* on the heartstone alloy to open the chains?

Would Rsiran be ready?

He pushed away the thought. If Josun were able to escape, he would have by now.

"Why are you here?" Firell asked. "What do you want with Shael?"

Rsiran squeezed Jessa's hand. "There is something Shael knows about. But since you don't seem to know where to find him, I think Jessa is right. It's time for us to be going."

He prepared to Slide them out of the cell. Rsiran didn't know where they'd go. Probably back to Elaeavn at this point, regroup, and then confront Josun again. If he *did* know how to find the Forgotten, Rsiran would see that he helped them.

And then Firell lunged at him.

Rsiran Slid off the to side, pulling Jessa with him. Firell's momentum into empty space sent him sprawling. He pushed up slowly and turned to face them.

"Don't. Please, Rsiran. Take me with you. I need to find Lena. I don't know what he did to her. She's too young… can't withstand him on her own… not without any abilities."

Rsiran hesitated. Could he leave Firell here tormented by the loss of his daughter? Firell had betrayed them, but had he done it by choice or force?

He looked over at Jessa. She nodded.

Rsiran faced Firell again. "You will stay with us until I release you. If you try anything that might hurt Jessa, or me, trust that I'll hide you where no one will ever find you. And I won't do anything to find Lena."

Firell studied him for a moment before nodding. "I think they underestimated you, Rsiran."

Rsiran hesitated. "What?'

Firell didn't get the chance to answer.

An entire wall burst open, light spilling into the cell. Firell threw himself back against the wall, moving out of the way.

Rsiran spun toward the door, holding Jessa's hand tightly in his. Six men stood facing them. One had a thick beard covering his face—something never seen in Elaeavn—and forked at each corner of his chin. Two holding swords, another pair with crossbows.

All were aimed at Jessa.

Firell had betrayed them again.

Rsiran readied to *push* his knives. He only had five on him, plus the pair of knives Jessa carried. If he acted fast enough, he could drop the attackers and get them to safety.

Or he could Slide. Nothing blocked him from Sliding. He could hold onto Jessa's hand and Slide to safety. Traveling a short distance would take little more than a thought to reach safety. And then he could take them to Elaeavn.

But if he wasn't fast enough?

A crossbow bolt might hit Jessa. He'd seen what could happen if he didn't Slide quickly enough. One of the Elvraeth had grabbed onto him during a Slide to Della's. If they did the same, or if the crossbow fired quickly enough, Jessa would be hurt.

Rsiran had another reason for hesitating. If these were the Forgotten, didn't he *want* to know why they had attacked?

When he didn't disappear, one of them stepped forward. He was startled to see it was a woman. She had black hair tied back behind her head. A tight-fitting jacket that flared at her waist, and loose-fitting leather pants. As she stepped into the orange lantern light, eyes flashed a deep green.

She smiled. "You're a hard one to find, Rsiran Lareth." Her voice had a deep quality to it, almost drawing him toward her.

Rsiran flicked his gaze over to Firell. How much had he told them about his abilities? Would they know he could *push* lorcith?

He listened for a moment, sensing for lorcith. Two of the men carried knives—his forgings even—made of lorcith. Unlikely they knew then.

It gave him an advantage.

"You know my name, but I don't know yours." As he spoke, he shifted so that he stood more in front of Jessa. He could still Slide them to safety this way, and she would be less likely to be injured.

The woman didn't move, only spread her hands. A steel sword hung from one hand and she nodded. "Mine no longer matters."

One of the Forgotten. The comment practically admitted to it.

Were all of these men Forgotten?

Something about the way she spoke made him realize that she tried to Push him.

Rsiran ensured his mental barriers were in place, infusing them with lorcith. If Readers were among them, he didn't want to risk someone learning anything more about him.

"Why are you holding Firell?"

The Forgotten glanced at the smuggler. He still cowered against the wall. Rsiran realized he may not have been any more a willing participant than he had with Josun. That didn't mean he didn't have a choice.

"I needed to see if what he said was true."

"And what did he say?"

"That there is a dangerous man who can Slide, one not Elvraeth."

She moved in a flicker, appearing suddenly in front of Rsiran. Sliding.

Rsiran tensed. She'd Slid faster than Rsiran could blink. Faster than he'd seen Josun Slide. Rsiran didn't think he could move that quickly, especially not with Jessa.

"I've met another who can Slide," Rsiran offered. "He killed someone I care about."

She leaned forward. She smelled of sweat and grease and something else. A familiar odor Rsiran couldn't quite place.

"Where is he?"

Rsiran didn't move. This close, he could sink one of his knives into her without moving if he needed to, but he needed to know more before he attacked her. Was she the only one who could Slide or could any of these others? And where were the rest of the Forgotten?

"Somewhere he won't harm anyone I care about again."

She studied Rsiran for a moment and then laughed. "Confidence. Interesting from one not born to the Elvraeth." She nodded at Firell. "He tells me you have another impressive ability."

Rsiran held his breath. If Firell had told them of his ability to *push* lorcith, any advantage he had would be gone. Of course, Josun already knew of that ability of his. He could have told any of the Forgotten before Firell needed to.

"About how you escaped from Elvraeth chains." She turned back to Rsiran. "Said you even Slid into the palace. I would like to know how you managed to do that."

Rsiran shook his head. "I can't explain what I do. I just can."

A wide smile spread across her face. "That's how you injured Josun the first time. Damn near killed him. Had he not had a ready supply of tchinth, he would have been gone. The Great Watcher knows it's a good thing you didn't finish him off sooner, or else we never would have found you."

"And why would you want to find me?"

She leaned into Rsiran's ear. Her breath was warm and smelled of faint spice. "Because you're going to help us."

CHAPTER 26

THE WOMAN HAD MARCHED RSIRAN to a room above the cell, leading them up a narrow staircase. A low ceiling forced him to duck as he made his way along the halls. The air smelled damp and musty, stinking of wet earth. Strange carvings marked the wood as they passed, written with marks that reminded him of what they'd found on the crates in the warehouse and those within Venass.

Small lanterns hung on hooks along the wall, staggered far enough apart that shadows still filled the space between them. When they reached the top of the stairs, Rsiran and Jessa had to duck to move through the door, as if it were made for a much shorter person.

And then they were in a wide room. A fire pit filled the middle of the room. Thick smoke rose toward a hole cut in the ceiling overhead, and thick logs crackled with heat. Two long tables filled the rest of the space, with benches along either side. Another narrow door led out the other side of the room.

The woman motioned them to sit, and Rsiran did, glancing to one of the men carrying a crossbow behind him. He eyed it briefly, noting that it seemed tipped with lorcith. Were he quick enough, he could deflect the bolt before it hit them, but they didn't seem interested in injuring them anymore. No longer did he fear for Jessa's safety. More than anything, he felt curiosity.

She Slid to a seat across from him. Four lanterns hung on posts around the room, spilling bright orange light around them. She leaned forward, the line of her sharp jaw catching the shadows between lanterns in such a way that her face seemed longer than it should. Bright green eyes looked out at them.

Jessa sat next to him, clutching tightly to his hand. She leaned toward him, as if claiming him as hers. She hadn't said anything since they left the small cell, abandoning Firell to whatever fate the Forgotten had in mind for him. After betraying them a second time, Rsiran struggled to feel any pity for him.

"Is this more comfortable?" the woman asked.

Rsiran glanced around the room. Other than the tables and the fire pit, not much else occupied the room. There was a faint scent of bread and meat. A sheen of grease smeared across the table. This was a barracks of some kind.

"You think to hold us here?" he asked.

She smiled. "From what I hear, you've shown you can't be held." She set her hands atop the table and leaned back, thrusting out her chest. A smile hadn't left her face since she appeared before them down in the cell.

Rsiran shrugged. "You can try."

She snorted. "Seems that would not serve any purpose, now would it? Besides, how can I convince you to help if I mistreat you?"

"What makes you think I'll help? After what Josun did—"

Darkness flashed across the woman's face. "That one acted on his own more often than not. He was useful, in his own way, but careless. He thought he could act alone."

"And do what?" After what happened in the palace and how Firell and Shael worked for Josun, Rsiran had thought all the Forgotten worked with him. But Josun had denied it, claimed he only wanted to find the Forgotten. What was the truth?

She arched an eyebrow. "Don't play the fool with me, Lareth. You saw what he wanted."

Rsiran resisted the urge to look over at Jessa. He wondered what she thought of this woman. With her Sight, she always picked up cues he missed, even without Reading. By the way Jessa leaned into him, he sensed jealousy from her, an emotion he'd never noticed from Jessa.

"I know what Josun claims he wanted, but I'm not sure I know what he really wanted."

The woman flashed her teeth, looking briefly like some kind of wild thing. "Fair enough. Tell me what you *do* know."

He debated answering honestly. He didn't think she could Read him—not with his barriers in place—but that didn't mean she couldn't Read Jessa. Or that she hadn't heard from Firell or even Josun what he'd done.

"He claims he searched for the exiles." Confusion flashed across the woman's eyes and then was gone. "That was why he wanted to poison the council. He called it a demonstration, but it was more than that, wasn't it? And he shipped lorcith out of the city. Since you have Firell, you would know that."

"You didn't poison them?"

The way she asked made it seem as if she really didn't know.

He shook his head. "I think I would have. But no. I didn't poison them."

Rsiran watched the woman. Her eyes narrowed and her brow furrowed slightly. One hand scratched at her face as she ran a hand through her hair.

"Why would he claim he can't find you?" Rsiran said.

The woman hesitated before answering. "He can be a bit short-sighted. Comes from his abilities, I suppose. Well, that and the fact that he's never worn the chains like others of us—" She cut off sharply and forced a smile onto her face.

Others had worn the chains? There would only be one reason they'd need to wear them. "How many of you can Slide?"

"You're no fool, are you, Lareth?" the woman asked. "Josun made a mistake with you, I think. He should have brought you here rather than trying to push you."

"Josun didn't push me. He killed one of my friends."

"That is unfortunate. Doing so did nothing but draw attention to us. That's something we don't want yet."

Yet.

"Why attack me in Elaeavn? Why come after me already?"

The woman flicked her gaze to one of the men behind her before turning back to him. "As I said, we want you to help."

"That's no way for you to convince me to help," he said. Lorcith moved somewhere behind him, and he resisted the urge to turn around.

"You haven't said how many can Slide," Jessa said.

The woman looked over to Jessa and frowned. It was the first time she'd spoken.

"Or your name. If you're asking Rsiran to help, the usual course would be to give your name. Draw him into your trust before you start making requests."

Her smile faltered for a moment, long enough that Rsiran noticed. Then it widened again, splitting her mouth.

"Ah, the sneak. We've heard about you as well. A thief of some skill. We could use your talents as well."

"We. You've said that before but shown no signs of anyone other than these men with you."

She nodded toward the pair of men standing behind her, practically hovering over her shoulder. Both carried crossbows. Swords would be nearly useless against someone who could Slide, but crossbows… they could damage before he had a chance to get them away.

"And you've given no indication that you're anything but Elvraeth tools."

Jessa laughed at that. "Elvraeth? You're actually suggesting that we might be *helping* the Elvraeth?"

The woman tipped her head and her eyes widened slightly. "That's exactly what I'm suggesting."

"We live in Lower Town. We couldn't be further from the Elvraeth if we lived here."

"Really?" She leaned back and turned to Rsiran. "You think yourself so separated from the Elvraeth that you're essentially exiled?" She laughed darkly. "Yet you still live within the city, enjoy the same protection of its walls, never fearing you'll be dragged away from your intended Slide as we fear. And you have one among you who visits the palace with enough regularity that he might as well live there." Her smiled disappeared. "Do not tell me you are separated from the Elvraeth."

If what she said was true, the Forgotten didn't just live in exile, they lived in fear. But of what?

"Who pulls you while you Slide?" he asked. "How many of you are there who can Slide?"

Something changed about the woman's face. It was as if it softened, the edge and the hidden anger fading. Rsiran didn't know if it was an act, or if she simply showed her true emotions.

"You really don't know, do you?"

Rsiran shook his head.

"This is not the first time you've left the city. You came to Asador. Took one of the smiths."

Rsiran nodded carefully.

"You didn't feel any… influence… while you were away from the city?"

"Influence?"

The woman let out a breath and shook her head. "You did not. Great Watcher, you really *are* a dangerous man, Lareth. You Slide without knowing the dangers. You travel without fear. And yet you do so safely. These are things we should like to understand."

Rsiran knew from what Della had told him—and shown him— that his Sliding could be affected by those able to sense him Sliding. She hadn't thought there were many with that ability. But from what he'd seen of Venass, they had some ability to influence his Sliding, especially if they managed to pull him into the Tower. But he'd needed to be close for them to do that, hadn't he?

"What dangers are you talking about? How many can pull you from a Slide?"

"So you know about that. Not as ignorant as you would have me believe."

"I know a Slide can be influenced. I've met someone with the ability."

"Where? Not in Elaeavn. That ability has been long dead, but there are those who study, who begin to understand—"

She cut off before she finished, but she didn't need to for him to understand what she meant. Venass.

Rsiran didn't say anything and hoped his barriers were stout enough that the woman couldn't Read him. If she thought the ability long dead, then it was better for Della. "Not as dead as you might think." He wouldn't tell her that he had been to Venass. Not yet.

The woman laughed. "Fair enough. But it's the reason we wanted to know about your ability. If you can safely Slide outside Elaeavn, there must be a reason. We would like to learn what that is."

"Why only outside the city? What makes Sliding within Elaeavn any safer?"

"The Elvraeth make it safer."

"I thought the Forgotten wanted to push the Elvraeth out?" Jessa asked.

"Is that what you think? There are some who feel that way. You've met one. Most of us don't care for the Elvraeth, not after what they did to us, how they either exiled us or our families, but most understand they serve a purpose."

"And what is that?"

She shook her head. "I can't believe you still don't know. The Elvraeth protect the city and its people. That's their purpose, why the Great Watcher chose them to rule."

Rsiran shook his head. "They don't do anything but collect lorcith and sit within the palace."

The woman smiled. "For the most part, that's true. But the council, at least, knows of their other purpose and guards it closely. It's why exile is such a punishment. Haven't you ever wondered why the Elvraeth banish people from the city? What kind of punishment is that unless there is something about the city that would benefit them?"

Rsiran hadn't considered it, but it made sense. "What kind of protection?"

She shook his head. "We don't know the details. Those of us who've lived outside the walls of Elaeavn know some of the effects. We've seen how Sliding can't be consistently used. It's a rare enough ability, but one that—outside of Elaeavn—is dangerous to utilize." She smiled, studying Rsiran. "Or, is for most of us."

"What of other abilities?" Jessa asked. "Sight or Reading?"

"For those recently exiled, there is no change."

"What of others?"

"They fade. Within a generation, abilities begin to slip. Over enough time, there are only weak abilities." She nodded toward the men holding the crossbows. "Naeln and Maven were both born to parents whose parents were banished."

Rsiran looked at the two men and only now realized the color of their eyes. They had faded green eyes that looked even paler than what Brusus projected when he Pushed. Rsiran had never seen eyes so pale. Within Elaeavn, they would be very weakly gifted.

He looked at Jessa before turning back to the woman sitting across from him. Rsiran noted the color of her eyes, the depths of the green. "Were you banished?" He didn't say Forgotten, worried he might offend her.

"I was born in Elaeavn. When my father was exiled, I went with him. There could be no evidence of him passing on his lineage."

Rsiran wondered about the woman's mother. As he did, he realized why Brusus's mother would have left him in Elaeavn. Now it made sense. Had she taken Brusus with her, his abilities would have faded.

Rsiran had come looking for the Forgotten, and found more than he expected. How much did Brusus know? How much did Haern? He'd wandered outside of Elaeavn more than any of them. Did his visions tell him what happened to the Forgotten?

And if Brusus knew, why hadn't he shared that with Rsiran?

"You see why we'd like to know how you can safely Slide?"

He shook his head.

"Because we're under attack, Rsiran Lareth. We have been for centuries, only now the attacks have grown stronger. And the Elvraeth will do nothing to help."

"Under attack? From who?"

The woman shook her head. "There are those with abilities that rival those gifted to us. They would steal from us, claim a desire to learn from us."

"You mean Venass," Rsiran said. Which meant that the Forgotten and Venass *didn't* work together.

She sighed. "You were a fool to come here, Rsiran Lareth. It is fortunate you did, but you were a fool."

Something struck the back of his head and he fell forward.

The last thing he felt was Jessa squeezing his hand.

Chapter 27

Rsiran awoke but didn't. Not really.

He felt a haze around him. Colors swirled as if he were Sliding. He smelled nothing like the Slide, though, and had no sense of movement.

Vaguely, he remembered what had happened. The back of his neck hurt and his head throbbed. He tried to move but couldn't.

Panic started through him, making his heart race. As far as he could tell, nothing bound his arms or his legs. He simply could not move.

Rsiran tried to force calm upon himself and focused on his breathing. He'd been trapped before and escaped. If he could sense lorcith, he would be able to Slide and free himself.

The air smelled damp and different than it had been before. A sweet edge hung to it, almost nauseating, like the edge of rot. The air didn't move, still as his limbs.

There was no light. That, more than anything, sent fear coursing through him.

Lorcith thrummed nearby, pressing on his senses. He felt his knives still strapped to his waist. They hadn't bothered removing the knives, thinking that he couldn't do anything with them if he couldn't move. It was a start.

At least his ability to sense the lorcith was not taken from him as it had been the times he'd been trapped before.

He listened for other lorcith, finally feeling it distantly. There were knives he'd made and others he had not. The crossbow tip he'd sensed earlier was somewhere nearby as well. A few lumps of unshaped lorcith, large enough to forge into swords, were near.

Rsiran ignored all of it, pushing it away.

He listened for a small piece of lorcith, one dear to him.

For long moments, he couldn't sense it. During that time, Rsiran felt afraid. He'd failed Jessa again, brought her into danger himself. And now the Forgotten would do what Josun first tried to do to him.

A sound came from behind him. Or above. Everything lost meaning as he lay unable to move. A dark shape hovered nearby. Rsiran smelled the sweet rot more strongly.

"Awake already?"

The Forgotten woman. As much as he wanted his freedom, he wanted to know who she was. What she wanted from him.

"This should help. Can't have you Sliding away before we get a chance to know how you escaped the chains."

Rsiran tried to open his mouth to speak, but it didn't work and sleep overwhelmed him again.

* * * * *

When he came around again, light streamed all around him. As much as he tried, he still couldn't move. His neck throbbed where he'd been struck, and his head ached. Other than that, he felt nothing else.

He could still hear.

Someone rustled nearby. From the occasional grunt, it sounded like a man. Rsiran listened for lorcith, and found he still wore his knives. There was more lorcith in the room, a long, slender blade. And not one he'd made.

Could he still *pull* on it?

He reached for the lorcith and tried. At first, he thought he touched the lorcith, that it would respond, but then it slipped away. He could sense lorcith but do nothing more with it.

A deep laugh came from where the person worked. "Can't be usin' your abilities, now can you?"

Rsiran would have lunged at Shael had he been able to move.

"Don't be worryin' about your girl. She be fine. And she'll stay fine so long as you help."

Rsiran tried to speak but couldn't move his lips. Sound escaped anyway, something that sounded like a low growl.

Shael laughed again. He came closer, splitting the bright light so it bent around him. "I do be rememberin' how you got out of the chains. Not going to make the same mistake again, am I? This be better. Can't escape if you can't move, now can you?"

Rsiran smelled the sickly sweet scent that was edged with rot again and began to understand.

They poisoned him.

Only enough that he couldn't move, but it was enough that Rsiran couldn't touch his abilities, either. They separated him from his gifts as surely as the Elvraeth chains.

"Need you to rest a bit more now, Rsiran. Do be needing to give them more time to work." He pulled on something. Rsiran realized he took his knives from his waist, but didn't find the others he had hidden on him. "You won' be needing these anymore, now will you? Probably fetch a few silvers for the pair."

Rsiran swallowed. His tongue moved, not much but some. "Why?"

The question came out as a croak, nothing more.

Shael leaned toward him, the sweet stench growing stronger, and laughed again.

* * * * *

He lost track of how many times he started to come around, only to be dosed again. Most of the time, it was the woman. He'd come to hate her visits and the satisfied smile she wore as she looked at him.

In some ways, Shael was worse. The man had already harmed him once, and that was when he was supposed to be his friend. Now he allowed Firell to be trapped as well.

This time, Rsiran awoke slowly. Blackness swirled around him laced with grey and deep green. His neck still throbbed, but it was distant, less than before. His head ached, pulsing with a steady pain that reminded him of what he felt while in Venass. Rsiran shivered with the memory.

He could still sense the knives on him and tried to *push* them but failed.

Was Shael still here?

He heard no sign of the smuggler.

Shael knew of his secrets, knew enough to poison him to keep him from moving, but why would they want to keep him immobilized if they needed to know how he Slid into the palace? He still didn't understand how they could learn anything if he couldn't move.

But they didn't need him to move to Read him, did they?

He pushed up his barriers, and found it more difficult than usual to do. As he did, he became aware of a crawling in his mind, subtle but clearly a Reader.

Would they learn all of his secrets? That he could move lorcith, and the way heartstone answered him as well? Would they learn how much Jessa meant to him, or that he would do anything to see that she came to no harm?

Rsiran felt violated in a way he never had before. Drugged so they could access his mind.

He focused on his connection to the lorcith. He might not be able to *push* it, but could he use it to support his barriers?

With an effort, he strained to push them into place, trying to seal out the Reader. The Forgotten woman, he had no doubt. Lorcith infused the barriers as he squeezed, pressing them into place. Slowly the sense of another presence, the crawling sensation he felt, disappeared.

Rsiran's breathing quickened as he held onto the barrier. Years spent living with his sister—a Reader of only minor skill—had taught him to keep his mind barricaded, but not in the way that he needed to around the more powerful Readers, those Elvraeth and Forgotten. And he didn't know how to maintain the connection even when asleep. When they dosed him with their poison again, he worried that the lorcith-infused barrier would fall again.

He heard movement. A door and then soft footsteps. Someone leaned close.

Rsiran feared it was Shael again, but he felt a warm breath and smelled a mix of spice.

The woman.

"You won't be able to keep me out indefinitely," she whispered. "Already, you have given me much." She crouched, leaning over so he saw her as little more than a vague shadow. "I confess I thought Shael had inflated his claims of what you can do with metal. After what I've learned, I see he didn't know everything, now did he?"

Rsiran tried to slam heartstone into the barrier in his mind, but wasn't sure he succeeded.

He smelled the sickly sweet scent, and then he went out.

CHAPTER 28

RSIRAN AWOKE TO AN ABSENCE OF PAIN. He didn't know what it meant that he felt nothing. No throbbing of the back of his neck. No pulsing of his head. Not even the ache from lying on the floor. Simply… nothing.

He still couldn't move.

And he was alone. No one made any sounds around him, not like there had been before. The air smelled only damp, none of the sickly sweet scent he'd come to associate with the poison.

His heart hammered in his chest. That they'd left him alone meant they'd likely gotten what they wanted.

But what did they want?

He checked the barriers in his mind, but they were still in place. Somehow he'd held them while the poison worked through him, keeping him from moving. Rsiran was no longer sure that meant anything. What if the woman could crawl past his barrier, even infused as it was with lorcith? Why hadn't he pushed heartstone into it? Then he remembered that he had.

Rsiran tried to swallow but couldn't. How long had he been here, separated from Jessa, trapped with the Forgotten?

Long enough to feel the effects of the poisoning over and over. Too many times to keep track. And long enough for them to learn everything about him.

He had thought to fear Venass, but they had not tormented him the same way the Forgotten did.

He was comforted by the thought that knowing how he Slid past the heartstone alloy didn't mean they would be able to do it. Unless they had others with his ability to sense lorcith.

But then what?

If that was all they wanted from him, they could have it. Knowing his abilities didn't mean they actually use them as he did.

Except he was trapped here. As long as they kept dosing him with the poison so he couldn't move, there was nothing he could do to escape.

And what of Jessa? Where was she? Shael claimed she was unharmed, but once they got what they needed from Rsiran, what reason would they have to keep her alive?

He had to think there was some reason; otherwise she'd already be dead. Maybe they wanted Josun back. And if they'd Read him, they already knew where Rsiran had left him. They might not be able to safely Slide—if what the woman told him was even true—but there were other ways to reach the mine. And once Josun was free, he would come for vengeance.

If only there was something he could do.

When Shael had captured him the first time and put him in the Elvraeth chains, he'd been cut off from lorcith. When he could reach it again, he'd been able to escape, freeing himself. That had been a different sense of hopelessness. This—the ability to sense and hear the lorcith but not *push* it—was a failure of his abilities.

Rsiran felt the lorcith of the knives he had strapped to his calf. There was a misshapen item an arm's length from him. Somewhere nearby were the knives Shael had taken off him. And then there was the charm.

He felt it differently than the rest, attuned to it in a way he wasn't to the knives. It was more like the sense he had with the sword, but different at the same time. If only he could anchor to the charm and pull himself as he had when he'd been trapped in Venass, but the poison kept him from being able to focus on the metal long enough to anchor.

Rsiran did nothing but listen to the charm. After a while, he realized it moved. If the charm moved, it meant Jessa lived; he refused to consider any alternatives.

The charm seemed to be closer than before. Were they taking her somewhere?

He wished he had some way of communicating with her. If only he had some of Brusus's abilities, he might be able to send her a message. Instead, he had to lie there motionless and wait. Eventually, the Forgotten woman would return, or Shael, and they would dose him again. And then he'd awaken, unable to move, cycling through again and again.

The charm came closer.

Rsiran felt his tongue loosen a little. Had they forgotten about him?

He managed to swallow. And then blink.

He prayed to the Great Watcher they gave him enough time. Maybe they'd miscalculated the effect. If it wore off before they returned, could he Slide to safety? Somehow grab Jessa on the way?

There was a sound near the door.

His heart hammered faster and louder. He blinked again, willing his body to move, but it didn't obey. Would it be Shael this time, or the woman? At least he'd discovered that Jessa still moved. Hopefully that had been Jessa.

A *click* came from near the door, soft but distinct.

Rsiran reached for lorcith, trying to anchor and Slide, but failed.

He moved his tongue, trying to work moisture into his mouth and his lips. It didn't work as it should.

The door pushed open with a soft burst of air. Did he smell something sickly and sweet or was it only his imagination? Then the door shut with another soft *click*.

Footsteps sounded softly across the floor. Too light for Shael. That meant the woman. The Forgotten. Would she push past his barriers this time or did it no longer matter?

A shifting of shadows crossed over his eyes, not enough for him to see. He waited. There was nothing else for him to do.

And then the voice. "Rsiran?"

Jessa.

He listened frantically for the lorcith of her charm. It dangled just over him, close enough to reach if his arms worked. He tried to make his mouth work, but it refused.

A fearful thought crossed his mind. What if this was another trick? What if she was Compelled?

"Rsiran? Can you move?"

He thought she touched him but couldn't be certain. He felt nothing other than his tongue, and it felt thick and swollen in his mouth.

The lighting shifted. He realized she lifted him, propping him up. Rsiran didn't know what she intended. He was too heavy for her to carry.

"We have to move. I don't know how long we have before they find I'm missing."

He licked his lips, moving his tongue slowly, and swallowed. "Jessa."

Her name came out more like a grunt, but he heard her sigh.

"I don't know what they gave you. Something to weaken you and prevent you from moving. Shael has come to me several times and said that if I told them where you'd hidden Josun, they'd let me go. The *other*"—she practically spat the word—"said he didn't matter. They wanted to know how you managed to reach the palace. There's something there they want."

Again, Rsiran listened for lorcith around him. He sensed the knives still hidden on him. Jessa wore the charm, but no longer had the knives she'd carried when they first came. If he could find the lorcith knives Shael had taken from him, he would find Shael.

He felt it close by. How much longer before Shael discovered Jessa was gone? How much longer before he came for Rsiran? Then she would be poisoned as well, left immobile as he was, unable to do anything. They would both be trapped.

"Shael."

It was the only word he could get out.

"I know about Shael, Rsiran. We need to get you moving. Can you Slide?"

He blinked and tried to move his head. Did it twitch? He couldn't tell. "No," he grunted.

She swallowed. "Whatever they gave you keeps you from your abilities. They know the Elvraeth chains won't hold you. No other way to keep you here."

Rsiran didn't think that was the real reason they poisoned him. At least, it wasn't the entire reason. They wanted his defenses down. They wanted to Read him.

"Read me," he said.

Jessa leaned toward him. He knew from the way the charm moved against his senses and that he could smell her. All he wanted to do was pull her close and hold her, but they'd taken that from him.

"What do you mean?"

His vision seemed to be returning. Shapes blurred in front of him. The dark shadow that was Jessa now had hazy borders, lines that made up her face.

"Read. Me."

She didn't move. And then she gasped. "They poisoned you so they could Read you?"

He tried to nod but didn't think his head worked.

"What do they want?"

Rsiran worked his tongue over the inside of his mouth again. "Same. Venass."

She leaned closer. He imagined she hugged him but couldn't tell. There seemed to be a little pressure this time, as if she pressed against him. Rsiran let out a slow breath, wanting nothing more than to put his arms around her and Slide her to safety.

But he couldn't.

They were trapped because his ability failed him.

"How. You." He didn't know if she would understand but at least his words came out more clearly than they had before.

"How did I escape?"

He tried to nod again. "Yes."

He didn't think she'd been Compelled but still didn't know for sure. If they poisoned him to Read him, there was no reason they wouldn't do the same to Jessa to Compel her.

"After they attacked us, I woke up, locked up, the same as you. They didn't think I was as much of a threat. I've not been poisoned, at least that I know. It took a while, but I managed to pick the lock on my door. Once I figured out how, I waited until I knew I'd be alone for a while. The guards come by on a schedule. Then I came looking for you."

"How?"

She laughed and pushed closer to him. This time he definitely felt it.

"The necklace," she said. She laughed again. "They took everything I had on me. My knives. The lock-pick set." She said that with more than a hint of anger. "But they left the necklace. They didn't think anything of it, I guess. But the shape worked well for a lock pick. Did you know that when you made it?"

Rsiran licked his lips. His tongue didn't feel as thick as it had. "Yes."

Jessa moved so that her face was directly in front of him. Now he could see the contours of her cheeks, the set of her jaw, and the way her hair swept back from her forehead. A blurry bruise discolored one cheek, severe enough that he could see it in spite of the poisoning.

"Liar," she whispered. She kissed him.

Rsiran kissed back, thankful he could feel her lips.

"How long will the poisoning last?" she asked.

"Don't. Know." He swallowed, feeling stronger by the moment. "Think it's… wearing off."

"How much longer until you can Slide us out of here? I'm a good sneak, but I don't know if I can get us out of the building on my own, especially not if I'm carrying you."

"Don't. Know," he said again. "I'll. Try."

He listened for lorcith to anchor. It would be easier than trying to Slide without an anchor. But he didn't want to Slide a great distance in the shape he was in. Shorter distances were easier, and he wasn't even certain he would be able to reach Elaeavn until the poison completely cleared his system.

While he sensed lorcith around him, he didn't have anything he felt safe using as an anchor. Most of it was likely with the Forgotten. Any that was not, he didn't know if he dared use in his current state.

But if they were in Asador, there was another place he could try. It was a place familiar to him only because he'd been there before when tracking down his sword. He'd found lorcith there, both his sword and unshaped lorcith. Could he anchor to that?

He listened for unshaped lorcith. At the edge of his senses, he heard it, as if calling to him. Rsiran held to it and tried to Slide.

But failed.

"Can't Slide. Yet."

"Keep trying," she said. "I'll keep us safe while we wait."

There came a soft sound of metal against metal. The door opened again.

"Not sure how you be doing that."

"Shael," Rsiran said weakly.

Jessa leaned over him, blocking him from Shael. "Leave him alone, Shael. Why are you doing this? I thought you were our friend!"

"Friend? I do be telling Rsiran before it's about coin, not friendship. When Brusus do be having the coin, then I be your friend."

He stepped closer. Rsiran smelled the sweet scent of the poison he carried with him. The knives he'd taken from Rsiran were tucked into his pockets.

"Now these folk do be having the coin. An' you be the reason I keep workin'."

Rsiran had seen how Shael had some talent, the way that he had once prevented him from Sliding. Rsiran had finally managed to surprise Shael when he'd used heartstone as his anchor.

"Now, you be going back to your room. I be tellin' Inna it time to use slithca syrup on you too. You be more compliant then."

He started forward. Rsiran felt it in the knives more than heard it.

"Stop."

Shael laughed. "You caught me askance once, Rsiran, but you be doin' nothin' to stop me in the shape you be in now. Don' be movin', you see." He laughed again.

Jessa lowered him back down. Then she lunged at Shael.

She moved in a blur, kicking off from next to him.

Rsiran felt the lorcith knife in her hand that she'd taken from his calf.

Shael grunted and then Jessa cried out before thudding loudly against the wall.

Rsiran turned his head to try to see if she was okay, but only saw her legs. They didn't move.

Shael crouched next to him. A hard hand pressed down on his chest. That Rsiran could feel it at all told him the poison was wearing off.

"You be restin' again, Rsiran. Almost got what they need."

"Stop." He said the word again with more force. He still could barely move his head and couldn't do anything against Shael without his abilities.

Shael laughed. "You're not gonna talk me out of this now. I'm not your friend."

Rsiran looked over and saw Jessa's legs. They moved, but not much. "I. Know."

He focused on the sense of the one lorcith knife still strapped to his calf.

"Don't make me do this," Rsiran said.

Shael chuckled. "Slithca lingers, Rsiran. Not much you *able* to do." He hesitated. "Besides, what you be thinkin' to do?"

Rsiran *pushed* on the lorcith knife. He used every bit of energy he possessed, pressing on it as if physically doing it.

At first, he didn't think it would matter. The knife wouldn't move.

Rsiran *pushed* harder. Nothing happened.

For Jessa's sake, he reached deeper, drawing from the memory of where the knife was mined, the lump of lorcith it once had been, the song it had sung to him before he'd forged it. They came to him in a flash, the connection strong as any.

Rsiran imagined the weight of Ilphaesn around him as he *pushed*.

Then it moved.

He felt the movement at the same time as Shael did. The smuggler grunted and reached for the knife, but was too late.

It tore through Shael. Rsiran had no way of knowing where, only that it did.

Shael coughed and started toward Rsiran again. He reached for the other blades Shael carried and *pushed* them with the same force, that of the memory of Ilphaesn. The knives sliced through him and sank into the wall with a loud crack.

Shael collapsed next to him.

Wetness pooled around Rsiran. He couldn't move away from it and lay next to Shael as his blood seeped out.

CHAPTER 29

"Jessa?"

She groaned. At least she still lived.

"Jessa!"

He said her name more urgently. They needed to move or the Forgotten would come next.

Rsiran felt his arms regaining strength and pushed to sit. He blinked and his vision cleared. How much time did they have?

Shael lay next to him. The knives had torn through his gut. Blood streaked across the floor, dripping a trail from where the knives had flown through the air after going through him. His chest rose slowly but still moved. Rsiran wondered if he should care whether Shael lived or not.

He dragged himself away from where Shael lay and toward Jessa. He found her resting at an odd angle, her back bent and twisted with her legs flopped over a box. For a moment, he thought Shael had broken her spine. Then she rolled, moving her legs with her as she did.

"Jessa. Can you move?"

She pulled her legs in and moved into a crouch. Her hair hung in front of her face. One hand clutched her side. "Probably still better than you." She tried to laugh, but it turned into a cough. Jessa got to her knees and looked past Rsiran. Her eyes narrowed as she saw what he'd done. "What happened with Shael?"

"I didn't want to," Rsiran said.

"Better than the bastard deserves. He was supposed to be our friend. And then he does this to us?"

It wasn't the first time Shael had hurt them, but Jessa hadn't been there when he'd put Rsiran in chains.

She stood, still holding her side, and limped past Rsiran. Rsiran watched as she knelt over Shael and looked at his injury. Then she picked up a long vial with a needle attached. Thick yellow liquid oozed inside. She made as if to plunge it into his arm.

"Wait—"

She looked over. "I don't want to risk him coming after us."

Rsiran pulled himself toward her, trying to stay away from the growing pool of blood around Shael. "Not sure he can. Might need that."

She frowned, looking at the needle, but nodded. "Can you Slide yet?"

Rsiran focused on the far part of the room to test whether he could Slide. Usually, he had to step into the Slide to make it work, though he had Slid without moving while in Venass. If he could drag himself forward in the Slide, he might be able to do it.

It felt as if he started to Slide, but failed again.

He looked at Jessa and shook his head. "Not yet."

Rsiran managed to move his legs. Relief spread through him as sensation began to return. Pain mixed in, the sense of thousands of needles stabbing into his flesh all at once, but he welcomed that sensa-tion. Anything was better than the absence of feeling.

Jessa hurried over to him and leaned down.

He moved one arm, resting on the other, and pulled her toward him. He still didn't have much strength, but years of working at the forge had made him strong enough to pull Jessa down to him. Holding her against him, he inhaled her scent. They sat like that for a moment.

"Thank you for coming for me," he told her.

She shook her head. "You still had to save me."

"You're doing the work. I'm just tagging along. You might have to sneak us out of here until I can Slide again."

Jessa flicked her eyes toward the door. Her jaw jutted forward and she nodded slowly. "If I don't have to carry you, we might be able to sneak out." She pointed to her side. "Think I broke a rib when Shael threw me. Gonna hurt for a while."

Rsiran snorted. "We make a perfect pair then."

"We always did." She smiled and took his hand. "If they catch us…"

She didn't need to finish. Rsiran knew as well as Jessa what would happen. There would be no hesitation to keep them fully sedated from now on. This would be their only chance.

"Then you'll have to be really good."

She punched him lightly in the shoulder. "I *am* really good."

He smiled and took a deep breath. "I need my knives."

"Can you just… you know… pull them?"

He tried, focusing on the three that were sunk into the wall. He was too weak to move them. Rsiran shook his head.

Jessa limped toward the wall and grunted before returning to Rsiran. "They're too deep."

"How deep."

"Buried into the stone."

Rsiran swallowed. He'd not had much strength to *push* as Shael nearly injected him with the slithca syrup so he'd focused on Ilphaesn. How had that given him such strength? He doubted that he'd be able to use the same to *pull* the knives back to him. "Guess I'm not getting them back."

Jessa laughed.

"I need something to use."

She nodded and started around the room. When she came back, she had the broken knife Firell had in his cell, as well as the one she'd thrown at Shael. "These are all I can find that's lorcith."

"You keep the good one," he said. Better for Jessa to have the whole knife. Rsiran took the broken one. It would work as well as anything. And if he could *push* with enough force, even the broken tang could do damage. "Help me stand?"

"Are you sure you're going to be able to?"

He shook his head. "Not sure about anything anymore."

Jessa studied him a moment and then slipped an arm around him and pulled. She grunted again as she did, the strain likely pulling on her injured ribs, but she pulled him up.

Rsiran nearly toppled over before gaining his balance. He wobbled for a moment and then tried taking a step. His legs felt weak, but they held. Jessa made certain to stay next to him, keeping her arm around him as they moved.

"We aren't going to move very fast… this way," he said, still working his tongue in his mouth. "Maybe you need… to go on without me. Get help."

She looked over at him and frowned. "If I leave you, you're as good as dead. And it's unlikely we'd ever find you again."

"But you'd be safe."

She shook her head. "You can be so stupid sometimes, Rsiran. What makes you think I want to be safe if you're not?"

He leaned and kissed her on the cheek. "Time to show me… how skilled you are."

She kissed him back, this time on the lips. She still tasted of mint. "I think I've already shown you."

They made their way toward the door. With each step, Rsiran felt his strength returning. By the time they reached the door, he felt strong enough to stand on his own.

"There's a long hall running outside the door. One end leads to steps. Upper level is where we were before. Other way is toward Firell's cell."

"I think we have to go up."

Jessa nodded. "Won't be easy. If there's anyone in the dining hall, then we'll be stuck. And we don't know anything about what's on the other side of that door. We could get through only to find another dozen guards on the other side. We can't sneak through there."

Rsiran frowned. The odds weren't in their favor if they went that way, not with only the two of them, and not with him as weakened as he was. "What if we had help?"

"Who's going to help us down here?"

"Firell."

She shot him a look. "That bastard is nearly as bad as Shael. He could have warned us about what the Forgotten planned."

"They've got his daughter."

"Josun has his daughter."

Rsiran nodded. "And I have Josun."

Jessa took a deep breath and then sighed. "I don't like it, Rsiran."

"Do we have another choice? Besides, if he looks like he's going to betray us again, then we just sink the needle with the syrup into his neck. Let him sleep for a while."

Jessa looked back to where Shael lay on the ground before glancing toward the door. "Are you strong enough to stop him if he tries anything?"

Rsiran didn't feel particularly strong yet, but each moment his strength improved. "I can subdue him if needed." He held out the broken lorcith blade and *pushed* on it. It hovered briefly in the air before dropping back into his hand. He'd need to *push* much harder than he was accustomed to if Firell tried betraying them, but he could stop him if it was needed.

Jessa shook her head. "I still don't like it."

Then she pulled open the door and slipped into the hall, heading toward Firell's cell. Rsiran followed after. Jessa moved silently with the practiced steps of a sneak. Rsiran tried to mimic her but didn't have the same ability to move quietly. He hoped he wasn't the reason they were discovered.

Lanterns staggered on the walls cast a soft glow. Rsiran had to duck as he moved along. The low-lying ceiling brushed the top of his head. Jessa stopped at the next door and looked back at him. When he nodded, she slipped the charm off her neck and used it to turn the lock on Firell's cell door before placing it back around her neck.

The door opened silently and they slipped inside. Rsiran closed the door behind them.

A single lantern glowed inside. Next to it, Firell rested.

Firell looked up. "You already got what you need from me—" He cut off and frowned. "Shael send you?"

Jessa shook her head. "Shael's dead."

A dark emotion flashed across his eyes. Disappointment? Anger? Then it was gone.

"How?"

"He poisoned me," Rsiran said, stepping past Jessa. "Gave me something that suppresses my abilities."

Firell sniffed. "Explains why you're here."

"Does it?" Jessa asked.

Firell looked at her. Rsiran thought he was Sighted, but what if Firell had another ability as well?

"I don't know another way out of here," he said. "They covered my head before they brought me down. And if the poison is the same as they give me, I don't know how long it will last."

"You can move."

Firell frowned. "You couldn't?"

Rsiran shook his head.

"Maybe they give me a weaker dose. Just enough my Sight don't work. Leaves me blind here in the dark." He shivered. "Nothing but the rats to keep me company. That and other things."

"We need your help," Rsiran said. "We don't know how many are out there."

Firell snorted. "Too many to slip past, that's for damn sure." He looked at Jessa. "I know Brusus thinks you're a skilled sneak, but this is beyond what even you can safely do." He shook his head. "Best hide until Rsiran can Slide again. Then you can get out."

"We don't know how long that will be. And we aren't waiting until we're caught again."

Firell shrugged again. "Why you think I'd help you?"

"Because I can get you to Josun."

Firell tensed and looked up at him. "Why would I want to see him again?"

"You want Lena back, don't you?"

Firell shook his head. "She's gone to me no matter what I do. Don't matter if I find Josun."

"You're giving up on her?" She didn't bother to hide the disgust in her voice.

"Not giving up. Practical. You're in my line of work long enough, you learn when it's time to be practical. I know what he's done to her. If she still lives, she's too far for me to find anyway."

Jessa turned back to Rsiran. She made no effort to disguise the anger flashing on her face. "I thought we knew him better than this."

"I thought I knew Shael better," Rsiran said. He hadn't suspected either Shael or Firell to betray them, but both had.

"Shael was a fool," Firell said. "Always thinking about coin, never looking beyond that. Never could trust him."

"Seems to me you're no different from Shael," Rsiran said.

Firell leaned forward and gripped his legs. "I like having coin, but that wasn't what motivated me. I always did what I could for my family. Except it wasn't enough." He shook his head. "Not when the Elvraeth got involved. Nothing I did could keep them safe, no matter what I tried."

Jessa didn't look back at him. "He's not the Elvraeth. *They're* not the Elvraeth. They're Forgotten, and I'm beginning to think there was a good reason for it." She started to turn away before pausing. "Doing nothing hurts them more than if you tried and failed."

She moved past Rsiran and into the hall.

Rsiran looked at Firell, wishing there was something he could say that would make him change his mind. Though he'd betrayed them, Rsiran couldn't bring himself to hate Firell the way he did Shael. At least Firell had a reason for his betrayal, one Rsiran may not agree with, but could understand.

"You should have told us," he said.

"Would it have mattered?"

"Not now, it doesn't. But had you told us before, you know Brusus would have done anything to help you. We're his family too. We would have been there for you."

Rsiran turned to follow Jessa out into the hall. They'd wasted enough time with Firell.

Firell called after him. "What do you know of family?"

Rsiran hesitated at the door. "When they learned about my ability, my own family stopped caring about me. They banished me. Brusus took me in." He turned and looked back at Firell. "He helped me understand what it means to have a family. And family is the reason I risked myself coming here. Because I would do anything to keep them safe."

He stepped out of the room and closed the door, leaving Firell behind.

CHAPTER 30

JESSA STOOD BETWEEN THE SHADOWS cast by the lanterns hanging on the walls. She tipped her head forward, though wasn't quite tall enough to brush the ceiling as she walked, not like Rsiran.

"We've wasted too much time on him," she whispered.

Rsiran wondered. Firell wasn't like Shael. He hadn't *wanted* to betray them. "Still think you can sneak us out?"

"Still not able to Slide?"

Rsiran focused on a spot two steps in front of him and attempted a Slide. It happened slowly, like moving through mud, and a foul odor filled his nose as he emerged, but he Slid. Then he collapsed against the wall.

He struggled to catch his breath. "Hard. Works, but hard."

Jessa bit her lip. "Then we sneak."

They made their way along the hall. When would the next guards come through? Had Shael sent them away as he came in to dose Rsiran? It seemed unlikely. More likely he'd come ahead of the Forgotten woman, the one he'd called Inna.

They wouldn't have much more time before she came looking for him.

And what about Jessa? She was supposed to be locked up as well. If one of her guards discovered she'd escaped, they'd come after her.

Rsiran paused at the door to the room where he'd been kept. Shael looked to have moved. The pool of blood smeared across the ground, different from when they'd been there. He lay more on his side. His split stomach heaved with each breath. Glassy eyes looked over at them.

Shael opened his mouth as if to say something. Rsiran didn't wait to hear what it was. He *pushed* the broken knife at Shael's head, catching him between the eyes hard enough to leave an imprint, then *pulled* it back to him.

Jessa glanced at him before looking into the room and nodding.

The effort of *pushing* on the lorcith lessened, giving him hope that they might get away.

They reached the stairs. The door atop the stairs was closed.

Rsiran grabbed Jessa's hand and held her from climbing. She frowned at him, but he ignored her. Instead, he focused on lorcith. In the room above them, he sensed a knife—possibly one of Jessa's—and a crossbow bolt. Probably two guards, but there might be more.

"What is it?" Jessa whispered.

"Two, I think. Can't tell if there are others."

She nodded. "You'll have to go first. I'll use the needle if I need to."

Rsiran slipped past her and climbed the stairs, careful with each step so they didn't creak under his weight. At the top, he paused to listen.

Muted voices drifted through the door. Rsiran listened but couldn't tell how many were on the other side. Possibly more than two. He'd have to be quick.

He shifted his focus to the lorcith in the room, holding an awareness of it in his mind.

Then he pushed the door open.

"Finally come back from beating on him…"

The guard looked over, and his eyes widened.

Rsiran *pushed* the broken knife at him, striking him in the chest, then quickly *pulled* it back.

Another guard jumped to his feet. He pulled a crossbow up with a swift motion. Rsiran was faster, *pushing* on the bolt, sending it flipping up from the crossbow to sink into the man's shoulder. He cried out, but it was silenced as Rsiran again *pushed* the broken knife, sending it directly at his head.

That left the knife he'd sensed before entering. It was moving in the room.

Rsiran sensed the knife and gave it a slight *push*. Someone grunted.

He turned in that direction. Near the fire pit a man crouched, working his way toward them. His eyes flashed a deep green. Rsiran gave the knife another *push*, but the man vanished before it could do any damage.

"Damn," he whispered. He hadn't expected someone able to Slide. "Anyone else?"

Jessa looked around the room. "No one I see. Just these two?"

He shook his head. "A Slider. Disappeared before I could turn his knife against him."

Jessa clenched her jaw and nodded. "Time to move quickly."

"So much for sneaking?"

She breathed out a laugh. "Not sure it was ever going to be about sneaking."

He hurried to the wooden door on the other side of the room and leaned against it to listen. Not for voices, but for lorcith. He heard nothing.

Rsiran *pulled* the broken knife back from the second guard. They needed to hold onto the few weapons they had.

He grabbed the thick iron handle on the door and pulled. It opened slowly and, thankfully, silently.

The hall on the other side of the door was nearly dark. A single lantern hung far down the hallway, spilling only a small circle of light around it. The air smelled different, like wood shavings and dirt.

Where were they?

"Can you see anything?"

Jessa leaned against him and peered down the hall. "Nothing. It turns at the end where that lantern is. Can't see anything beyond there."

Rsiran moved carefully as they started forward, but they needed to be quick as well. If the Slider reported they'd escaped, others would come. How many before Rsiran couldn't handle them all?

As they reached the corner, he hesitated. Light came from around the corner. He listened.

"Rsiran!" Jessa hissed.

She grabbed his shoulder and pulled him back.

Wind whistled past his face. Lorcith suddenly bloomed nearby. A knife, and one he'd made.

The outline of a shadow appeared near the corner. It flickered briefly. Another Slider, maybe the same one from the dining hall.

He *pulled* on the knife and then *pushed* it at the shadow. It missed, sinking into the wall before it could hit. Jessa coughed and he spun. The shadow had her gripped around the neck, pulling her back.

If they Slid, he might have no way to find her.

He *pushed* on the knife she held and sent it twisting around her. It caught the Slider on the arm and he released her, crying out as he did.

The broken knife came next, whistling toward the Slider's head. But he missed, the person Sliding too quickly for him to catch.

Rsiran *pulled* both weapons back to him.

"We can't stay here," he said, pulling Jessa toward him. "I can't hit him, and I don't think it's the same person as before."

"How many can Slide?"

Rsiran wished he knew.

"Rsiran!"

The Slider had reappeared.

Rsiran slipped the knife back into Jessa's hands. The Slider might be Sighted, leaving him at a disadvantage in the dark. At least Jessa could throw the knife. Rsiran could always retrieve it.

She sent it flying over his shoulder.

He looked back to see the Slider disappear. Rsiran *pulled* the knife back to him.

He wouldn't be able to keep them safe like this. Anywhere he could Slide, the person could follow.

But… not everywhere.

With a force of will, he pushed away all sense of lorcith and listened for heartstone alloy. He could anchor and draw them to safety.

"Rsiran?"

The Slider had returned.

Rsiran felt alloy and reached for it. He didn't know where this was—not the palace—but it didn't matter as long as it wasn't here.

The connection was weak at first, but grew stronger the longer he held onto it.

Jessa jerked him down. Something whistled over his head. With lorcith pushed away, he couldn't tell if that's what the attacker used. Rsiran held onto the sense of the heartstone alloy and pulled as he Slid.

At first, nothing happened.

He felt a moment of fear. If a single Slider had them nearly incapacitated, what would happen if another arrived? Could they follow him along a Slide? What if the alloy didn't stop them either?

Rsiran threw everything he had into the Slide.

Hot air whispered past his face carrying the strange sweetly bitter scent of the alloy. A wash of colors oozed past. And then they emerged, stumbling forward.

Jessa crouched as she spun around. When satisfied they were alone, she stood slowly and helped Rsiran to his feet.

He took a deep breath and stood, unsteady as he did. They were in a wide room. Faint blue light gave enough for him to see by. Twin tables rested against each other in the center of the room. Walls were lined with shelves that had books stuffed onto them. The blue light came from a dimmed lantern hanging from a hook near the center of the room. A woman sat underneath the lantern in a plush chair, a book propped in her lap.

Rsiran blinked. "Della?"

CHAPTER 31

THE WOMAN TURNED AND LOOKED AT HIM. Her eyes had the same bright green intensity and her face wore wrinkles from age, but her face had none of the soft affection Della always wore.

She set the book down and looked at him. "How did you get here?"

Rsiran glanced around before his eyes settled on the woman again. He couldn't shake how much she looked like Della, but wasn't.

"Where are we?"

She frowned and looked from Rsiran to Jessa. "You don't know where you are."

Rsiran shook his head. He felt the heartstone alloy that had pulled him here, but couldn't see it.

"Then how did you…" Her eyes narrowed. "You traveled here."

It was a phrase he'd heard before, but Rsiran couldn't place where.

"We were being attacked."

The woman pushed off the chair and stood, then started toward them. She moved slowly but with a grace to her steps. She weaved around the tables until she stood before them, looking up at Rsiran and over to Jessa. "You should not be able to travel here."

Rsiran frowned and then listened for lorcith. There was none around. He pushed the sense of the knife Jessa carried and the charm she wore to the back of his mind, clearing lorcith from it. Then he listened.

The sense of heartstone alloy came from all around. It practically infused the walls, reminding him of the way the walls in Venass were infused with lorcith. Something else hummed against him more strongly than the rest, but he couldn't see what it was.

"I'm sorry we came," he said.

Rsiran shifted, pushing Jessa behind him. The Slide had taken much energy from him, but already he began to feel better. All he needed was to focus on lorcith, and he could anchor well enough to Slide them to safety, but with all the heartstone around him, would he be able to find an anchor?

The woman took a step toward him. She had a curious expression on her face. The set of her jaw made her appear almost angry. Silver hair twisted behind her head into a tight bun pinned with a long metal rod.

Rsiran frowned again. Even that was heartstone.

"Tell me again how you managed to reach me here."

He shook his head and stepped back. Something told him that he didn't dare turn his back on this woman. "A mistake. I'm sorry. We'll be going."

"A mistake? The Great Watcher makes no mistakes. If you were meant to come here, so be it. I should only like to know how it is you managed to reach me."

He swallowed, and the words came out in a tumble. "You're right. I Slid. Traveled. Whatever you want to call it. It was a mistake. I anchored to the first thing I could sense…"

Rsiran cut off his words, recognizing what happened. The woman Pushed him.

He pushed his barriers into place, infusing them not only with lorcith but with the heartstone. Always before, it had seemed that he pulled on the sense of heartstone from somewhere, but this energy seemed to come from all around him. This woman had been subtle. As had been the case with Thom, Rsiran hadn't even known she was Pushing on his mind. Much longer and he might have said anything to her. Already he'd probably said too much.

Her mouth twisted in a hard smile. "Who taught you that trick?"

He shook his head, unwilling to answer.

Jessa moved behind him until they backed against one of the long tables. Rsiran looked down at it before turning his attention back to the woman. She hadn't moved any closer. As small as she appeared, she exuded strength and control. This was a woman accustomed to getting what she wanted.

"You will tell me what I ask."

"Who are you?"

Her eyes narrowed, flashing a bright green. "Rsiran Lareth?" A smile parted her mouth. "The smith who can Slide. I have heard of you."

She hadn't Read him. With the barrier in place, he didn't think she could. But that didn't mean she couldn't Read Jessa.

"And you are Jessa Ntalen." Her face darkened. "You should not have left your parents."

Rsiran looked over at Jessa. Her face had gone white.

"I see you have not told him everything. Interesting."

He touched Jessa's arm. She jumped but didn't pull away. He hoped he could reassure her but wasn't sure he could without revealing too much to this woman.

239

"If you can Read her, you know how I feel about her. Be careful what you say to me."

The woman laughed. "He has teeth. I had heard you were one to watch."

Rsiran steeled himself. He released his connection to the heart-stone and listened for lorcith. He felt a moment of surprise when he couldn't.

The woman watched him. "Very interesting. From what she shows me, you access the lorcith fully." Her lips pressed into a thin line. "Not just a smith then."

Rsiran checked to ensure his barrier was still in place. As far as he could tell it was, but how would this woman know what he had done? "How do you know that?"

She turned and waved her hands around the room. "You think all this a curiosity?" She laughed. "You aren't the first to be able to access the ore, only the first I've met in many years."

The woman fixed her gaze on him. As she studied him for a long moment, something changed about her face. "Not just the lorcith. That is how you managed to squeeze your way in here." She laughed and shook her head. "I did not see that. And not only here, but other places as well. Useful."

The way she said it made Rsiran realize she meant it the same way Haern spoke of Seeing. This woman was Elvraeth. Or had been, once.

"When were you banished?" he asked.

The dark expression slipped over her eyes again and then was gone. "You speak of exile as if you know of such things."

"You speak of me as if you know of me."

She frowned at him before laughing again and turning away. "See? Teeth. I will find you interesting to observe." She took a seat in her chair.

Rsiran considered grabbing Jessa and Sliding from the woman. His strength had mostly returned, the effects of the slithca syrup finally worn off, and he would be able to get them safely away. But this was one of the Forgotten, and different from those who'd attacked him.

He could get answers.

"Why did Inna Elvraeth attack me? Why were we attacked in Elaeavn?"

The woman looked up sharply. "You should not have been attacked. That is early—" She stopped herself and smiled.

"Tell that to Inna. She dosed me with slithca syrup."

A cloud passed over the woman's face. "Foolish girl. Thinking the only way to get what she wants is by force."

"And how do you think to get what you want?" Rsiran asked.

"Persuasion."

"You won't be able to Compel me."

"No. I do not think I will."

Jessa moved around him. The lorcith knife they'd taken from the Forgotten pointed at Rsiran's chest. Her eyes were wide and her jaw worked as if she tried saying something.

Rsiran backed up a step. "Release her," he said to the woman.

A feral smile twisted her mouth. "Tell me about your other ability. You can manipulate heartstone?"

Jessa took a step toward him. The knife came close to his chest. Rsiran didn't want to move too far from her and risk not being able to Slide them to safety, but if she kept the knife where it was, he might not be able to reach her. Della might be able to clear what this woman did… at least, he hoped she could. But what if she couldn't? What if the Compelling held even when they were away from her?

"Release her, and I'll answer your questions. As long as you'll answer mine."

The woman grinned in a wolfish flash of teeth. "Fair enough."

Jessa blinked and lowered the knife. "I'm sorry, Rsiran. I couldn't control what I was doing. It was like there was another mind inside me, making me…"

He pulled her to him and wrapped an arm around her. "I know. And we'll make sure she didn't do anything permanent," he whispered.

The woman pointed to a chair. "Sit while we talk. That way, I'll know you won't travel from here."

Rsiran checked to ensure his barriers were in place and fortified with heartstone. She didn't know he could Slide without moving. Perhaps she hadn't stolen that knowledge from Jessa. Or maybe Jessa didn't know.

Rsiran pushed a heavy, wooden chair toward the woman and sat in front of her. He cleared his mind of lorcith as he did, focusing on the heartstone all around him. If he needed to Slide, he wouldn't be able to anchor to lorcith here, not if he couldn't even sense lorcith outside the walls. Heartstone might work and allow him to slip past it.

Jessa stood beside him. She clutched the knife in her hand, holding it against her chest. One hand rested on his shoulder, gripping the fabric of his shirt tightly. If they needed to quickly Slide, the connection made certain she came with him.

"Where are we?" Rsiran asked.

"My question first."

Rsiran took a deep breath before answering. She might know if he didn't tell the truth. If she could freely access Jessa—if she could Read her as well as she Compelled her—then he risked angering her if he didn't speak the truth. But he didn't want to share everything with her, either.

"I can hear heartstone."

The woman frowned. "Hear?"

He nodded. "Lorcith has a… a call. A voice of sorts."

"Some who hear it call it a song."

Rsiran nodded. The boy from the mines had called it that. "It calls to me."

"The original smiths all heard lorcith. They were chosen by the Great Watcher to work the metal. It is not surprising that you can hear it."

Della had once said the same, but had never shared more than that with him.

"Yet you claim you can hear heartstone. I have never known anyone with such a gift."

Rsiran again debated how much to share. She already knew he could hear heartstone if he listened. It didn't matter what else he told her of it. "Mostly the alloy. I think it's the connection to lorcith I sense."

The woman leaned forward and placed her hands on her knees. Long fingers bore wrinkles from age. Her pale skin had blotches of brown in places. "But there is none of the alloy here."

Rsiran frowned and listened, trying to ignore the wild thumping of his heart. Hadn't he sensed the heartstone alloy? He'd never sensed pure heartstone before, though had never really tried.

What he sensed in the walls *did* feel different from the alloy. And the pin holding her hair up was not really the alloy.

Could he be sensing pure heartstone?

"You didn't know."

He shook his head. "Always before it was the alloy. That was how I managed to forge it."

"It is said that only a rare smith can work an alloy of lorcith, even when the smiths were revered. In your city, those who can are no longer smiths."

It took a moment to realize what she was telling him. The alchemists. That meant they could hear lorcith as well.

"Who are you?" Rsiran asked.

The woman leaned back in her chair and crossed her hands over her chest. "Which of my titles would you like?" she asked. "For I have many. I am the Eldest. The Mother. The Watcher. The Leader. The Exile. Forgotten."

"What is your name?"

"Ah. That is a different question. Mine first. You hide something of your ability with lorcith from me. What is it?"

It didn't matter if he answered. The Forgotten had already seen what he could do with lorcith, if Shael hadn't told them already. Likely, it was the reason Inna waited until they were seated and practically disarmed before attacking.

"I suspect you already know the answer."

She waited.

"I can *push* on lorcith. It listens to me."

She frowned. "And obeys?"

Rsiran had never really tried to explain how he *pushed* lorcith, only that it worked. The metal followed his commands, but only lorcith. He could *pull* on the alloy, but wasn't that the lorcith in it that responded to him? He'd never really tried with heartstone.

He took the broken knife they'd taken from Firell and *pushed* on it. With barely any effort, it hovered in the air, spinning end over end before he let it drop.

The woman watched the lorcith until it fell back into Rsiran's hands. "I am Evaelyn. Can you do the same with heartstone?"

Rsiran shook his head.

Her eyes flickered to Jessa's necklace. The chain of heartstone alloy. "Try."

He listened for the heartstone. With it all around him, infusing the walls of the room, it was easy to do. Rather than focusing on Jessa's necklace, which was made of the alloy, he pulled on the pin holding the woman's hair.

The response was different from that of the lorcith. Lorcith moved immediately or not at all. This felt slippery, as if he couldn't fully grip the heartstone.

And then it moved.

It slid from her hair and across the distance to him. Rsiran caught it.

The pin was a dull grey and harder than the heartstone he used to make the alloy. That was soft enough he could imprint it with his thumb. This felt firmer, but still less solid than lorcith. Lines twirled around the length of the pin, spiraling in a pattern that blurred his eyes.

"I will have that back now."

He looked up at Evaelyn. Her face was an unreadable mask, but emotion split it enough for him to see the concern she wore. The corners of her eyes wrinkled slightly.

Rsiran *pushed* on the strange pin. Again it felt slippery, as if he couldn't get a good grip. He had the distinct sense that he wouldn't have the same control with it as he had with lorcith, that if he squeezed too hard, the heartstone would slip away from him in a direction he didn't intend.

With a cautious *push*, it crossed to Evaelyn. She pinched it carefully and rolled it in her hands, running her eyes along the length of it before slipping it back into her hair.

"It seems you can control heartstone as well. It makes you dangerous. Others will wish to know how you manage." She looked to Jessa and her eyes narrowed. "And it seems they already know of your ability."

Venass.

"The scholars wish to learn as well," he admitted.

She sniffed. "Scholars? Is that what you think of them? Perhaps you should live outside Elaeavn for a time, see if you still think of them as 'scholars.'"

"What are they, then?"

She shook her head. "You called me a name when you first saw me. What was it?"

Rsiran hesitated. She'd already heard him say it, so why would she ask? "You looked like someone else I know. A woman in Elaeavn."

She tilted her head, waiting.

Rsiran took a breath. "I thought you were a woman I know as Della."

Evaelyn nodded slowly. "Could she really think she's found the blood of the smith?" she said to herself. She fixed Rsiran with an appraising eye. He felt a momentary assault on the barriers in his mind, but they held. With heartstone, he made certain that they held. "That is what I thought I heard. It is a name I haven't heard for many years."

"You know her?"

"That is your question?"

Rsiran had dozens of questions, but it was the one he suddenly wanted the answer to. "Yes."

"Very well. I knew her. I no longer claim that I do."

"How?"

She shook her head. "Why did you come here?"

"I came looking for Shael."

"Shael?" She frowned. "He is the smuggler? Why would you risk coming here for the smuggler?"

"That is my business, but I wanted answers."

"Then you will get no more answers from me."

Rsiran glanced over at Jessa. She shrugged.

"Shael asked something of me once. I wanted to know why." And he had thought that the exiled Elvraeth and Venass were connected, but he saw that wasn't the case. The exiles would not prevent Venass from summoning him again.

"That is all?"

He ignored her follow up question. "What did Inna want?" Rsiran asked.

Evaelyn laughed. "You're learning," she said, touching her hair where the heartstone pin rested. "She wants the same as most. To return. What did Shael ask of you?"

"That's not what Inna wants," Rsiran said. "She wants into the palace. Why?"

"What did Shael ask of you?" she said again.

Rsiran considered pushing, but he wanted to know why Inna wanted into the palace. "He wanted me to forge something for him. What is within the palace?"

"Memories," she said. "What did this Shael ask you to forge?"

"Some kind of device. What are the memories that Inna wants?"

Evaelyn hesitated. "I think we are finished with our questions."

Rsiran shook his head. "No. I don't think we are. What is it that she wants?"

"It is time for you to leave. If you traveled here, you may travel away again. Do not return."

"Wait—why won't you answer?"

She looked at him. "Ask Della."

"Della? Why would she know the answer?"

"Because she's the reason I am here."

Evaelyn pushed up from the chair and started away from him. She reached the far wall and pushed open a hidden door, disappearing from the room without saying anything else.

CHAPTER 32

R SIRAN LOOKED AT JESSA. "WE SHOULD LEAVE."
"Can you get us back out?"

Rsiran listened for lorcith but couldn't hear anything to anchor to. Even heartstone alloy was blocked, only the walls of heartstone surrounding him pressing on his awareness. With enough time, he might be able to push past it, but he didn't want to remain here any longer than was needed. Not after what Inna had tried.

"Not this way."

"Then we go through the door."

"Once we're past the heartstone, I can try Sliding." For the first time since they became close, he hesitated explaining more and telling her how the heartstone interfered with his abilities. He'd probably told her before, but if Evaelyn could use her against him—could Compel her as easily as she'd seemed—then she could Read her. It put them both at risk.

Jessa frowned at him a moment before nodding.

Rsiran almost explained more but did not.

Jessa started toward the door where Evaelyn had just left. As they reached the wall, he looked back and considered the wall of shelves all around them. A library, but one unlike he'd ever seen before, one that exuded formality and wealth. Could the Forgotten have a palace the same as the Elvraeth? If that was the case, were the cells where Firell had been held in the same building or different? And why would they want to return to Elaeavn?

"Rsiran?" Jessa held one hand on the door. Once they were through the door, he would try Sliding them again.

He shook off the questions and stepped into the hall.

Massive walls stretched on either side of them. Pale white marble reached high overhead, arching with a smooth grace unlike anything he'd ever seen before. Deep etchings worked into the stone in various carvings. Light spilled through colored glass overhead, leaving the carvings on the wall awash with color. A few lanterns hung from high overhead, glowing with a steady blue light.

Rsiran had never seen anything so beautiful.

Jessa pulled on his arm. "Can you Slide?"

He blinked and released his connection to the heartstone. The sense faded, but not before he felt where Evaelyn had gone, how she made her way far down the hall. He considered *pulling* on the heartstone pin and dragging it back to him, but doing so would likely anger her. What would she do to him—to Jessa—if he tried?

Then he listened for lorcith. It called all around him, practically a chorus of sound. After being separated from it within the Forgotten library, the suddenness of it nearly overwhelmed him. Most was unshaped, massive amounts that reminded him of Ilphaesn. Others had distinct shapes. If he listened long enough, the lorcith promised to tell him all about what it could become.

"Rsiran?"

"It's everywhere," he whispered.

She frowned. "What is?"

"Lorcith. It's in the walls, in the windows, in everything here."

Jessa shook her head. "Why?"

"I don't know. But I think Evaelyn does."

Jessa gave him a dangerous look. "You can't go after her. You saw what she did to me. I had no control over myself. If she'd wanted, I would have stabbed you with that knife."

"You would never have stabbed me."

Jessa sighed. "I don't know that I could have stopped her."

"I would have *pushed* the knife out of your hands," Rsiran added.

Jessa turned to face him and punched him on the shoulder.

He shrugged. "Then I would have dragged you from here and back to Della to fix your mind. I have a few other suggestions for fixes she could make while she's working."

She looked as if she might punch him again. "Can we go?"

Rsiran nodded. "It will be easier if we can get outside these walls. The lorcith interferes with my connection to the smithy."

It didn't, not entirely, but he wanted to see more of the Forgotten palace before they left. Now that he sensed lorcith, he had no fear of Sliding. It would be as easy as anchoring to… well, to anything.

Jessa took his hand.

He Slid them down the hall, emerging at the far end, thankful that his ability had returned. The walls towered over them, still the same white gleaming stone. The carvings in the wall were different here, and the colored glass overhead made of a pale blue rather than orange. The hall ended in a steep stairway leading both up and down.

"Which way?" he asked.

She looked back. "I don't know. Should we go down?"

He held her hand and Slid. They emerged on a massive stair landing. Polished stone gleamed under his feet. The stairs continued down. Rsiran Slid again.

Each Slide took them farther and farther down. The light streaming through the colored glass high overhead began to fade, leaving them with only the glowing blue Elvraeth lanterns hanging over their heads. And then they emerged onto a wide landing.

A massive arched metal door—pure lorcith, he noted, just like in Venass—was closed in front of them. Shadowed halls led away from the stairs in both directions. The lanterns down those halls were dim, the blue light barely visible.

"Have you noticed?" Jessa asked.

"Noticed what?"

"There's no one here."

Rsiran had been thankful they hadn't encountered anyone else. Had they come across more of the Forgotten, he didn't think he was skilled enough to get them to safety. Not after what happened when they were trying to escape after being held captive.

"We didn't find out where we are. Where the Forgotten are hiding."

"That's what you wanted to know? Is that why you don't just Slide us out of here?"

"Part of it," he admitted.

Jessa turned to him and pulled him close to her, wrapping her arms around his neck. "You're keeping things from me."

He swallowed. This close, her breasts pressed against his chest and he felt her heart beating. He could no more lie to her than he could Slide from the library upstairs. "What if they use what you know against us?"

She laughed softly and kissed his cheek. "I have faith in you, Rsiran. Even if they know what we know, they can't do what you can do.

It's why they want to capture you. Why Venass wants to study you. The Great Watcher has given you a great gift."

He hugged her tightly and nodded.

"Can we go home?"

Rsiran sighed. "We need to talk to Della. She needs to know what happened here. And I have a question for her."

Jessa pulled away, letting her arms slip apart as she ran her hands down his arms. "I don't trust anything that woman said to us."

"I don't, either. But she knew Della, and we need to know why."

Jessa frowned. "Why would you believe what Evaelyn said? Della has only wanted to help us. That's all she's ever done."

"The Forgotten want into the palace. Venass wants to know how I can Slide past the alloy. That's the only connection, isn't it? They want something there."

"Does it matter?" she asked.

"Knowing can keep us safe. It's the not knowing that's dangerous. Right now, it feels like we're always getting chased, always a step behind and always in danger. If we know what they're after, maybe there will be something we can do to keep ourselves safe."

Jessa kissed his cheek. "That's what I love about you. Always thinking you'll find safety."

"You don't?"

Jessa shrugged. "I've seen enough of the world to know safety is fleeting." As she said it, steps echoed toward them, the first sound they'd heard since leaving the library. Jessa looked up at him and smiled. "See?"

Rsiran Slid them just past the doors, leaving the Forgotten Palace.

* * * * *

They emerged in darkness. The air had a familiar bitter scent of unmined lorcith.

Jessa pressed against him. "Why did you take us to Ilphaesn?"

He shook his head. "I didn't. I meant to Slide us just past the doors."

He turned, listening to lorcith around him. It created a sort of map within his mind, painting the image of tunnels all around them. It was just like Ilphaesn, only no part he'd ever visited.

Could his Slide have been altered? That was what Inna feared, the reason Sliding was so dangerous for the Forgotten, but Rsiran had never worried about Sliding outside of Elaeavn. Did he need to fear where he'd emerge?

He hadn't anchored his Slide. Could that be the difference?

"This looks like when you took me to Ilphaesn. Like when *he* took me to Ilphaesn."

Rsiran tried listening to the lorcith. Could they be in another mine, one he hadn't come across while working in Ilphaesn? As massive as the mountain was, it seemed possible. But how would the Forgotten Palace hide here as well, this close to Ilphaesn?

Unless his Slide *had* been altered. It was the only explanation that made sense.

"I told you how Della influenced my Slide? How she pulled me toward her?"

"You did. Said she could sense when you were Sliding, sort of how I can see it, the slight shimmering as you begin your Slide."

"What if someone pulled us here?"

"Or pushed?"

"I guess."

"Why here? Why would they bring you to Ilphaesn, unless it's only to show you that they can."

"But I already know my Sliding can be influenced."

"That's the reason the Forgotten fear Sliding too."

"Yes, but *who* is influencing it? Della didn't seem to think there were many with that ability."

"Does it happen when you…" she paused, searching for the word "…when you anchor?"

He shook his head. "Not then."

"Maybe this is another mine. Someplace other than Ilphaesn."

If that were the case, then why would Josun have gone to such effort to mine lorcith from Ilphaesn and sneak it from the palace?

"Can you Slide us from here? Can you find another anchor with all this lorcith around?"

Rsiran took a deep breath and listened. The lorcith called to him, some asking for him to pull it from the walls around him, others seeming to tell him what the nugget could become, as if bargaining with him. Rsiran pushed it away, ignoring the sense of the unshaped lorcith.

With as much as he sensed around him, it was difficult to do.

This was not the same as Ilphaesn.

"Where are we?" he muttered.

Jessa gripped his hand, tensing. "Not Ilphaesn then."

He shook his head. "Within the mines, I can sense other lorcith. This is different."

"How?"

"I don't know. But it's not Ilphaesn."

But where had he ended up? And how could this place have as much lorcith as in Ilphaesn? Did the Forgotten have their own mines? Why would they have needed what Josun mined if they did?

Without knowing where he was, he hesitated Sliding blindly. Likely, he could get them back to Elaeavn. He knew it well enough that he could Slide there without an anchor, but what if someone influenced his Slide again? What if the next time, they ended up back with Inna? Or in Venass?

No—he needed an anchor to Slide them safely. With it, he didn't think he had to fear outside influence on his Slide. But how to reach an anchor with all this lorcith filtering his ability to sense one?

He'd need to use a different type of anchor. The alloy. As he'd used the lorcith-forged sword before, could he use the heartstone alloy-forged sword as an anchor as well? If he could sense it, he could get them back to Elaeavn, and finally back to his smithy.

He pushed away the sense of lorcith he felt all around him, focusing on his breathing. When he had control of the lorcith, when it was pressed into a corner of his mind, he listened for the heartstone alloy.

Not pure heartstone. That he could sense it like he sensed lorcith still surprised him. He had none of the same connection to heartstone, not as he had with lorcith. Except, he had been working with it more often. As he'd folded the heartstone into the alloy, he'd worked it. How was that any different from how he first worked with lorcith, slowly growing his connection to it?

The alloy in Jessa's necklace called to him first. He pushed it away and listened.

For long moments, there was nothing. Silence. Rsiran wondered if it would even work or if they would be forced to Slide blindly through the mines searching for a way out.

Then he felt a distant thrumming on his senses, like a pinprick of light burning in his mind. Could this be his sword?

Rsiran grabbed onto it and pulled it toward him.

As he felt himself Slide, he realized he might have made a mistake.

What if the alloy he felt was from the Floating Palace? What if he Slid them back to Elaeavn only to end up in the palace?

255

CHAPTER 33

SLIDING WITH THE CONNECTION TO THE HEARTSTONE alloy was different from his usual Sliding. That was a blur of motion and colors and a hint of lorcith. With the alloy, movement seemed slower. The colors more vivid. The scents around him different. Rsiran didn't know why that would be.

They emerged from the Slide into shadows.

He tensed, releasing his connection to the alloy and listening for lorcith as he readied the broken knife. Lorcith bloomed around him, but different than it had within the mines. Unshaped lorcith stacked together. A row of forgings—all done by him—were nearby.

They were back in his smithy.

Jessa let out a shaky breath and let go of his hand. "That was… different."

"The Slide?"

"What did you do that time?"

He looked around, his eyes slowly adjusting. Using what he felt of the lorcith as markers for him, he made his way toward his bench and fumbled until he found the Elvraeth lantern. Flipping it open, blue light spilled around them.

Rsiran shifted a pair of boards in the floor and lifted the heartstone-forged sword out from where he'd hidden it. "I used this as an anchor." He carried the sword to Jessa.

She took it carefully and twisted it. "This isn't the one you made before. This is different. The color is wrong and the metal feels," she frowned, turning the sword, "slippery and warm." She looked up at him and handed it back to him. "Why would you make another sword?"

Rsiran wasn't sure how to explain the reason that he'd felt compelled to do it. He had wanted to see why Josun wanted the sword, to learn what the heartstone blade might do, but now?

When he put the swords together, they had a strange connection, like they were paired, meant to exist together. He didn't have an explanation for why that should be.

He took the sword from Jessa and slipped it back into place beneath the boards. Hidden alongside the sword were four cubes of heartstone, each large enough to mix into a large nugget of lorcith for the alloy. Once, he'd thought the heartstone he had precious, that the metal was rare. What he'd seen in the Forgotten Palace made him wonder if that was true.

A tapping at the door startled him.

Jessa looked over and jumped to her feet. She grabbed a pair of knives off the bench and turned to the door. "Who would come looking for us? Brusus wouldn't bother until we searched for him. And Haern… well, Haern finds us when he wants to," she whispered.

"I'll check."

"Be careful."

He smiled but nodded in agreement, *pulling* three of his small blades from the bench to him and pocketing them. After what happened with the Forgotten, he didn't want to be caught unprepared again.

Rsiran Slid, emerging atop the roof of his smithy.

Moonlight shimmered around him, filtering through thick clouds. The air felt heavy and damp, smelling of rain. Waves crashed against the shore, the sound carrying well. Gulls cawed as they circled. A cat yowled somewhere nearby, a single cry.

Rsiran shivered.

He crept forward, using the slope of his roof as cover. The thick tiles were damp, and he had to move carefully so he didn't tumble off. Rsiran didn't dare Slide to the edge, not certain whether he would emerge safely.

When he reached a point where he could look down, the alley below was empty.

Rsiran frowned. There *had* been tapping on the door.

He looked up the alley. Most of the buildings were abandoned, no one but squatters living in them anymore. That was the reason the smithy remained hidden. Nobody would report the sounds of his work to the constables for fear of being discovered themselves.

The moonlight didn't reach far enough for him to see well. Water pooled along the alley where the cobbles were pulled up. Shadows stretched outward, growing thicker the farther away from the smithy they went. Something moved below, small and slipping between the shadows. Likely the cat he'd heard.

But he saw no sign of whoever tapped on the door.

He should have brought Jessa. At least her Sight would have penetrated the darkness.

Crawling back up the slope roof, he Slid back into the smithy.

But emerged in Della's house.

He blinked. Fire crackled warmly in the hearth. Mint tea steeped in a steaming pot. Della sat in her chair facing the fire, a striped scarf wrapped around her shoulders and a cup of tea held between both hands.

She looked up, unsurprised at his appearance.

"Sit, Rsiran. I've got tea for you."

Rsiran shook his head. "Why did you pull me here?"

She smiled. "Brusus has already gone to fetch Jessa so you needn't worry for her. You and I need a few moments to speak."

"You knew I'd returned?"

She tipped her head toward her cup and inhaled deeply. "I knew you'd returned. I knew when you left. I felt it each time you Slid while you were away."

"You can feel me Sliding from a distance?"

She nodded toward the empty chair.

Rsiran sighed and sat. With Della, he always felt like a child. How many times had he now sat before her fire, either injured or getting advice?

"Can you feel lorcith from a distance?" Della asked. She handed him a pale white mug. It had a slight crack along the side, but it still held.

"Usually. Unless something blocks me."

"Such as heartstone."

He frowned. "Heartstone doesn't block me, not anymore, but sometimes, I need to have something to anchor. When I was in Venass, the walls were infused with lorcith. This is what made it difficult to sense other lorcith."

"Infused?"

He shook his head, trying to come up with a better word. He hadn't explained to Della what he'd experienced while in Venass. "It was like

259

lorcith was worked into the rock itself, but that isn't how lorcith is found in the mines. There, it's only in lump form."

Della took another sip of her tea.

"Could you tell where we were?"

She shook her head. "That's not how it works. I can sense the changes from your Sliding, but not where it takes you."

"Then how do you influence it? How did you pull me here?"

She set her tea down. "It is imprecise, at least for me. I can draw you to me, but beyond that, my control is limited." She shifted the shawl around her shoulders. "Did you find what you sought?"

"We found Shael. We found the Forgotten."

Her brow furrowed. "Dangerous times if they've chosen to reveal themselves. What happened to you?"

"I didn't want to hurt him. He was poisoning me. Using slithca syrup on me."

Della turned slowly to face him. "Are you certain that's what he called it?"

He nodded. "The Forgotten were trying to incapacitate me, to break down my defenses so they could Read me. They wanted to learn how I was able to reach the palace."

"How you could Slide past the barrier?"

"Yes."

"And did you tell them?"

Rsiran wrung his hands together and looked over to the fire. "I don't know what I told them while the slithca syrup worked through my system. There was one woman—a Reader—who might have learned everything in my mind while I was incapacitated."

Della shook her head. "A foul thing to do, especially to one like us. Few know how to make slithca syrup. And a good thing. Low doses pull you away from your connection to the Great Watcher. Higher doses…"

"I couldn't talk or move. I couldn't Slide." He shivered, thinking of how helpless he'd been. Had Jessa not come for him, he didn't know what would have happened.

"As I said, a foul thing. And to use it to Read you while under its effects?" She shook her head.

"I'm not sure how well they were able to Read me. I could still sense lorcith."

"Your were able to shroud your thoughts?"

Rsiran noted she used the same term as Brusus for blocking his mind. "I don't know. I infuse my barrier with lorcith to strengthen it."

The twitch of a smile told him she knew he also used heartstone. "There's that word again. Do you know how you do it?"

He shook his head. "It doesn't feel any different than when I pull on lorcith to move it."

Della watched him for a moment and then took another sip of her tea.

"Shael injected me with the syrup. I think… I think he waited too long between injections. I was able to use my lorcith knives."

Della closed her eyes and sighed. "You had no other choice, Rsiran. Shael chose a dark path, one that carried with it many risks. Perhaps darker than you even realize."

"I still regret what I did."

She opened her eyes and looked into the fire. "You wouldn't be you if you didn't."

Rsiran took a sip of the mint tea. A wave of warmth washed through him. "There was another person we met."

She sighed and turned, meeting his eyes. "That is why I called you here."

Rsiran gripped the cup tightly. Had Della Read him, even with his barriers in place? "You know Evaelyn?"

Della nodded. "I knew her many years ago."

"Who is she?"

Della turned back to the fire. "I don't know what she considers herself these days. She always had an inflated view of what the Great Watcher had in mind for her, but always wanted to put herself before others. That is why she was exiled."

"How did you know her?"

"She didn't tell you?"

Rsiran shook his head. "She said you were the reason she was exiled."

"That is partly true."

"Then who—"

He didn't get the chance to finish. The door to Della's home opened and Jessa rushed in, hurrying over to him. Brusus followed after and closed the door behind her.

"Are you—"

"I'm fine. Della wanted to remind me that my Sliding wasn't always safe."

"We already knew that from what happened when we Slid from the palace."

Della frowned at him. "You returned to the palace?"

Brusus leaned against the wall. Since his poisoning, he hadn't seemed entirely the same. A weariness worked across his face as if he still hadn't shaken the effects of what happened. One hand fingered the cloth of his pants, twisting it around the ring he wore. "I thought you went to find Shael."

Rsiran looked up at Brusus and nodded. "We did. And we found the Forgotten."

Brusus's hand stopped moving. "You found them. Where are they?"

"Asador probably. But more than that, I don't know." And Rsiran wasn't about to go searching for them again. They had been lucky to escape this time.

Brusus looked from Jessa to Rsiran. "How did you find them if you don't know where they are?"

"When we were escaping from where I was poisoned—"

"Excuse me?"

Rsiran glanced at Jessa. "You didn't tell him?"

She shrugged. "Thought we'd tell him together."

Rsiran laughed softly. "When we were escaping, I grabbed onto the one thing I could sense. It took us to this… palace. Like the Floating Palace, only different."

Della sighed. "And that is where you met Evaelyn."

He nodded. "You said you knew her, but how? Who is she?"

Della took a sip of her tea. "Evaelyn is my sister."

Rsiran nearly dropped his tea. "Your sister?" But he reminded himself that the resemblance between them had been enough that he'd confused Evaelyn with Della when he first saw her.

"She said you were responsible for her exile!" Jessa said.

"As I said, partly true."

"How?" Rsiran didn't ask about how it meant Della was Elvraeth or why she no longer lived in the palace. Those were questions for another time.

"As I imagine you learned, she is not without abilities of her own."

Rsiran nodded, remembering how she Compelled Jessa to nearly attack him. Jessa touched his shoulder and looked straight ahead. "I was able to block her from Compelling me," Rsiran said.

Della smiled. "I wonder how she handled that?"

Jessa's face darkened. "She twisted my mind so that I nearly attacked him."

Della nodded toward Rsiran. "If you are able to keep her from Reading and Compelling you, your friends become your weakness."

Rsiran swallowed. That was what he'd feared, the reason he hadn't wanted to share with Jessa his plan. But it left him feeling empty.

"But your friends are also your strength. That is something I am not certain she understands."

He looked up to Jessa and took her hand.

"It felt like someone else was in my head," Jessa said.

"For that type of influence, you need to exert more direct control. It is never subtle," Brusus said.

"Is that what you do?" Rsiran asked.

Brusus's eyes flashed a bright green. "I have never Compelled you. I have only made suggestions."

"How is that different?"

"Trust that it is."

Jessa nodded. "What Brusus does is nothing like what *she* did to my mind."

"Would Jessa know if she were being Compelled again?" Rsiran asked.

Della shook her head. "It depends on how strongly Evaelyn chooses to influence. If it is only a subtle influence, you might never know."

"That's why she was exiled?" Jessa knelt next to Rsiran's chair, keeping close to him.

Della nodded. "She used her abilities to Compel another of the family, a young man she desired."

The family. Della had practically admitted she was Elvraeth before, but this was a more direct admission. "What happened?"

"She is not the only one with skill," Della said. She sighed. "When I tore her from his mind, it was nearly too late. Little could be done to help."

"I don't understand."

"Pray to the Great Watcher that you never have to understand, Rsiran. When I knew Evaelyn, she did not have the control I suspect she now does over her abilities. She delved deeply—too deeply—into his mind, forcing him into an action that was anathema to who he was. With such force, she destroyed his mind."

Rsiran shivered thinking of what could have happened to Jessa. Had Evaelyn tried forcing her to attack him, would that have been enough to tear apart her mind? Would she have tried to fight, only to end up changed?

"She said you know what they're trying to find."

Della frowned. "And you believed her?"

Rsiran thought about how angry Evaelyn had become when he asked. It was when the questions had stopped. "I had no reason not to believe her."

Della looked at him and took another sip of her tea.

"Della?" Brusus pushed off the wall and took a step toward her. "What do they want?"

Rsiran answered for her. "Both the Forgotten and Venass are interested in knowing how I can Slide past heartstone alloy." They hadn't asked him the same way, but that had been the purpose. Other than the barrier Rsiran created around his smithy, there was only one place with enough alloy to make Sliding difficult. "What do they want in the palace?"

Della glanced at Brusus before turning to regard Rsiran with a weary gaze. "There are many things the Elvraeth hide, Rsiran. But there is only one thing both Venass and the Forgotten would both seek. And it is something they cannot be allowed to have."

"Della?" Brusus asked.

"No, Brusus. This is not my secret to share. There are things in this world greater than me. I've never hidden the fact that I don't trust those in the palace, but they serve a purpose."

"What purpose?"

"Knowing will only draw you deeper," she said to Rsiran. "That is my fear. As one with the blood of the Watcher, you are at greatest risk."

Brusus frowned. "I don't understand."

"And you should not."

"And not knowing?" Brusus asked. "What does that do to us?"

She didn't answer, instead, she turned away from them, and sipped at her tea.

Rsiran couldn't shake the frustration he felt at Della not sharing with them. After everything they had been through, everything that it seemed the Forgotten and the scholars had gone through to bring him to this point, he felt as if her not sharing placed them at increased risk.

What was he to do, though?

CHAPTER 34

RSIRAN STOOD BY THE ROCKS overlooking the shore. Jessa stood next to him, staring at the sunrise. For long moments, neither spoke. He had been thinking about what to do ever since leaving Della, and kept coming back to the same answer. It was the only thing that would bring them any sense of closure, any sense of understanding, but it was something that could be avoided if only Della were willing to share.

"I need to go into the palace again," he finally said.

Jessa shook her head. "No. That's not the answer. You heard what Della said."

"Della said that the Elvraeth hold secrets. We already knew that. But she won't share what those secrets might be."

"Rsiran, if you go there, if you do that—"

"But I'm the only one who can. Della won't tell us what they want, and we can't be safe without knowing." As much as he tried, he hadn't been able to convince Della to share what might be hidden in the palace or learn why she might hide it from them. If there was something there that could help them, why wouldn't she share with them?

"And then what?" Jessa asked. "What do you think you can do?"

"They won't stop. Not until they find out how to enter the palace." And here he had thought the key had been the warehouse and what had been stored within it. Instead, *he* had been the reason the Forgotten began moving. The reason Venass wanted him. And they all wanted a way into the palace.

Even mentioning it made him anxious, but more than that, he had the urge to get moving. To begin. Once he knew what everyone wanted, he might finally be in a position to stay ahead of them. Maybe then they could be safe.

Could he really Slide into the palace? The alloy didn't stop him as it once had, and he wouldn't need an anchor to get in and back out. With all the time he'd spent Sliding, he didn't think such short Slides would even require much energy. Then there was the added benefit that he'd already sensed some of his forgings within the palace. He could use them, anchor to them, and reach any place in the palace as easily as Sliding into his smithy.

The only problem he had was that once he was there, he had no idea what he was looking for. He suspected that whatever the Elvraeth kept would be hidden deep within the palace. Getting there meant risking exposing himself. Doing so would put him in more danger, but wasn't he already in danger? Simply being in Elaeavn put him in danger.

For too long, he'd blamed Brusus for what had happened to him. The more he thought about everything, the more he realized his choices had led him here. It had been his choice to leave the mines. He likely would have died had he stayed, but leaving set off this chain of events. It had been his choice to go searching through the warehouse when he learned of the heartstone. That led him to Firell's ship and to the alchemists. And it had been his choice to go after Jessa.

Knowing what he did now, he would not change any of them.

He could do nothing and wait, but already he'd been sought out. First by Venass. And the Forgotten knew about him now too. Who would search for him next? The palace Elvraeth? The alchemists? Or someone else?

At least in making a decision, he still had a choice.

Jessa had been watching him, and she took his hand, squeezing gently. "You don't have to do this, Rsiran."

"And if I don't, who do I have to fear next? Where can we hide?" Once he would have thought that leaving the city would keep them safe, but it seemed that only put them in more danger. At least here they had friends. They knew the city. Outside… outside there were the exiled Elvraeth *and* Venass. How could he keep them safe from both?

"There's always something that will happen. Fearing what will come does nothing to change it. You just need to trust the Great Watcher knows what he's doing."

"And if not?"

Jessa shook her head. "You can't think like that."

"When have I ever had reason to think otherwise?"

"You think you suffer such hardship? That others don't know what it's like to suffer?"

"I'm sorry. I know that you've been through a lot—"

"No more than you. Mine is different. Had Haern not brought me back to Elaeavn… I don't know what would have happened. I've heard the stories, though. I know how they use women outside of Elaeavn. For that, I thank him."

"What does this have to do with the Forgotten? With Venass?"

"Only that we all have suffered, and we've survived. We'll survive this too."

Rsiran thought of the helpless way he'd felt when he'd been in Venass. He'd felt it again with the Forgotten. He'd felt it his entire life, from the moment his father learned of his ability. He was ready to no longer feel that way.

"I need to know," he said softly.

"And what will that change?"

Rsiran shook his head. "Maybe nothing. Or maybe it begins to give us answers, leverage, so that we might understand why everyone has been trying to use me. Isn't that worth it?"

Jessa took his hands and sighed. For a moment, she said nothing. "Just you? You're not going to leave me behind on this. You can try, but I've already shown you I know when you're going to Slide. I'll come anyway."

He pulled her to him and smiled. "You know I wouldn't have it any other way."

CHAPTER 35

THEY STOOD IN SHADOWS NEAR THE PALACE WALL. A cool breeze gusted from the north, carrying the hint of lorcith with it. He wondered if he was the only one who noticed it. The wind rustled against the dark grey clothes he wore, so similar to what he'd once worn while working in the mines. These were different enough that they couldn't be confused for them; Brusus had made certain of that. The embroidery running down the sleeves was far to rich for the mines.

The shirt covered the leather wrap around his waist where he'd fitted a half-dozen of his slender knives. They were all placed so they could be easily *pushed* away from him. Rsiran felt a certain reassurance with their presence.

Jessa stood next to him. A blood-red flower tucked into the charm hanging over the deep brown shirt that clung to her chest. She caught him looking and smiled, nudging him with an elbow. Tonight, she wore a thin leather belt with loops for the pair of lorcith knives she carried. The lorcith lock-pick set was tucked into one of her pockets.

"I still think this is stupid," Jessa whispered.

The wall loomed in front of them. They'd walked from the smithy rather than Sliding. Emerging from a Slide so close to the palace might draw attention and neither of them had wanted to risk it.

Rsiran snorted softly. "Probably. Do you have any other ideas?"

She fixed him with a hard stare. "None."

"Once we find out why they want to break into the palace, we can prepare for what they plan. Don't you think that's worth it?"

"But if you break into the palace, and if whatever we find there is well protected and we *still* fail to reach it, how does that help us with the Forgotten? With Venass?"

Rsiran sighed. "Then we'll know that I can't help them. That's worth something, as well, don't you think?"

"And if we get caught?"

If they were caught, Rsiran suspected the worse that would happen to them would be that they'd be exiled. Forgotten. No longer did he fear that as he once had.

"We'll just have to make sure we're not caught."

"Do Brusus and the others know you plan to do this tonight?"

Rsiran shook his head. "Brusus can't know or he'd try to come. He's still too weak from the poisoning." What Rsiran hadn't said was that there wasn't anything Brusus could do to help anyway. And Rsiran didn't want the strain of trying to Slide more than himself and Jessa through the palace.

"And Haern?"

"What about Haern?"

Rsiran spun. The scarred man stood leaning against one of the eareth trees that grew only near the palace. He had a long knife in his hand and used it to pick at his nails. He studied Rsiran with an amused expression that didn't quite reach his eyes.

How had he sneaked up on them?

Rsiran flicked his eyes to the knife. Not lorcith, though after their experience prior to the last time Rsiran Slid into the palace, he didn't really expect Haern to carry any of his knives unless he wanted Rsiran to know he was there.

"Haern," Rsiran started, but didn't know what else to say to him. How would he explain that he hadn't planned to tell him what he wanted to do?

Haern shook his head. "Don't, Rsiran. That's not why I'm here."

Rsiran frowned. "Then why *are* you here?"

Haern laughed softly. "Just because you don't tell me what you're planning, don't mean I can't See it."

"I thought you couldn't See anything when it came to me?"

Haern's brow wrinkled, twisting the long scar across his face. "And I still can't." He pointed his knife at Jessa. "But I've known that one too long not to look after her. You might be able to protect her, too, but that don't change the fact that I watch after her."

Jessa took a step toward Haern. "What do you See when you look?"

Haern flickered his eyes from Jessa to Rsiran. "That you'll need help."

"You… you don't want to stop me?" Rsiran asked.

Hearn flicked the knife, and it disappeared so quickly, Rsiran almost hadn't seen it happen. "Not sure I could if I wanted to." He shook his head. "Your gifts make you dangerous, Rsiran, but you got a good heart. That much I've seen. I trust you'll do what's right. And if this is the only way to find out what the exiles and Venass want, then I think we need to do it."

"This is just for information. I'm not going to steal from the Elvraeth," he said.

Haern grunted. "Wouldn't help you if you did."

Rsiran frowned. "Why is that?"

Haern nodded to where the palace loomed over them. This close, it no longer looked as if it floated like it did in Lower Town. Here, it jutted out from the rock the city was built upon, rising high overhead. A few lanterns glowed in windows, pale blue light shining. Heartstone lanterns—what he used to call Elvraeth light—though Rsiran still hadn't learned the trick of making them.

"Is it any better for us to have whatever's stored there?" he asked. "If it's so valuable that the exiles *and* Venass want it, do you think *we* can keep it safe?"

"Do you know what the Elvraeth hide?" Jessa asked.

Haern fixed her with a hard expression, his lips pressed tightly and his eyes tightening. "The one curse of my Sight. I See the potential of what's in there. And the dangers."

"That's why you came. You thought we were going to take it."

"I said that I wasn't."

"Then what?"

"Far as I know, the Elvraeth have protected this power for hundreds of years. At least since our people left the Aisl. But others know of it as well, or suspect they do, others with visions as strong—or stronger—than mine. While the Elvraeth know how to protect it, I'm not so sure we do." He fixed Rsiran with a hard stare. "Were you to take it from the palace, you think you can keep it from the Forgotten? From Venass? From any other thief who might think to sneak into wherever you end up storing it?" He snorted. "Least the Elvraeth have kept it safe all this time."

"They both want to use me," he told Haern. "Venass and the Forgotten. I need to know why. See if there's anything that we can learn from it. I'm doing this for information only."

Haern nodded. "You're different. Don't know what it means, but your abilities—the combination of your gifts—is different from anything else I've ever heard of. Makes you strong. And, like I said, dangerous. That's why they want you." He grunted softly and finally stepped away from the tree. "Not sure Josun Elvraeth knew that when he first thought to involve you in his plans. When you didn't kill him then… well, then he must've decided he'd use you in a different way."

Rsiran shook his head. "He only wanted a sword."

Haern grunted again. "Why do you think he wanted a sword?"

Rsiran hadn't discovered that answer yet. "I don't know."

Haern studied Rsiran. "No, I see you don't."

"You see or you See?"

Haern shrugged. "Told you—I don't See anything with you."

Rsiran looked at the palace wall. Standing and talking to Haern didn't get them any closer to what he wanted—and needed—to do. "I don't think I can Slide all of us around the palace," he told Haern.

A dark smile twisted his mouth. "Don't need you to take me. Can you get me past the wall?"

Rsiran nodded.

"That's all I need."

"What if you get caught?"

Haern laughed softly. "I won't get caught. Besides, you need someone to draw the Elvraeth away. That's why I'm here."

Jessa sucked in a breath. "Haern!"

He fixed her with his hard gaze. The light from the moon and nearby lanterns made the scar on his face seem to stretch. "Haven't you seen me get out of worse?" he asked.

"Let Rsiran and me do this. You don't need to put yourself in danger."

"We're all in danger now. Doing this don't change that."

He looked at Rsiran and waited.

Rsiran took Jessa's hand and grabbed Haern by the sleeve. Then he Slid.

They emerged on top of the wall. The wall here was nearly two feet wide, but Haern wobbled. Rsiran held him tightly. Haern's face had gone white and his jaw clenched. The palace loomed larger now, the darkened grounds sweeping out below them. The last time Rsiran had been here, he'd almost lost Jessa. That time, he'd come thinking he might need to harm the Elvraeth. This time, he had a different plan in mind.

"Are you all right, Haern?" Jessa whispered.

"Don't care for that."

"You've never Slid with him, have you?"

"Only once. Didn't like it then, either."

"You were barely awake. Had I not Slid you out of there, you would have been captured by the alchemists."

Haern nodded once. "Didn't say it wasn't necessary. Only that I didn't like it." He turned, shifting his weight so he crouched near a pool of shadows atop the wall. He scanned the palace grounds quickly.

"Looks like a pair of guards," he said.

Jessa nodded. "Same as the last time."

Haern frowned. "Same?"

She nodded.

He grunted softly. "Then we're missing something. Elvraeth are nothing if not careful. Not smart to go jumping in somewhere without having a better idea of what they've changed."

"I don't plan to walk across the yard."

Rsiran stared at the dark building near the center of the palace lawn that he knew to be made almost entirely of lorcith. The last time they'd come, he'd used one of his knives to gain access. Would he be able to Slide this time?

"And then what?" Haern asked. "You plan to walk through the palace? You aren't dressed well enough to go unnoticed."

"That's why he brought me." Jessa crouched next to him and watched Haern. "You think me incapable of such a sneak?"

"You're incredibly skilled. But where you're going, they know how to sniff out sneaks. Rsiran's ability masks him somehow. I'm not sure it carries over to you."

"He's not going without me."

Haern flickered his eyes over to Rsiran. "That's how you feel? Knowing you might not be able to protect her once you get into the palace?"

"I need her with me, Haern," Rsiran answered softly.

Haern took a slow breath, his eyes losing focus as they did when he attempted a vision. "Go. I'll do what I can to give you time. But be safe. There are things even I can't See about the palace, but I—" He cut off, his head snapping around to the left. "Go!" he hissed.

Rsiran followed the direction of his gaze. One of the palace guards moved through the shadows toward them, as if he knew where they were.

"Haern—"

Haern shook his head, already moving down the wall, fading into the shadows. Rsiran didn't understand how he managed to move so stealthily.

Without waiting, he squeezed Jessa's hand, focused on his target, and Slid.

CHAPTER 36

THEY EMERGED INSIDE THE LORCITH BUILDING. Rsiran had been here before, making the Slide less dangerous than it otherwise would have been. The air stank of dampness and bitter lorcith. Muted sounds drifted toward him, but he couldn't tell if they came from the other side of the door or down the stairs. Very little light made it to him, leaving him again in the dark, nothing but the lorcith to guide him, much like the Ilphaesn mines.

"Do you see anything?" he asked.

"Stairs. Move carefully. I'll guide you."

Rsiran pulled against her hand. They could walk, but doing so meant they would spend more time in the palace. More time for the Elvraeth to learn he'd come. And Haern was right. What had they changed since he last had come? Someone would have learned of their presence, and the Elvraeth already knew Sliders existed. Would they have moved walls and created unfamiliar barriers, or didn't they know about the need for some familiarity with a Slide?

More than that, he had no idea where in the palace he planned to go. Did they wander, searching for places that might be heavily fortified indicating the Elvraeth hid something? Della suggested what they sought would be deep within the palace and heavily guarded. But how would they find that?

Every step sounded loud in his ears, as if he thundered through the palace.

How long until they were discovered?"

If they wandered blindly, how long would it take to find what they needed? Too long, he decided. Long enough that he didn't dare wait.

That left searching a different way. Rsiran thought he might be able to find where he needed to go, but not without focusing.

"Wait," he whispered to Jessa.

"What are you doing?"

"Trying to learn where we need to go."

She said nothing. He listened to the lorcith, letting the sense of the metal call to him. All around him, it practically pressed upon him, an oppressive sense different from what he'd grown accustomed to while working in Ilphaesn. At least then, he hadn't really known what he felt. Over time, his connection to lorcith had strengthened to where he could pinpoint the smallest of his forgings from a great distance. Even unshaped ore he could feel from a distance.

This was different.

The lorcith here seemed a physical sense. Heavy and demanding his attention.

Rsiran closed his eyes and focused on his breathing. As he did, he pushed away the smaller sense of lorcith near him. That of Jessa's charm or her knives. The sense of the knives he wore. More distantly, the sense of the sword and other forgings he'd made. Some of those forgings were here in the palace. That realization nearly made him lose his focus.

But he pushed them away.

It left him with the yearning call of the lorcith building.

Rsiran listened to it, slowly understanding what it wanted.

And then he pushed that away as well.

Once done, he felt emptiness around him.

Pushing away the sense of lorcith was dangerous. Haern could See him when he did which meant the Elvraeth could also. But it also left Rsiran more attuned.

He listened.

At first, he heard nothing. Silence. Only the sound of his breathing and the beating of his heart. There was a distant awareness of Jessa, but he'd had to push that away as he cleared his mind, or the lorcith she carried with her would have overwhelmed him.

Then, distantly, he had the sense of *something*. Not the alloy. That was a hard clash of awareness when he recognized it. And not lorcith. That was softer, eager, and one he could ignore.

Was it pure heartstone?

This was warm and welcoming and seemed to draw him forward. If he followed it, there was no telling where it would take him. Possibly out of the palace and away from his goal. But without knowing another way, he worried they wouldn't find what the Elvraeth hid in the first place.

Intruding on that sense was the distant awareness of lorcith moving toward him. His forgings within the palace.

They had to move.

"Hang on," he whispered.

"Where are you Sliding?"

He appreciated that she didn't question otherwise. Jessa trusted him.

"I don't know."

She squeezed his hand tightly around hers.

Then he focused on what he sensed and Slid.

The feeling was nothing like a normal Slide. That was colors and movement and a hint of bitterness that reminded him of lorcith. And it wasn't anything like what he experienced pushing through the alloy. That was hard, and he felt it as he squeezed through the barrier it created.

This felt warm and welcoming and strangely vast. Rather than a sense of movement, he felt as if he shifted. The only thing he could compare it to was the way he'd had to Slide in Venass.

As he Slid, Jessa was torn from him.

At first, she was holding his hand, Sliding with him, and then she was not.

He tried calling out her name in the middle of the Slide but nothing came out.

And then it was done.

He emerged surrounded by blue light that reminded him of the heartstone lanterns. This glowed differently, deeper and purer than that light. It blinded him.

Rsiran stumbled, sprawling across a warm floor, one cheek smacking against it. As it did, Rsiran lost the concentration he'd been holding. The sense of lorcith flooded back into him, almost enough to overwhelm him.

It was everywhere.

The sense was different from before and not the oppressive sense he had when he Slid into the palace building. This was vast like the ocean rather than like Ilphaesn. And he sensed no voids as he did within the mines, nothing he could use to guide his steps.

He pushed up, rubbing at his eyes to clear them. Slowly, the soft blue light began to fade, and he could see the space around him. He stood in a massive room, so large that he couldn't clearly see the walls. Overhead, lights flickered, as if stars twinkling in the sky. The air was warm and smelled familiar in a way he couldn't quite place. He had the vague sense of welcome.

Five distinct orbs rested atop pedestals within a ring in the floor. Each glowed with that pure light. One pulsed slightly, drawing his eye. What was this?

And how could he get back out? He might have Slid here, but he didn't know if he could find his way back out. And Jessa was nowhere to be seen.

His heart hammered. When first learning to Slide with her, he'd worried about what would happen if he lost her during the Slide. Where would she end up? Would she carry onward to where they traveled or would she emerge along the way?

He listened for the lorcith in her charm and knives, but with lorcith all around him, he couldn't focus well enough.

Rsiran tried to steady his breathing, but failed. He couldn't clear his head enough to listen for her. She might be stuck, trapped somewhere in the palace. Or worse, caught in that place between Slides.

The glowing orbs surged brighter with one still pulsing slightly, beckoning him toward it.

The pedestal seemed made of twisted wood, almost like vines… or roots of some great trees… weaving together to hold the orb almost at eye level. The blue light came from deep within it, vibrant and pure. If he stared too long, Rsiran felt as if he might be drawn into it.

He started to turn away, but paused.

Isn't this what he came for? Didn't he *want* to know what the Elvraeth protected?

Nothing about this was like anything he'd ever encountered. And he knew with a deep certainty, the Forgotten and Venass could not be allowed to reach here. Had he not had the ability to sense lorcith—and the heartstone—he doubted he would have been able to find it. Which meant that *they* wouldn't be able to find it.

No longer did he want to remain. He wanted to return, find Della and ask about the orbs. And after that, he hoped Venass wouldn't reach him. All he wanted was to live in peace, Jessa at his side.

First, he had to find her.

But how? While he felt lorcith all around him, he had no way of sensing her.

He tried to Slide a step away from the glowing blue lights and failed.

Sweat slicked his hands, and he wiped them on his pants. He was trapped.

Chapter 37

R SIRAN LOOKED AROUND THE ROOM, searching for some other way to go back. If this room was in the palace, then it made sense there would be some way to access it other than Sliding, especially given the way the Elvraeth had protected the palace against Sliding.

He moved away from the softly glowing orbs. The nearest one still pulsed slowly. If Rsiran stared too long, he felt he would be drawn to pick it up and slip it into his pocket. After everything he'd been through over the last few months, the last thing he wanted to do was take something like that from the Elvraeth.

A high wall rose overhead in the pool of shadows at the edge of the light. The air felt different, stirring with a soft breeze that touched his cheeks and cooled him. Rsiran touched the wall and found it warm like the rest of the room. Shapes were etched into the wall, but he couldn't see through the shadows to discern what they were, whether writing or simply decorative. He traced his way around, following the wall, trailing his hand along as he went.

Rather than running straight, the wall circled the room. He didn't find any other access. No doors interrupted the wall. Nothing that would provide a way out.

He looked up. The distant lights that twinkled in the darkness above could be open sky, but he had no way of reaching it. And without being able to Slide, he couldn't escape.

Panic sent his heart racing. The Elvraeth would find him. And then what? Would they force him to tell them why he'd come? If he couldn't Slide from here, they must have some method of restricting abilities, more than what the Elvraeth chains had managed.

Or did they?

Rsiran looked back at the lights. He'd managed to Slide here. Had the Elvraeth blocked his ability, they would have prevented him from reaching this room. But they hadn't.

He slowly looped around the ring that surrounded the pedestals. Each glowing orb looked the same, resting on a similar pedestal made of the same twisted wood. But when he stared at them, actually studied them, subtle differences slowly emerged.

At first, he saw a difference to the light in them. He'd thought the blue glow coming from them the same, but the more he studied them, the more he realized there was a *texture* to the light.

Rsiran frowned, trying and failing to understand what he saw.

Could the *shape* of the orbs be different as well? Without touching one, it was hard to tell—the light glowed too brightly for him to know—but he suspected the shape had something to do with the light.

He continued in the circuit around the orbs, finally stopping before the one that pulsed. The light from this one was definitely different from the others. But why? What about this orb made it different?

Rsiran circled the pedestal. The twisting wood looked no different from the others, so it was not a measure of the pedestal that made the orb different. In the moments when the light pulsed lower, he almost saw the shape of it.

As he studied it, it pulled on him.

Before knowing what he was doing, his face was barely a hand's width from it.

This close, he felt warmth radiating from it and knew the orbs were the reason the room felt so warm. It even had a distinct odor, a little like lorcith, but sweeter. Something about it reminded him of Jessa.

Rsiran needed to get out of here and get to Jessa.

But there was nothing that would help him escape.

Nothing but these orbs.

He steadied his breathing, hoping to slow his pounding heart, and wiped sweaty hands on his pants. Then, without thinking too much about what he did next, he grabbed the orb he'd been studying in both hands and lifted it from its pedestal.

And then he held his breath.

The blue light within the orb faded, leaving only a white, almost colorless pulsing light. It began pulsing more rapidly, faster than he could blink. Rsiran felt himself drawn forward—*pulled*—almost as if Sliding.

But he had no other sense of movement. No flashes of color as he was accustomed to seeing as he Slid. No scent of lorcith. Just a feeling of movement.

And then blackness all around.

The orbs had all gone dark. The air turned cold. He realized he still held his breath and forced himself to suck in a breath. It was cold and tasteless.

Then white light flashed below him, distantly. He no longer saw the floor, the ring, the orbs.

For a moment, Rsiran had no idea what he saw, but as he became aware that the sense of the lorcith all around him had faded, he realized what he saw below him was the ore itself, not just sensing it as he always had before but seeing it, in its raw, almost brilliant form but from high above.

Some of the lights he saw were massive. One in particular seemed incredibly vast, and he wondered if it was Ilphaesn. But how was he seeing this?

There were other lights below him, some nearly as large. Above what he suspected was Ilphaesn—to the north, he supposed, though direction had little meaning where he was—there was another bright light. He frowned. Could that be Asador? To the east was another, as bright as the last. That would be Thyr. Dozens of other lights flashed. Some he had no idea of what they would represent, and others were separated by great distances, as if separated by the sea.

How was he seeing this?

And did it really represent what he thought it did or was this simply some vision of the orb?

"What is this?" he asked aloud.

He didn't expect an answer, and none came.

The lights shifted, dimming until he couldn't see them anymore. Slowly, new lights appeared below him, a deep blue that both resembled the light from the orbs and could not compare. As before, some of the lights burned brighter. One in particular, not near where any of the others had been, glowed with a steady, deep blue, nearly the match of the light of the orb he still held in his hands. Within the darkness, Rsiran couldn't tell where this would be—or even what the lights represented. There were others, though most were smaller, only a pale blue, with the vaguest similarity to the orb. There weren't as many as the white lights he'd seen before, and he had no sense of location as he had with the other light.

Then they faded.

The light of the orb he held faded with it.

Rsiran was cast into darkness so profound, he felt it in his bones. He shivered.

Because of the time spent in the mines, he hated being in the dark. It left him with a crawling sensation at the back of his mind, like someone crept up behind him. This time was no exception, but the sense came from all around.

Rsiran turned, looking for who might be near him.

There was nothing.

He held out the orb, wishing for light to spring from it again, but it remained dim and grew cool in his hand.

The presence neared. Rsiran didn't know what he felt, only that he knew he was no longer alone. And whatever approached was enormous.

Then it stopped.

Rsiran held his breath again.

Moments passed. Time had no meaning. There was only the sense of the other nearby.

The air warmed suddenly. The orb sprang back to light.

For a fleeting moment, he thought he saw someone standing next to him. Pain shot through his head, blinding him. When it cleared, whatever he'd seen was gone.

Rsiran blinked tears from his eyes. He stood in the middle of the circle made by the pedestals, and blue light glowed brightly from them once again. He'd been holding one in his hand, but somehow it had returned to its pedestal and no longer pulsed with different light from the others. He had no way of telling which one he'd held.

The orb had given him a strange vision, but nothing else had changed. He was still trapped in the room, separated from Jessa.

Rsiran sank to the ground.

There was nothing else to do but wait for the Elvraeth to find him.

CHAPTER 38

RSIRAN SAT ON THE STONE, warmth radiating through him. The sense of lorcith surrounded him again, nearly oppressive. Within the ring of orbs, the light glowed so brightly, he couldn't see anything else.

As he sat, he steadied his breathing, focusing on the lorcith.

While he felt it everywhere around him, he began to wonder if he could listen for lorcith he'd forged. Always before, it pulled on him differently than the mined ore. Could he distinguish it from what he felt around him?

Time passed as he listened. Rsiran had no idea how much.

He breathed, listening, hoping that he could find Jessa. She could be trapped anywhere. He still didn't know if she'd been lost in the space between the Slide or if she'd been captured by the Elvraeth.

But, if he couldn't escape from this room, he would never find her. His priority was finding a way out. Once out, he would track her using the lorcith knives she carried.

Then, slowly, like a tickle at the back of his mind, he had the vague, familiar sense of forged lorcith. Something about this particular lorcith called to him strongly.

Rsiran grabbed onto this distant sense and held it. At first, he did nothing else.

It became more distinct the longer he held onto it. Something about it changed. Not just the sense of lorcith, but there came a sense of warmth and light that reminded him of the vision he'd had while holding the orb.

Rsiran almost lost his connection.

He steadied his breathing again and listened.

This time, as he reestablished the connection to the lorcith, he *pulled* rather than using it to anchor. It was the same as what he'd done when trapped in Venass. This time, he had the same sense of movement. There came a flash of blue and the sweetly bitter scent he smelled while holding the orb, and then he emerged.

Rsiran sat in a darkened room without windows or lanterns to give him any light. Lorcith burned nearby, the sense more acute than anything he remembered having before. He didn't move for a long moment, listening for other lorcith.

It was all around him, but this time it seemed to come from distinct locations. The knives in the leather he wore around his waist. Another knife, somewhere close. And then the charm.

"Jessa?" he whispered.

It had to be her. He'd made the charm for her, made certain she wore it, hoping he could use it to anchor and find her if she went missing. This time, he had been the one who'd gone missing.

A hand touched his face and ran through his hair. He smelled the flower she wore and when lips touched his, he kissed her back, pulling her down onto his lap. She tasted sweet, like mint. He didn't stop until someone cleared his throat nearby.

"Have you had enough?"

It was Haern.

"Haern?"

He grunted.

"Where are we?"

"Better question is where have you been?"

Rsiran shook his head, but had no way of knowing whether they could see the motion. "I tried to Slide into the palace…"

Jessa tensed atop him, and he put his arms around her, holding her close.

"What happened when we were separated in the Slide?" he asked. At least she hadn't been trapped in the place between the Slides. Rsiran wasn't sure he would have been able to find her again.

"You were holding my hand when you Slid, but I slipped away."

It had felt like they were torn apart to him. At least she was safe. Whatever else happened, he could get them to safety.

"How did you find Haern?"

Haern grunted again, softer this time. "Not too hard. She was standing just inside the door."

"Where are we?"

"You don't know?" Jessa asked.

"I can't see anything."

"Still a babe," she whispered in his ear.

"We're in the palace. Too many guards coming by for us to move safely. Jessa said to find a place to hide and that you'd find us. Didn't know if I should believe her."

"How long have you been here?"

No one answered.

"How long?"

"It's been the better part of a day, Rsiran. When I lost you… I didn't know what to do. I knew it wasn't safe for me in the palace. I traced my way back and reached the door when Haern pushed it open. We heard voices and knew we needed to hide. This was the first door we found."

"A day?" he repeated. "How have I been gone a day?"

"That's what I keep asking Jessa."

Rsiran looked toward Haern's voice. The darkness had faded somewhat, and he thought he could make out a shadowed outline crouching nearby. "Why did you stay here?"

"Where else would we go?" Jessa asked. "If we returned to the palace yard, we would have to make it up the wall before the guards found us. I wasn't sure we could manage without getting caught." She squeezed him and seemed reluctant to let him go. "So we waited."

From the edge of tension in her voice, he could tell how difficult it had been for her to wait. Jessa prided herself on her ability as a sneak, and waiting meant she didn't think she could manage to escape on her own.

But what would have happened had he not been able to escape from the room with the orbs? Would they have tried to get out on their own eventually?

Rsiran didn't want to think about that. He *had* escaped, though he still didn't know what the vision meant that he had while holding the orb. And what did it mean that he'd twice managed to Slide without taking a step?

"What's in here?" With the darkness, Rsiran couldn't see anything and again wished he had some of Jessa's Sight.

"Boxes."

The darkness around him continued to fade, but not enough for him to make out anything but lines, gradients of shadows. "Boxes? Like the crates in the warehouse?"

"Pretty much. These are smaller. I can't really tell what's in them. This is even too dark for me, and I don't dare step out to find a lantern."

"How haven't you been discovered?"

Haern grunted. "Damn lucky." His voice sounded closer. "Did you find what you were looking for?"

Rsiran took a shaky breath. "I think so."

What he'd seen in that room could be nothing else. Lorcith all around, the blinding blue glow, the strange pedestals made of a twisted wood, and the massive room with starlight for a ceiling. What else would it have been?

"I found what they want." This time, he said it with more conviction. "I don't know what they think to do, but I've seen it. Hopefully Della can provide answers." He had the sudden memory of the sharp pain stabbing through his head. When he managed to clear his vision, the orb had been back atop the pedestal. "I'm not sure they can even take what's there."

"Could you reach it again?" Haern asked.

He tried to remember the sense he'd felt when he cleared his mind, the sense he'd focused on as he Slid to where the orbs were kept. This time, he managed to clear the sense of lorcith away quickly. He felt the heartstone chain around Jessa's neck. If he listened, he could hear the alloy of the bars within the palace, the heartstone all around him.

Rsiran pushed this away as well.

He was left with emptiness. It reminded him of the blackness that had surrounded him after touching the orb.

Then he felt… something. Warm and powerful and calling to him…

Rsiran let it go before it pulled him back. He didn't know if he'd have the strength to return to Jessa.

"What is it, Rsiran? You almost Slid again."

"You felt it?"

She shook her head. The shadows around her had cleared enough that he could now make out the outline of her face. "I saw it. The swirl of colors that usually surround you when you Slide. But you stopped. At least, I think you did."

"I stopped." He took a deep breath. "I found what the Elvraeth protect."

"What? What did you find?" Jessa asked.

"Some kind of orbs of power," he said. "I felt connected to the Great Watcher himself when I was there. I think I could reach them again if I tried. When I was there, one of them pulsed softly. I couldn't find a way out of the room. I couldn't Slide, and there was the sense of lorcith all around me, like this building in the palace. So I touched it."

Haern leaned toward him. "You held one?"

Rsiran couldn't tell if there was accusation or a question to what he said. "I didn't know what else to do. I couldn't get out of there, and it seemed one of the orbs *wanted* me to hold it." That was the only answer he'd been able to come up with for why the orb had stopped pulsing after he touched it. If only he knew what that meant.

Haern leaned back and rocked on his heels. Had the room grown lighter or had his eyes finally adjusted to the dark? Now he could practically make out the look on Haern's face, the way his jaw clenched while he contemplated what Rsiran had said.

"Can you get us out of here?" Jessa asked.

"I think so."

"Better hurry," Haern said.

Rsiran stood and readied to Slide. As he did, a heavy pounding came from a nearby wall.

He looked toward Jessa and Haern. The Elvraeth knew they were here.

"Haern—"

Haern stepped over one of the boxes on the floor and grabbed Rsiran's hand. Rsiran held Jessa close. He tried taking a step and Sliding but couldn't.

"Rsiran…"

He tried again. Again he failed with his Slide.

"I don't know what's wrong. I can't Slide us."

Jessa tensed next to him. Haern only grunted.

Chapter 39

Y OU WERE ABLE TO SLIDE TO US, WEREN'T YOU?" Jessa asked.

The pounding came louder and now mixed with a scraping sound. Rsiran imagined the door slowly peeling away until they were exposed.

"I did, but it was different."

Haern turned to him. He still held onto Rsiran's hand, as if he hadn't given up on the possibility that Rsiran could Slide them to safety.

"Different?"

"Like in Venass," he explained to Jessa. "When the lorcith surrounding me kept me…"

He stopped and looked around. Lorcith surrounded him here much like it had in Venass. The only difference there had been that the walls seemed infused with it, whereas here, the walls *were* lorcith. He didn't know why that should prevent him from Sliding, but it seemed to work that way. When he'd been in Venass, he'd been able to listen for one of his forgings and use it to anchor, to pull himself rather than step into the Slide.

Rsiran focused on the lorcith around him as the pounding built louder and louder. As before, he pushed it away, ignoring the immediate lorcith. He was left with the sense of heartstone alloy coming from Jessa's necklace. Ignoring this, he listened for his forgings, knowing hundreds were scattered around the city.

The faint sense of one of his forgings pulled on his senses. Rsiran listened, trying to ignore the pounding that seemed almost in the room with him, as he focused on this forging. But he couldn't tell what it was. Possibly a knife—the Great Watcher knew he made plenty of them—or something small like that. Definitely not the sword, though he didn't know why he wouldn't feel the sword. Always before he'd been especially attuned to it.

Rsiran gripped Jessa and Haern and then pulled on the sense of lorcith.

At first, he didn't know if it would work. Then, as light pierced the darkness of the room, he felt them move.

The Slide was different, slow and thick, but picked up speed as they moved.

And then they emerged.

Rsiran blinked, looking around him, surprised at where they were. In spite of the darkness, there was no mistaking where he'd Slid them. The Barth.

They stood in the kitchen of the Wretched Barth. A massive hearth that usually burned brightly was cold and dark. Cook pots lined one wall. A shadowed counter stretched in front of them. The scent of stale bread and meat filled the air.

"Why did you bring us here, Rsiran?" Haern asked. He pulled away from Rsiran and made his way to a corner. He worked silently for a moment and then orange light spilled around the room from a small lantern. Haern held it out and twisted around.

Rsiran shook his head. "I had to use lorcith to anchor. This was the first thing I sensed."

Haern turned the lantern toward him. It nearly blinded Rsiran, and he put his hand up in front of his face and turned away. "What?"

The bowl he'd once made Lianna hung on the wall near them. That was what he'd sensed, what he'd used to anchor to. Rsiran pointed to it.

Haern lifted the lantern to look at the bowl. He grunted again. "Couldn't just take us to Della's house?"

Rsiran shook his head. "I can now. But I think I'm lucky I was able to sense anything."

Jessa pulled on his arm. "Rsiran…"

He turned toward her. The lantern light played with the shadows across her face, leaving her looking lean and haunted. Her dark brown hair fell past her shoulders. The flower she'd been wearing had faded.

"There's someone else here," she whispered.

Haern's head snapped around. "You saw something?" He spoke softly and set the lantern on the counter in a swift motion, another knife appearing in his hands as he did.

Jessa shook her head. "Movement only."

Rsiran listened for lorcith, using his ability to try to determine whether they had anything to fear. He couldn't sense any lorcith other than what they'd brought with them.

But there was something else.

He almost missed it, and realized nearly too late what it was: heartstone.

Not the alloy, though. This was pure heartstone like they'd found in the Forgotten Palace.

Rsiran quickly worked to clear his mind of lorcith. It was the only way he knew to sense heartstone. As he did, he knew Jessa was right. They weren't alone.

The heartstone was behind him.

Rsiran turned, twisting with Jessa to take advantage of her Sight. As he turned, he grabbed two knives from his leather belt, and held them ready.

A deep laugh echoed from the shadows near the door.

"Impressive."

A figure stepped forward and Jessa gasped softly.

Thom.

"You were dead," Rsiran said.

Thom smiled. The long scar tracing up the side of his face twisted with it. "Was I?"

An image surged in Rsiran's mind, that of Thom lying on the ground, blood pooling around him. He'd been *Pushed*.

Rsiran released the sense of heartstone alloy, but not before realizing it wasn't somewhere near Thom. Rather, what he sense seemed to come from *within* him. He readied to use his knives.

"Brusus didn't send you to guard the house."

Thom's smile widened. "I never said he did."

Rsiran frowned, trying to think about what Thom said when they'd first met. Had Thom been the one to mention Brusus's name or had he?

"Why are you here?" Jessa asked.

Thom turned to her, his smile fading. "Why? The same reason as you, I suspect." His eyes narrowed as he studied her. "I know your secrets the same as I know his." He jerked his head to the side, to where Haern had been creeping closer. "And now it's time we know *his*," he said, motioning to Rsiran. "Consider this your summons."

Before Rsiran could answer, Haern stepped forward, holding onto his knives. "Most know my secrets," he said softly. "Much as I know yours."

Thom tilted his head. "You really think so?"

Haern frowned and pursed his lips. "They know about my past. Don't change what I need to do now, does it? Doesn't change that I can't let Venass summon the boy."

"No? Then it wouldn't matter to you if Brusus knew where you studied before you returned to Elaeavn?"

Haern grunted. "That's how you knew."

Thom tapped his head. "We're more alike than you know."

Haern shook his head. "If you've studied there, then you know we're nothing alike."

Thom smiled, his lips peeling back to show his teeth. "Perhaps." He turned to Rsiran. "You've been busy. When I met you near the Aisl, I never expected you'd be so... resourceful. I'll admit that I didn't think you would be the one to reach it, but the others thought you might. And when you traveled *within* Venass, then I was sent to watch." He laughed. "You've proven to be quite interesting, Rsiran."

"Rsiran?" Jessa whispered.

Thom didn't take his eyes off Rsiran. "If you are to refuse the summons, then I will have what you took from the palace."

"I didn't take anything from the palace."

Thom took a step toward him, moving in that dangerously graceful way that he had while one hand rested on the hilt of his sword. Rsiran had no doubt that Thom knew how to use his sword. He didn't know if he'd be able to reach him with his knives.

"We know you were in the palace. And then you weren't. Hand over the crystal."

Rsiran frowned. When he'd Slid to find the orbs, hadn't he still been in the palace?

But would he have known if he had Slid from the palace? The Slide had been different from any other he'd done.

"I'm not going back to Venass."

"You made a bargain."

"Consider it broken," Rsiran said.

Thom smiled. "What did you take from the palace?"

"We didn't find anything," Rsiran said.

Thom angled to keep Haern in view and twisted toward Rsiran. "Now I know you're lying."

Haern shifted and Rsiran glanced over at him. "How do you think you can stop all of us?"

Thom shook his head. "I don't have to stop all of you. Just one."

"There are three of us. I suspect you know what Rsiran can do, so you know how dangerous he is." Thom tipped his head slightly. "And you know my history."

Thom sniffed. "That's two. And this one?" He nodded toward Jessa, his hand still on the hilt of his sword. He hadn't tried to draw it yet and seemed completely at ease. "You think I should fear your sneak?"

"More than you know," Haern said.

He made a movement to come around Thom, but Thom raised a hand and wiggled a finger. "Didn't I say I only had to stop one of you?"

Haern suddenly jerked and stood up straight. The knives he'd been holding dropped from his hands, clattering to the ground.

Rsiran turned. Haern wore a blank stare much like when he had one of his visions. "Haern?"

Thom chuckled. "One down."

What had Brusus said about Thom? That he was a skilled Reader, one who could Compel even more strongly than Brusus.

Rsiran made certain his mental barriers were in place, drawing on heartstone to fortify them.

He grabbed onto Jessa. If he needed to Slide, he would at least make sure he got her to safety.

Thom laughed again. "You'd leave him behind?"

Rsiran didn't think he'd Read him, but didn't know for sure. Sometimes Della seemed to Read him even when he thought he'd fortified his defenses. "I'd get us to safety."

Thom smirked. "Thought I'd read you differently. I never expected you to be so callous." He took a slight step forward, edging closer as he did.

Rsiran *pushed* on one of his knives. "Don't. Not any closer."

Thom paused. "Are you fast enough?"

"With the knives?"

Thom shook his head. "Sliding."

Thom lunged toward Jessa, slender knives appearing in his hands.

Rsiran had been ready.

He Slid faster than he ever had before, anchoring to a knife in Della's home as firmly as he could.

Everything blurred as he tore Jessa through the Slide. Air whistled past his face, colors surged. The air smelled of burning lorcith.

He emerged long enough to drop her near the hearth. Della sat in her chair and looked up at him with a deep frown. Then he Slid back to the Barth.

He had moved quickly enough that Thom still moved in his lunge.

When Rsiran emerged, Thom spun, flinging one of the knives at him. Rsiran helplessly tried pushing on it, but it wasn't lorcith made. He hadn't expected it would be; Thom wouldn't make that mistake.

Rsiran Slid a step to the side, ducking away from the knife. It whistled past him and sank into the wall. Another knife followed and Rsiran Slid again, back a step.

He ended near Haern who still stood staring blankly.

Thom looked at him and as he did, Haern grabbed toward Rsiran's arm, gripping tightly.

"Haern!"

It had no effect.

Another pair of knives appeared in Thom's hands, so smoothly that it reminded him of Haern. Rsiran hesitated. As he did, a knife nearly struck him.

Then he anchored again and jerked Haern with him into a Slide.

Pain shot through his arm as he Slid. He glanced down to see a knife protruding from his upper arm.

Rsiran ignored it long enough to complete the Slide, emerging again in Della's home.

Haern let go of his arm and grabbed his neck with both hands, squeezing with a suffocating grip.

Rsiran tried pulling away, but couldn't. Between Haern's grip and the pain in his arm, his vision faded. He thought he heard someone call his name, but he couldn't be sure.

CHAPTER 40

RSIRAN AWOKE TO BLURRED VISION AND WARMTH. Pale blue light glowed somewhere nearby. For a moment, he thought he'd returned to the room with the orbs. Then his vision cleared. As it did, he felt the gentle pull of lorcith all around him.

He sat up quickly and looked around.

A lantern glowing with a deep blue light rested nearby. Unshaped lorcith filled a bin. His forgings practically spilled over the table along the far wall. His smithy.

But how had he gotten here?

"You're awake."

Rsiran pushed up. Pain shot through his arm, and he remembered Thom's knife hitting it as he Slid with Haern. He swallowed, feeling his throat burn as he did. An injury he hadn't expected.

He looked over to see Della sitting next to him, her legs tucked under her as she sat along side his thin bed. She sipped from a steaming mug. He smelled mint.

"Who let you in here?"

Della's eyes sparkled a deeper green for a moment. "You nearly die, and your first question is about the safety of your smithy?"

"Yes."

She nodded. "Perhaps that's good." She leaned toward him. Her silver hair twisted atop her head. A colorful scarf, slashes of blue and green and orange, twisted around her neck, the only colors she wore. Otherwise, a flowing tunic of white draped to her ankles. "I brought you here."

"With Jessa?"

He looked around the smithy but didn't see her. She was the only one with a key, though Brusus had already proven he could pick the lock. Except, when he'd left for the palace, Rsiran had barricaded the door, slipping the heartstone-forged blade in front of it to prevent anyone from sneaking in.

His eyes flickered to the door, and he saw the barrier remained in place. "Not Jessa," he said. Rsiran leaned back, shaking his head. His arm throbbed, and he wondered why Della hadn't simply Healed him.

"Not Jessa," she agreed.

Della laid a hand on his arm, and a sense of calming warmth worked through him. The pain persisted where he'd been struck, but he didn't fear pain.

"Did I Slide us here?"

"In a way."

Rsiran grunted. "You guided me. Like the time before."

She nodded. "It seemed safest. I cannot Slide on my own, but my abilities allow me to guide you as you Slide."

He remembered the first time it had happened. He'd appeared at Della's home unexpectedly. That was when he learned she could sense him Sliding. Not just sense it, but influence it. Another weakness of his abilities.

"How?"

She smiled gently. "I asked."

Something about the way she said it made him think of how he forged lorcith, the way he asked the lorcith to take a different shape than it wanted. It was how he'd made his knives, even before knowing what it was he did.

"What of Haern?"

Della's face tensed for a moment. "Haern will be fine. Brusus helped clear the compulsion."

"And me?"

"You will live. The blade was poisoned. Tchaln powder. Had we not already had the antidote…"

Rsiran blinked. That meant she used the antidote he'd been given in Venass, the one meant for Brusus. "You couldn't Heal me?"

"It is a fast-acting poison. I stabilized you, but without that antidote, even my skills wouldn't have been enough." She frowned. "I haven't seen tchaln powder used in many years. The making of it is mostly forgotten, a mixture of several different poisons, each with a distinct effect. Taken together…" She shook her head. "You are lucky."

Rsiran could think of a place where the making of such a poison hadn't been forgotten. A place where Haern—once an assassin—had trained. "It was Thom. When we left the palace, I couldn't Slide at first. Something blocked me. I anchored to the only thing I could sense and pulled us from the palace. We emerged in the Barth."

Della took a sip of her mint tea. When she set the mug down, she was frowning. "You did not have the same difficulty the last time you went to the palace?"

Rsiran shook his head, understanding what she was getting at. "I sensed the sword and used it as the anchor. And when we left the palace the first time, I used what I sensed in your home."

307

"You were less skilled then."

She was right. Rsiran's skill at Sliding had increased significantly since he first entered the palace. Now, even the heartstone alloy didn't limit him. But something had.

He thought of the way Thom had been waiting for them at the Barth. The idea that he'd been Compelled frightened him, but what else would explain it?

"Could Thom have blocked me?"

Della took a deep breath. Worry crinkled the corners of her eyes. "If he managed to Compel you to believe he was dead, it's possible that he managed to do other things as well." She hesitated. "I understand he pulled you there as a summons." When Rsiran nodded, the worry in her eyes deepened. "And you refused?"

"I'm not going back there," he said. "The last time… the last time, I was lucky to get free."

"Not luck, I think. But you made the right choice."

Rsiran sighed and rested his head back on the bed. "You know what happened in the palace?"

"I know what Jessa told me."

He turned to look at her, wondering if she would be disappointed that he hadn't returned with whatever it was the others sought. The source of power Della had told him about. He'd come away with nothing. It would have been better had he never gone. As it was, he'd risked Jessa and Haern for nothing. For him to be trapped in the orb room and to hold the orb and have a vision.

She studied him, as if expecting him to say more.

"I never planned to take anything from there," he admitted.

Della surprised him by laughing softly. "I know."

He struggled to sit up again. "You know? You didn't try to stop me?"

"Would it have mattered what I said? Had I told you that the crystals can't be removed but that they are the reason that Venass and the Forgotten seek your abilities? What would you have done?" She paused, and her eyes seemed impossibly green, depths there that he didn't fully grasp. "You needed to go, to understand. It is something that can only be experienced, not explained."

Rsiran blinked. Crystals. That was the same term Thom had used. "You knew I would go?"

"I suspected."

"And you've seen them."

She nodded. "I've seen them. And like you, I suspect, have held one."

He pushed the barriers up in his mind, but suspected he was too late. It probably didn't matter anyway. Della seemed to Read him regardless of what he did to protect himself from her. And if she could, did that mean Thom had Read him as well? Hadn't Brusus commented on Thom's skill?

"I think you already know what I did."

She smiled and sipped her tea. "I didn't Read you, if that's what you're asking."

Rsiran frowned.

Della set the mug down and fixed him with a direct gaze. "The great crystals are said to be items of power gifted to our people by the Great Watcher himself."

"What are they? What do they do?"

"Power," Della said. She took another long drink of her tea. "The Elvraeth call them crystals, but they are more than that." She glanced toward his forge. "As each of the Elvraeth are born with varying degrees of all the abilities of the Great Watcher, these... crystals... concentrate that power."

"I don't understand," Rsiran said.

Della smiled. "Few understand what they are. Even the council doesn't fully know what they possess. They are power, but more than that. They are a way to speak to the Great Watcher. It's why those who have held them call them sacred crystals."

Rsiran didn't know what to say. A way to speak to the Great Watcher. If true, he understood why the Forgotten and Venass would seek them. "And they think to reach them now—"

"Because of you." She set her mug down and met his eyes. "I am surprised you were able to reach the crystals," she said, her eyes flashing even darker before brightening again. Rsiran caught a hint of—surprise? Fear?—in her tone. "And with that kind of power… the crystals change you. Speaking to the Great Watcher changes you."

"But I didn't speak to the Great Watcher."

"Are you so certain? Do you think the Great Watcher would use words like you and I?"

Rsiran thought about his visions, the steady glow of the white lights in the distance that switched to the deep blue glow. And then the immense presence. Had he witnessed the Great Watcher?

"I see you aren't certain. That's good."

Rsiran sighed. He needed to share what he saw with someone, and Della would be the most likely to help him understand what he'd experienced. "When I held the orb—the crystal, I had a vision. White light, massive amounts, that spread below me. With the light, I could almost make out cities, as if the light represented people." Or something else. At the time, he'd wondered if the light represented lorcith. But that meant the dark blue light represented something else. Heartstone. And Rsiran didn't think there was any source remaining. "Then it was gone. I was left in darkness. Nothing but night surrounding me."

Della listened intently, nodding as he spoke. When he finished, she looked over at him. "When I reached the Heart, I saw the crystals likely the same as you." Her eyes went distant, reminding him of what happened to Haern when he had a vision. "This was many years ago. Much has changed since then, but I doubt the crystals are any different. There was one, different from the others, and it pulsed slowly, pulling me to it. It wasn't until I held it in my hands that the pulsing stopped."

Rsiran shivered. What she described mirrored his experience.

"And then… then I saw a vast expanse below me, as if I sat within the stars. I saw no glowing lights, nothing but darkness. As I sat there, I felt connections… I had no other word for it and still don't… form between me and distant places. Like you, I felt the presence. I did not see anything. When it was done, the crystal had returned to its place among the others. I remember standing among the crystals, uncertain which of them I held."

She fell silent and took another sip of her tea.

Rsiran thought about the similarities of their experiences. "Why do you think you spoke to the Great Watcher?"

Della smiled. "I don't think I spoke to him. I do not doubt that he spoke to me."

"And what did he say?"

"Those connections I felt, I feel them still. Every day, I am aware of the connections I first felt when I held the crystal."

"What are they?"

"They are people I'm meant to help. That was what I was shown. And given the ability to do so."

The words took a moment to settle into him. "Given the ability? You're saying your abilities changed after you held the crystal?"

Della nodded. "There is much about me I do not share, Rsiran, but I didn't always have the abilities I have now. Without that experience, without holding the crystal and feeling those connections form, I would never have gained them." She smiled at him. "I would never have been able to Heal you when Brusus first brought you to me. I would never have been able to Heal you when you Slid to me on your own."

"The Great Watcher *added* to your abilities?"

She shrugged. "Or simply allowed me to access what I already possessed."

"You think the same will happen to me?"

"I don't know the will of the Great Watcher, Rsiran. Few can claim they do. But I know what I experienced. It is the reason the crystals are so well protected and why Venass cannot be allowed to possess them."

"Just Venass?"

"I don't think the Forgotten would do anything more than what you were able to do. Even were they able to reach the crystals in the first place—which isn't possible for most—they would find that, like you, they wouldn't be able to remove them. The crystals are well protected."

"But Venass?"

Della's eyes narrowed. "Venass studies many things, twisting what the Great Watcher has made. The crystals… they are the purest form. I fear what would happen were they to possess even one of the great crystals. How they would twist what was meant to remain pure. And I fear that whatever Venass sent in those crates, whatever device they thought to bring into the palace, would give them the ability to reach them."

Had this been about Venass the entire time? If Venass managed to bring him toward Thyr, using Brusus's poisoning to convince him that he needed to Slide north, what else had they been involved in? Had they convinced the Forgotten that they needed to obtain the crystals?

Rsiran shivered again. Venass intended to use him too.

"You see the difficulty."

Rsiran nodded. "I'm not sure I can do anything against them. If they managed to Compel me…"

Della smiled. "That, I think, is why the Great Watcher chose you. Your specific combination of gifts protects you from them."

"But it doesn't. They drew me north. I was trapped within Venass—"

"Were you? Didn't you tell me you managed to Slide out of the cell they placed you in?"

He nodded slowly. "They let me go. Released me."

"They tried to bind you to them. They wanted to convince you that you needed to return." Della's eyes hardened. "I think the scholars knew they could not truly trap you. That's the reason they thought to convince you otherwise."

"If Thom Compelled me once, making me believe him dead, what keeps him from doing it again? What protects me from that?"

She sighed. "I don't think he Compelled you. Perhaps Pushed. I am not certain one such as you can be Compelled."

"What do you mean?"

"Only that nothing protects you other than the defenses only you know how to build. For you to be safe—for us all to be safe—you must learn to shield yourself at all times. But doing so is difficult and will make Sliding more challenging."

"You think I need to stop Venass from reaching the crystals?"

"Once I would not have thought it necessary. But now… now I think you're the only one who has a chance."

Rsiran thought about how hard it had been for him to even reach the crystal room. But if the scholars Pushed him, even if they didn't Compel him, he doubted he would be able to prevent them from using him to find it.

"What do I need to do?"

Della shook her head. What she said next struck fear through his heart. "I don't know."

EPILOGUE

R SIRAN SAT ON THE ANVIL, staring at the door to his smithy. The sword that he'd used to block the doorway now rested against the wall. He hadn't bothered to slip the lock. Since Della had left, he'd stared at the door, waiting for Jessa to return. What did it meant that she hadn't?

He didn't know what he needed to do, but felt that everything he thought he understood was wrong. The Elvraeth protected the crystals. After holding one—and now hearing Della's experience—he had to agree they should be kept safe. Who better than the Elvraeth, gifted by the Great Watcher with all the abilities?

Rsiran blinked. Beyond what had happened in the palace and the attack afterward, he'd promised Brusus he would help him find the Forgotten. Brusus wanted to find his mother, but attempting to find her exposed him to capture by both the Forgotten and Venass. Whatever Della might say, he wasn't as convinced he could escape if they managed to catch him again.

Finally, the lock turned and the door opened. Jessa slipped in followed by Brusus. Haern came in a moment later. Once through, Jessa slipped the lock back into place.

Haern approached slowly. The long scar across his cheek seemed tight and twisted as he made his way toward him. The blue lantern light reflected off the scar, sending shadows streaking down his face.

He stopped a couple of paces from Rsiran. "Need to apologize for what happened."

Rsiran shook his head. "I don't think you do."

"You brought me out. You could have left me."

"No. I couldn't."

Haern grunted. "Wish I could See you better, Rsiran. It would make all this easier for me, knowing what's to happen. Maybe then I would have been able to avoid Thom's control."

Rsiran watched Haern and came to a realization. "It's happened to you before, hasn't it?"

Haern blinked. One hand fumbled with a dronr, flipping it from finger to finger. He had the other hand behind his back. Finally, he nodded. "You remembered what he said."

Rsiran nodded.

Jessa came alongside Rsiran and put her arm around his shoulders. "What did he say?"

Rsiran kept his eyes on Haern. "Haern studied with the scholars. And so did Thom."

Out of the corner of his eye, Rsiran saw Brusus near the long table covered with his forgings. He stiffened with the question. Brusus already knew.

"What is it, Haern? More than just scholars there, isn't it."

He swallowed and then nodded. "More than just scholars." The dronr paused along his knuckles. "I wasn't born in Elaeavn, not like the rest of you. Not Forgotten either, but a generation removed. Venass keeps an eye out for those like me. Most of us want nothing more than to understand our abilities. When you don't grow up in Elaeavn, you don't really understand why you have these visions or this sight or…"

Rsiran nodded. "They offer to teach you."

"They offer to teach. But there are conditions attached. Some are born with abilities. Others get them over time. But even those with abilities can have them strengthened, augmented if you will."

"That's why you're such a strong Seer," Rsiran said.

Haern nodded.

"What did they do to you?" he asked.

"Not a what, so much as why," Haern began. "Forced me into lessons, always giving me more and more to learn, assignments that were increasingly difficult. Taught me about poisons and tactics and…" He touched his forehead as he frowned. "Don't matter anymore. That's behind me. Or was."

Rsiran thought of Thom and the heartstone that he'd sense within him. "Did they…" He hesitated, uncertain how to finish the question.

Haern tapped his scar. "Tried. Maybe it worked, but what do I know?" he asked. He fell silent and glanced over to Brusus. "Thought this was all gone. That I wouldn't have to think about this anymore."

"So did I," Brusus said.

"What does it mean?" Rsiran asked.

Neither answered. Rsiran realized that neither had an answer. That troubled him more than anything.

＊ ＊ ＊ ＊ ＊

Rsiran emerged from his Slide with Ilphaesn rising above him. The sense of lorcith swirled all around him, stronger than it had been before. Distantly, he felt other collections of lorcith. From the vision he had while holding the crystal, he could close his eyes and know where they were.

Other senses tugged at him, as well, ones he'd once had to clear his mind to focus on. Now he felt them easily. Heartstone, both pure and in the alloy. That was the other vision gifted to him by the Great Watcher.

But why?

Rsiran didn't have the answer. And maybe that was the point.

He inhaled deeply of the salty air, gripping the canvas sack of jerky and bread he'd brought for Josun. He'd debated leaving him trapped within the mines but decided that was no different from the torture the Forgotten had inflicted upon him. Rsiran would not be like them.

Jessa waited for him back in the smithy. He felt the lorcith charm she wore hanging from her neck. Had he wanted, he suspected he could pull on it from here. Strange how attuned to lorcith he now felt. And he had thought his connection strong before.

Rsiran Slid, emerging in the mine.

He looked around. Since holding the crystal, his Sight had improved. Now, along with the maze of lorcith he sensed within the walls of the tunnels, he saw shades of grey. Not as sensitive as what Jessa managed, it allowed him to see enough in the darkness that he could move safely through the tunnel.

Rsiran made his way toward where Josun would be hiding. As he did, he realized something was off. Heartstone alloy didn't pull on his senses.

As he reached the end of the tunnel, he looked around. Josun was gone.

Rsiran didn't bother searching the tunnels for him.

He Slid to the peak of Ilphaesn and looked out, listening for the alloy of the Elvraeth chains. He felt it distantly, like a bell tolling on his senses.

Without hesitating, he Slid.

When he emerged, he stood atop the deck of a ship. Wide sails swept open, the wind gusting against them. Spray spit over the bow, slicking the decking.

Firell.

"I'm sorry, Rsiran."

He turned and saw the smuggler looking at him. His face had changed during his time in captivity. Now it was drawn and worn under a stubbled beard. One eye streaked with red. A steel sword hung from his waist.

There was no lorcith on his ship. Only the chains.

Rsiran *pulled* them to him. They slipped across the deck, and he grabbed them from the air.

Firell's eyes widened.

"You released him."

"He gave me Lena back."

Firell nodded toward something behind him, and Rsiran looked over his shoulder to see a young girl, probably no more than twelve or thirteen, standing on the deck of the ship. She smiled as she stood with the air blowing against her face, her dark black hair fluttering in the wind.

"Do you know where he went?"

Firell shook his head. "I promised him the chains again if he ever came after me."

Rsiran didn't know if Firell could capture Josun to place him in chains, but smiled. Then he *pushed* the chains back to him. "Keep them. You need them more than I do."

"You're not angry?"

Rsiran shrugged. He could sense Jessa still in his smithy. Even if he couldn't, they had to make their own choices, as Firell had made his. "I'm glad you chose your family."

Firell looked back at Lena. "What are you going to do now?" Firell asked.

Rsiran could feel the pull of lorcith and heartstone. They glowed all around him in his mind. Then there was the change to his ability to Slide. He didn't understand what it meant—not yet—but he began to think that he would.

"They think they can use me," he started. "But they will find that I am not going to be drawn into their fight."

Firell glanced to Lena. "If only it were that simple, Rsiran."

"What do you mean?"

Firell sighed and shook his head. "With everything you've done… the palace, the smithy, the *lorcith*… the Great Watcher knows I probably don't know the half of it."

"What are you saying?"

Firell smiled sadly. "You don't see, do you? It's more than just a simple fight. War is coming. And you've already been pulled into it."

DK HOLMBERG is a full time writer living in rural Minnesota with his wife, two kids, two dogs, two cats, and thankfully no other animals. Somehow he manages to find time for writing.

To see other books and read more, please go to www.dkholmberg.com

Follow me on twitter: @dkholmberg

Word-of-mouth is crucial for any author to succeed and how books are discovered. If you enjoyed the book, please consider leaving a review online at your favorite bookseller or Goodreads, even if it's only a line or two; it would make all the difference and would be very much appreciated.

Others Available by dk holmberg

The Dark Ability

The Dark Ability
The Heartstone Blade
The Tower of Venass
Blood of the Watcher

The Cloud Warrior Saga

Chased by Fire
Bound by Fire
Changed by Fire
Fortress of Fire
Forged in Fire
Serpent of Fire
Servant of Fire

The Lost Garden

Keeper of the Forest
The Desolate Bond
Keeper of Light

Manufactured by Amazon.ca
Bolton, ON

19811171R00194